The Physics of Love

Where the past, the present, and the future collide

By Donna Schlachter

Cover Photo: Used by permission

ISBN: 978-1-943688-24-1
(c) 2016
Published by PLS Bookworks, Denver, CO

Where Publishing Dreams Become Reality

This is a book of fiction based in truth, as all novels are.
There has been no intention to harm or embarrass anybody
involved in the actual events or in the fictional events.

Many thanks to:
God the Father – for the story, the ongoing ideas, the time,
and ability to put this down in written form.
Dad – without you, there would be no story.
Bert Parsons, Town Historian/Archivist –
without you, the details would have been lost in history.
Mona, Court Reporters Office – for finding the
documents that fill in some gaps
Patrick and Barb – for the love and support
during the painful parts of writing this story,
for putting up with us as we spent hours traveling,
asking questions, and talking about this book.
James: father, grandfather, great-grandfather – without your
cashbooks and diaries, this story would never have come alive.

Book 1: Opposition

Was it love? No. For him, our coupling was the opportunity to one-up my father, the biggest fish in a very small pond. For three minutes. For me, I don't know that I really thought about anything. Except I did imagine the look on my father's face if he could see me now. And that stayed with me much longer than those three minutes, in the back seat of a 1933 Mercury coupe, on a beach in Newfoundland.

Book 2: Momentum

Was it love? Must have been. How else do you explain a childless couple in their fifties taking in a bastard child, to raise as their own, when everybody around them knew the truth? When they had so much to lose—the respect of their peers, their position in the church, the rung on that ladder he'd climbed so diligently. Of course, I don't remember how the story began—I was only six months old at the time. And the story has been told and retold so many times I don't know if the truth will ever be known.

Book 3: Convergence

Was it love? Yes. That's what family is all about, so the answer must be yes, right? But I've since learned that family is about a whole lot more than just love. There are complicated dynamics involved in blood relationships, marriage relationships, even those once and twice removed relationships. But one thing I know for certain: it is love now.

Donna Schlachter

Book 1—Opposition
Laura's Story

op·po·si·tion

[op-uh-zish-uh n]
noun
1. the action of opposing, resisting, or combating.
2. antagonism or hostility.
3. a person or group of people opposing, criticizing, or protesting something, someone, or another group.
4. (sometimes initial capital letter) the major political party opposed to the party in power and seeking to replace it.
5. the act of placing opposite, or the state or position of being placed opposite.

opposite
[op-uh-zit, -sit] adjective
1. situated, placed, or lying face to face with something else or each other, or in corresponding positions with relation to an intervening line, space, or thing: opposite ends of a room.
2. contrary or radically different in some respect common to both, as in nature, qualities, direction, result, or significance; opposed: opposite sides in a controversy; opposite directions.
3. being the other of two related or corresponding things: friendly with many members of the opposite sex.
4. Botany .
a. situated on diametrically opposed sides of an axis, as leaves when there are two on one node.
b. having one organ vertically above another; superimposed.
5. adverse or inimical.

March 29th, 1934

"You are unredeemable."

My father's words—spoken the previous night in a tone much more frightening than anger—echo in my head as my train speeds as fast as a branch line of the Newfie bullet can speed, toward St. John's, carrying me away from the two biggest mistakes of my life.

I had just given up my firstborn child.

And I hadn't stayed to prove my father wrong.

Perhaps he was correct.

Perhaps I *am* unredeemable.

Laura

Donna Schlachter

Chapter 1
October 15, 1921

Whenever I look at my father, I see Nebuchadnezzar: head of gold and feet of clay.

You might wonder how a girl of not-quite nine would even know of such a person as that great king, let alone be able to spell his name. Well, I am the oldest—and only—daughter of one of the most powerful businessmen in Carbonear, on the island of Newfoundland, a British dominion in her own right. Although I attend the local school, my father is determined to make a genteel lady of me some day.

I fear he will be greatly disappointed.

As I stare out the window on this blustery fall day, watching him stare down the street toward the cemetery, I think how queer that he has two reasons for his two clay feet.

One reason is the secret I know about him.

The other is the fresh grave in the cemetery where my mother lays, cold and dead in the ground. My ninth birthday is a week away, and we buried my mother yesterday. And while this is where I'm choosing to start my story, the tale doesn't start here.

The first clay foot starts in the late 1890's before my mother and father were married. Apparently my father was a bit of a rake in those days. And a gypsy. Explains me, I guess. I remember the talk Mother and I had about a year ago, when I was still just a kid..

The day was cold and stormy, and school was closed. Not the shop, though. Never the shop, except on Sundays and holidays. At first, the people she described were like characters in one of my action story books. Tales of men—and women—braving the ocean, travelling to unknown lands so many years ago. She wove such a tapestry of colors and names and places I could almost see events lived out in my imagination.

I sat at the kitchen table, the same table where my mother kneaded bread and gutted fish, cut out cookies and jumpers for me, where we took our meals when we didn't have company, and where we set the empty plates when we did. She sat across from me, and we sipped our tea. Well, she her tea. I was too young for tea. Might stunt my growth, she said. So I sipped cocoa from a dainty tea cup, holding out my little finger just as she did, learning the social graces I needed to marry a man of good standing. When we weren't holding our cups, our fingers worked at a puzzle I'd gotten for my birthday.

I never liked doing puzzles on my own, but any time spent with just my mother was a rare treat. I would have been satisfied to sit and listen to her talk, but she believed idle hands were the devil's playground, and so we slipped these little pieces of stiff colored cardboard into place, each one filling in a blank that would eventually make up the picture on the box.

Assuming I'd managed to find all the tiles after I dropped the box on my bedroom floor the previous week while looking for a book.

At any rate, there we were, me acting all grown up, Mother pretending to be interested in my schoolgirl prattle, the puzzle the only thing making any sense. When I finally ran out of playground tales, I settled in to let her talk.

If I'd known how little time we had together, I would have let her talk more.

"Your family on my side, the Abbott family, came here from England in the 1700's. Ours was a proud family."

I dared to ask the question I'd always wondered. Britain seemed such a regal place to live, at least compared to Carbonear. "Why did the Abbotts leave England?"

Her hand shook as she set the cup in its saucer, and a hard look passed over her face. "We were proud, but we weren't Anglicans."

I wasn't sure what that had to do with anything. I knew lots of people in town who went to the Church of England just up the road from our Methodist church. "Is everybody in England an Anglican?"

She smiled, one of those half-smiles where you know a person isn't happy, just trying to make you feel so. "At that time, so long ago, if you weren't Anglican, you didn't get on."

I nodded as if I understood, but I didn't. Not really. It's not like we were *Catholic*.

She continued. "My great-grandfather, along with his two brothers, sailed from Liverpool. They arrived in Newfoundland, and at first they settled in Brigus."

She went on to tell me tales of bravery and stout-heartedness such as I'd never heard before. Never even imagined. About how the Beothuck, the native people on the island, welcomed them. How hard the winters were, how short the summers.

But the fish. Cod, herring, capelin, salmon, halibut. And lobster. All there for the taking by the man who knew the fishing grounds and had a boat to bring home his catch.

Which apparently the Abbotts didn't. But they were good businessmen and soon had a company set up to supply fishermen with what they needed. Nets, traps, lines, all that sort of thing. A chandlery, they were called. Abbott and Sons Chandlery. And they moved to Carbonear.

Many years went by, and then my mother was born, the daughter of Isaac and Sadie. They doted on their Louise, at least according to my mother. Saw something special in her.

Which doesn't surprise me. Every time I look at her, my chest pains me. She is so beautiful. Sometimes I stand behind her at her dressing table as she fixes her hair, and I try to imagine my scrawny child's body with her lovely face instead of my plain face with the Cameron nose. Her nose is a tiny button, so small I wonder how she breathes. One time I scootchied down behind her so I couldn't see my face, only hers. I see why my father loves her so much.

And why he can't seem to tolerate the sight of me because I look nothing like her.

She paused in her story. I don't want her to stop. I want to hear how my mother captured my father's heart. I imagine her as the girl in the story of the fairy tale about the princess and the pea. My mother is so fine she would be certain to feel a pea beneath twenty mattresses. Surely she is royalty deserving of so much more than this life as a shop clerk in a small town on the coast of Newfoundland.

"And then I grew up and met your father."

I stared at her, pleading with my eyes for her to continue. The story can't end there. She had done such a grand job up to this point, painting the picture for me with words and hand gestures. Expansive waving of her delicate but work-roughened fingers as she outlines the house they lived in, the fine things her father had shipped in from England, the gowns their live-in seamstress had sewn for her. At the time, hers was the only family in Carbonear to have its own live-in anything.

Even at that age, my father had instilled a sense of class in me, a *knowing* that we were better than most people in our town. I don't think he'd ever said that in so many words up until then, but I knew. And for my mother to marry him, she must have seen something in him. Because as the son of a fisherman, he wasn't in her class. And never would be.

Unless she made something of him.

"And we got married, and then you came along."

She leaned over the puzzle again, her brow pulled down as she concentrated on the picture. I waited as she placed three or four pieces into position, expecting her to carry on with the story. For surely there had to be more than that. When she didn't continue, I shifted in my chair.

She paused, a puzzle tile in her fingers, and tilted her head toward me in question. "What else did you want to know, child?"

Her question caught me off guard. I didn't have any specific questions. I was hoping for a fairy tale story where she, the princess, fell in love with Poppa, the man who wanted to be a prince, and something tried to come between them and tear them apart, but their eternal, undying love for each other bound them together body and soul. Or something like that.

I stared hard at her profile, so unlike mine. So petite and defined with her high cheek bones, tiny nose, cherry-red lips, and a chin that wasn't too big, wasn't too small. I understood why my father fell in love with such a woman. What I couldn't see was why she would fall in love with him.

Except she hadn't said they'd fallen in love at all.

So I ventured the first question that came to mind. "Did you love him?"

She dropped her gaze from mine, and a faint blush rose to her cheeks. "I love your father very much."

Aha. Her avoidance of my question answered me more than a dozen volumes of letters. "And did he love you?"

She met my eyes. "Almost unnaturally so."

I had no idea what she meant by that, and I wasn't certain I wanted to know. So I went on with the next burning question. "Why did you marry him?"

She stared out the kitchen window for a bit, as if she were back in time. Several minutes passed before she returned. "Your father is a great man. He has a lot of potential. I guess once I got to know him, I wanted more for him than perhaps he even wanted for himself."

"What did he want?"

She set the piece she had held in her hand for the last however many minutes in place. "He loved his job with Royal's. He liked travelling all around the island, going to Labrador."

I waited, figuring she would continue if I gave her the chance.

She did. "I could see there was no future in that work. He wasn't family, and so would never rise above the position of head clerk. He would work out his days in a dreary office, perhaps here, perhaps in Quirpon or some other town out around the bay. In some ways, I think his earlier memories of those days clouded his judgment about the future possibilities available to him."

"Tell me some stories about his younger days. He never tells me anything."

Her mouth turned up in a half-smile, but her eyes carried a hard glint. "Your father is a man of diverse passions."

I understood the meaning of the word 'diverse'. We'd had that in a spelling bee just a week or so ago. I'd looked up its definition in the dictionary. But passions? I had a vague notion that word had to do with love and all that goopy stuff. I couldn't imagine my father having feelings like that. In fact, this conversation about marriage and me coming along was as close to talking about passions as my mother and I had ever gotten. Did I really want to ask for more details?

But there was no backing down now. "What do you mean?"

The hard look slipped away as she selected another piece to place. "He wasn't always the God-fearing man you see today."

The image of my father's pointed chin, dark brown eyes, and

furrowed brow filled my vision. He had a rigid sense of right and wrong, and even the smallest of infractions earned me a spanking and a lecture. He should have been a preacher. Quoting scripture at me with a tongue as sharp as a sword. I often saw him roll his eyes heavenward as if asking the Almighty what he was going to do with me. I caused him no end of heartache and worry.

But now to find out perhaps, beneath the skin, we were more alike than he cared to admit. Well, this was something to know. And might explain why he treated me so harshly. I was more like him than he cared to admit.

A recent admonition from him regarding gossip skipped across my memory, so, rather than encourage my mother to continue, I sat back in my chair and waited. She would tell me in her own good time. Hopefully today.

My patience won her over.

"When your father was young, before we married, he went to Labrador with his brother and father."

Oh, another fishing story. Not what I wanted to hear. But still, there might be something interesting. "Really?"

I chose another piece of puzzle and turned it this way and that, as if trying to visualize where it fit, when, in reality, I wasn't paying the slightest attention to anything but the story.

My ruse worked again.

"Yes. They went to fish in Quirpon. And Labrador was but ten miles away by boat, so they would row over there on a Friday night and stay the weekend."

"Who did they stay with?"

She set the piece into place and chose another. "Whoever would put them up. There was no difficulty in finding a billet."

"A what?"

She smiled at my lack of understanding. "A place to sleep for the night."

"Like a hotel?"

"No. Not a hotel. With whatever girl they fancied, I expect."

"They had wives?"

For me, that was the only woman a man ever spent the night with.

She snorted softly, very unladylike for my mother. "No, they weren't married to them."

I let her words sink in, swim around, and digest through me. What she was saying about my father sounded wrong. But my father didn't do wrong. He wouldn't. He couldn't.

So my idea had to be wrong. That was a very big understanding for a child of eight, and I knew my mother had just burdened me with a fact of great importance.

"What happened?" The words choked out as if my mouth were full of crackers. I wasn't certain I wanted to know the answer.

My reaction must have alerted her to the fact that this news distressed me deeply, because she smiled and set another piece of the puzzle on the table. "Oh, I could tell you tales of evil half-sisters and curses on the family, but I won't." She patted my shoulder. "That would sound too much like something from one of your storybooks."

I nodded, much too afraid to ask any other questions. I'd just learned something about my father that would forever change how I viewed him and how I viewed myself.

I was more like him than I wanted to be.

Chapter 2

The front door slams, and my father returns to the house that will never be the same again. My mother's words still haunt my memory. Perhaps now is the time to get things out into the open. He and I are in pain and shock from my mother's sudden passing, and all the singing and patting on the head from the folks around town isn't going to change that.

We are all alone, and I want to know where I stand with him.

I go down the stairs, holding the bannister rail tight, although the palm of my hand sweats and slips on the painted wood. The rich pattern of the runner on the stairs reminds me of my mother—bright colors, pretty, but hardworking and long wearing. He looks up at me as I descend, his eyes rimmed with red as if he'd gotten little sleep or been crying.

Or both.

I force a smile. "Poppa."

He nods and walks down the hallway toward the kitchen. "Come with me, child. There is plenty of food in the ice box. We can warm something for dinner."

I don't want to eat. I don't want to see another casserole or cold salad that the church women have brought in over the last three days. If I never see another jellied pineapple salad as long as I live it will be too soon. But I follow him anyway. We are alone but together, a strange sensation to be sure. We are all we have in this world. At least, that's how it feels to me.

In the kitchen, he chooses a couple of dishes from the icebox and sets them on the table. The same table where just two weeks ago, my mother cut out a new dress for me. I glance at the sewing machine in the corner. The red corduroy material lies in a heap on the table next to the machine, never to be completed. I can't sew. She never taught me. And I doubt my father will pay someone to complete a dress I would never wear.

If my mother didn't sew it, I didn't want it.

I go to the cupboard and take down a couple of plates and set them on the table. He spoons some gelatinous concoction from a bowl into a saucepan, then lights the fire in the stove, moves the coffee pot nearer the heat, and stirs the soup as he stares out the window.

The same window my mother stared out last year as she told me about my father and the girls in Labrador. Then I was young and naïve, but now I am older and much more experienced. Now I know the questions to ask. I've listened to the gossip in the schoolyard about the older girls who don't come back to school in the fall, who got married quickly and had babies almost as quick. I've heard my friends tell me about the things that go on between a man and woman, things their older brothers and sisters have told them.

Things I could never imagine possible.

We sit at the table and wait for the soup to warm. My father stares at his hands, folded on the table, his elbows resting on the edge. I think what my mother would say if she saw him, and I bite back her words to take his elbows off the table. It's too soon to speak for her, and I doubt he'd listen to me anyway.

He looks up. "Well, maid, it's just us now."

I nod. I want him to go on. I want to know that he loves me as much as he loved my mother. Eternal and forever. To hear those words from his lips, just once, would ease my heart on the way to healing.

"Your mother's loss is a great blow to me."

My heart aches so much I fear I will never draw another breath. I cannot speak, so I simply nod again.

"A great tragedy and the end of a grand career."

Is this all he can think to say?

"We had our lives all planned out, you know. She would run the shop, and I would work at Royal's. But the shop grew so quickly it seemed to make sense that she and I should work together. And then you came along."

I work some saliva into my mouth until I get my tongue to move. "Do I have an evil half-sister in Labrador?"

I don't know where the question came from, but suddenly I have to know. Perhaps I don't want to feel so alone any longer. Maybe if I can find this person, related to me through my father's *diverse passion*, I would have the family I long for.

Or perhaps I simply want to shock him out of his morose attitude, bring him back to me and our current dilemma.

Whatever my reason, I don't achieve my goal. Rather, he faces me straight on, his lips a thin line of disapproval.

Suddenly, I am a little afraid of my father.

Not afraid he will hurt me. No, rather I am afraid he cares so little for me that he might leave me and seek out this other family that I know nothing about.

And then I would be truly alone.

He rises and returns to the stove, where he pours soup into two bowls, his hands shaking a little. He slops liquid over the edge of the pot, and the broth spurts and sizzles on the hot stove, dancing along, until it evaporates completely. Much like my hope for the future.

He sets the bowls on the table, and we bow our heads to pray. His voice drones on and on as the smell of beef and vegetables fill my nose, turning my stomach with its ordinariness. My mother made wonderful soup, the best in town, and this is nothing like hers. I know I won't be able to force even a mouthful down.

Once he's done, he lifts his spoon and sips delicately at the broth, nods, and digs in for some vegetables and meat. "Mrs. Nickel makes good soup."

"Not as good as Mother's."

He raises his eyes. "That is true. But still good."

I glance at the sewing table. "I won't wear that dress."

He nods. "I know. We'll put it in the scrap bin for the rummage sale."

I know he is avoiding my question. I could let him have his peace, but something inside me wants to hurt him and to know the truth. I'm not certain which is more important to me. Hurting him or knowing the truth. I want to believe the truth is the real reason I ask again. "Do I have any relatives in Labrador that I don't know about?"

"Gossip is very unbecoming and very un-Biblical."

"Is it gossip when your mother tells you something that probably everybody else in town already knows?"

He sets his spoon down and stares at me. "I will tell you this one time, and then you are never to mention this again. Do you understand?"

His voice echoes across the kitchen, rattles around my head, and settles in my soul. I nod slowly, not certain I really want to know any longer, but knowing that he must say the words to keep peace in the house.

Between him and me.

Perhaps between him and God.

"When I was a young man, before I married your mother, I went to Labrador. I fancied a girl or two there. I did some things that I shouldn't have done." He paused as if searching for the words. "But I have accepted God's forgiveness, and your mother's forgiveness." He uses a forefinger to accent his words. "I. Don't. Need. Yours."

With that, he stands and drops his half-eaten bowl of soup in the sink. The china strikes the cast iron and shatters, sending shards onto the counter and floor. He walks away as if he'd heard nothing, although I know he had.

He must have. My sobs are enough to rouse the dead.

Chapter 3

Over the next month, our lives settle into a "much of a muchness", as Alice in Wonderland would say. Which suits me very well. I am still numb from my mother's passing, and every day I expect to hear her voice when I come home from school.

Because back to school I go. My father turns a deaf ear to my pleas that I be allowed to stay home one more week, one more day. No. He is back in the shop, of course, which means I must follow suit as his daughter. If nothing else, the Cameron family is not weak.

My mother's mother, Grandmother Abbott, stays with us for two weeks, cooking meals and cleaning and doing those things I am too young to have learned and that my father never learned. She is a good woman and puts up with my moodiness as only a loving grandmother would.

After she leaves, the house is empty except for me, Father, and Irena, our live-in girl. I think she is glad Grandmother has gone, leaving her to do her job. Irena was never much of a housekeeper before my mother died, but somewhere she dredges up enough interest and energy to keep the house in order and have meals on the table for us. I think she's trying to honor my mother's memory by doing now what she should have done then.

My ninth birthday comes and goes with barely a mention. My father is still in a fog, I think. Irena bakes a cake and helps me blow out the candles at dinner. Father is working in the shop. Of course.

Christmas comes around, and two days before, at breakfast, Father speaks to me for perhaps the first time in a week.

"I'll need your help in the shop on Christmas Eve."

I nod, a funny excitement in my tummy. He needs me. In the shop. To work. Alongside him.

I am truly starved for my father's attention. For his affection. For his approval.

Of course, my mother lavished much love and attention on me, constantly telling me how smart I was. She never lied and said I was beautiful, but would complement me on my penmanship, my needlework, my inept bungling at helping when she baked. We often sat in her casual chair and I would read to her, with her helping me over the more difficult words.

My father, for the most part, was either in the shop, poring over the shop books at the kitchen table, at church, or closeted in his office, the one area of the shop where I was never permitted.

Thus, the very idea that he needed me in the shop, to work beside him all the day before Christmas, was an invitation—or rather a summons—not to be ignored.

Two days later, unable to sit still long enough to eat breakfast or even gulp a cup of milky tea, I trot down to the shop beside my father. The weather has turned cold and damp, with dark clouds hovering out over Carbonear Island. Seagulls soar on updrafts above the public wharf, and the dank smells of salt water and rotting seaweed float by on the brisk breeze. I shrug down into my wool coat, wishing I'd taken the time to pull on earmuff and mittens.

Father unlocks the door and I step inside a world of adventure. The shop is filled to the rafters and beyond with articles and items of wonderment from every corner of the world. Today I might sell ginger from the Orient or salt fish from Royal's across the harbour. Perhaps a customer will want a yard of paisley to sew up some curtains, or two yards of plush velvet for a gown for the New Year's Eve ball at the Cricket Club.

The possibilities seem endless, and I stroll the aisles as Father pulls a barrel of salt meat from the rear of the store to the cold room. Here, customers will use the trident hook to choose which piece they will take home to cook with their Christmas dinner. As I wander the store, refreshing my mind as to where everything is, my mouth waters at the sight of the cinnamon sticks, the molasses candy we call kisses, and the bull's eyes, fresh in from Purity Factory in St. John's. Surely there is no better place to spend the day than here, with my father.

He steps behind the long wooden counter and ties on his white apron that hangs below his knees. It's the same faded piece of muslin my mother wore over her work clothes, and I feel a pinch at the bridge of my nose as I recall her asking for my help to tie the strings. Of course, she didn't really need my help.

And apparently neither does he.

It seems to me that being nine years old is a particularly useless age. I'm too old to cuddle, and not old enough to do a day's work. I'm too big to dress in pinafores, but too young to wear bloomers.

"Can I unlock the door, Father?"

I desperately want to be useful.

"You can, and you may."

Chastised at my poor use of English, something my father abhors, I turn the knob on the deadbolt and test the door to ensure the lock disengaged, as if the open door is a magic lure for customers, drawing them into the shop to buy.

Except that this is Christmas Eve, and no lure is needed. My father's shop is the biggest and best at this end of Water Street. For someone to shop in a larger store, they would need to travel to the far end of the street, past the public wharf, a twenty-minute trek in the cold. Or they could choose to walk in the opposite direction about the same distance.

Mrs. Wilfred Noel and Mrs. Joseph Long, enter first. I smile and step aside as they sweep in, pulling the cold air with them. Mrs. Noel's cheeks are red from the chill wind, and her shopping basket bangs against her Milton-wool coat. Mrs. Joe, as my father calls her, fixes her eyes on the turkeys hanging in the front window.

"Mr. Cameron, I need a turkey."

He turns from the cheese slicer where he's been carving a chub of sharp cheddar into slices and wipes his hands in his apron. "I have several to choose from. See one you like?"

While she surveys the choices hung on hooks, their goose-pimply flesh pale in the morning light, he leans his elbows on top of the candy display. Inside this cabinet is loose candy, licorice shoe strings, and peppermint sticks. I press my nose against the glass case at the end of the counter that holds a couple of other cheese rounds that he's going to slice, imagining the smooth texture and creamy taste of the samples I might beg from him.

"No. I need something bigger."

"Yes, Mrs. Joe. How big?"

She holds her hands about two feet apart. "Twenty pounds or so?"

My father nods and heads toward the cellar beneath the store where the perishables are stored. Old Man Tucker came in a couple of days ago with about a dozen turkeys. As we wait, Mrs. Noel roams the aisles while Mrs. Joe fingers a bolt of pale blue taffeta that came in last week. Father returns a minute or so later, carrying his prize to the scale and sets the turkey on the platform. He studies the numbers. "How is twenty-two pounds?"

Mrs. Joe touches her chin with a forefinger. "Well, I don't know."

He smiles and wraps the bird in brown paper, then ties a length of butcher string to secure the ends. "I'll let you have it for the price of a twenty-pound bird."

She nods, a smile pushing her spectacles high on her cheeks. "Fine. You drive a hard bargain, Mr. Cameron." She glances at me, then lowers her voice and leans over the counter toward my father. "How are you doing since Louise left us?"

She makes my mother sound like a runaway wife, and I clench my fists in anger. I watch my father's face, and I see her words have touched something still raw in him, too. His Adam's apple works up and down, and his jaw tightens, the muscles rippling beneath the drawn skin. I hadn't noticed before, but I believe he looks older today than he had before my mother's death.

Everything goes back to her death. A sudden, silent killer. Stomach upset one day, in the hospital the next. Father coming home from the hospital all smiles. And the day we expect her to come home, she is scheduled for emergency surgery. Appendix, they said. A week later, she is dead. And three days after that, buried. Nothing left to mark her existence on this earth except a fresh pile of dirt, a small headstone in the cemetery, and a huge void in my heart.

The silence between Mrs. Joe and my father builds, and then he breaks the moment by stepping away from the counter and resuming his cheese-slicing, smacking the fresh slices on the parchment paper a quart pound at a time before beginning a new layer. Mrs. Joe casts her gaze on me, and I shrink behind the counter, busying myself with straightening the bottles of molasses so the labels all face forward.

She harrumphs and pushes out the door, her turkey in her basket, and is instantly replaced by Mrs. William Butt and a lady I don't recognize. They hustle to the back of the store where several drawers of shirts and ties reside, and soon all I can see are hunched backs bent to their task.

Mrs. Noel walks behind me, and our eyes meet. I dip my head in deference to her age, and she nods in my direction.

"May I help you find something, Mrs. Noel?"

"Yes, I'm thinking of getting some hair ribbons for my Sally. She's about your age. What do you like?"

Hair ribbons are something I know a good deal about. I have a basket of ribbons and barrettes on my dressing table. And I know Sally. She's in my class at school. "She has a lovely blue dress you recently had made for her. I think she'd like ribbons to match." I lead the way to the corner where the sewing notions and hair things are stacked, and I pull out a tray with spools of satin and silk ribbons, some grosgrain, some with eyelet edging. I hold several to the light. "I think some of these."

Mrs. Noel agrees and purchases a yard of each of the ones I'd chosen. "And she has a red dress, but reds are so different, don't you think?"

She is asking my opinion, and I'm flattered. "Yes. So perhaps some white ribbons? Or maybe some silver or gold?"

She fingers each of the colours I suggest. "How much is the silver?"

"Three cents a yard. The gold is the same. And the others are two cents a yard."

She thinks a moment, then nods. "Christmas comes but once a year. I'll have a yard of each."

I carefully measure each ribbon, adding an extra two inches onto the length, as my mother taught me, then I roll each ribbon carefully so as not to smudge or crease the fabric, and carry them to the cash register. "Will that be all, Mrs. Noel?"

"Yes, thank you." She digs into her reticule and withdraws a dime and a nickel. My father rings up her purchases and returns her coppers in change, and she leaves the store, a satisfied smile covering her face.

He turns to me. "She bought more than she planned."

I am pleased he noticed, and more pleased he chose to voice his thoughts. "I'm a good helper, aren't I, Father?"

His brow pulls down and his mouth forms a hard line. "We are here to provide what they need and what they want, and no more. To encourage people to buy something they don't want would be a sin, no matter how much profit is in the transaction. Once they get home, they will be unhappy with their actions and with our complicity, and they may feel we tricked them."

His words scald my heart like a hot iron, and words of defense spring to my lips. But he'd said his piece, and he turns away, dismissing me as if I were nothing.

Which is how I feel at that moment.

I cannot remember much about the rest of the day, as the bell above the door played a merry melody every time someone enters or leaves the shop. Even the door seems to spin on its hinges, admitting shoppers, then spitting them out into the cold again. I believe every person who lives in Carbonear comes into our shop at least once, and two or three show up several times.

Noontime comes and goes, and Father slices off some ham and cheese from the stock and we nibble delicately between customers. He is full of energy, up and down the ladder to the shelves behind the counters that form a horseshoe shape around the inside of the store. I greet people, assist them in finding what they want, but am very careful not to make suggestions about what they should buy.

"Once bitten, twice shy", as the saying goes. I do not want to risk my father's wrath another time today.

Dinner comes, and Irena slips in through the door with a tray. She has brought us a pot of tea, which I am dying for. My head aches with all the chatter and questions and gay Christmas wishes I've endured all day. Father pours tea with extra milk for me, and I take advantage of a lull in the customers to down the cup in one gulp, sitting on a barrel of apples where he has set me.

His eyebrows descend again in disapproval as I swipe my mouth with the back of my sleeve. I sigh. I never seem to measure up to his expectations.

I hop down when the bell over the door rings yet again. Reverend Clarke enters the store, and I groan to myself. He is a *twacker*, that most hated of persons to a shopkeeper. He looks and looks, touches the goods, wants to see everything, but never buys.

Perhaps today will be different. After all, it is Christmas Eve.

My father nods in greeting, and the minister asks to see some chocolates. Preferably something imported. We carry only imported chocolates. Purity Factory makes candy, but not chocolate. We order Rowntrees and Hersheys directly from England. Several boxes are placed on the counter, and he hefts each in his hands before shaking his head and setting them back. My father returns each to its place on the shelf.

"Perhaps some handkerchiefs? This is for my good wife, you know. Something special. Nothing common for her."

Yes, nothing common. I'd heard my mother talking about Mrs. Clarke with some other ladies. She was a spoiled woman, my mother said. I didn't quite understand what she meant. I'd heard of spoiled meat and spoiled milk, but in regards to a person, that was quite beyond my years. I thought Mrs. Clarke a nice, if quiet, woman. A perfect minister's wife. She plays piano at the church, smiles at him as he preached, and never raises her voice in Sunday School.

But something about her was spoiled. Perhaps her nose? If he wanted to buy her handkerchiefs, maybe her nose ran. Or if he couldn't find chocolates she would eat, perhaps her taste buds were off.

That was something I'd heard my mother say about old Mrs. Penney. She'd gotten sick and died of food poisoning because she couldn't taste anymore.

But no, not her nose, because the reverend shakes his head and moves on. He has no intention of buying anything. More likely he'll tell his wife he tried and tried, but Cameron's just didn't carry anything good enough for her. Which, of course, was a lie. We carry lots of things good enough for the best person in town. My mother shopped here all the time, and she was a princess as far as I was concerned.

And so the day goes. The long hours wear me down, and I am glad to see ten o'clock rounding the bend. Except my father has no intention of closing the store so long as customers are willing to shop. I don't understand. What about our Christmas tree? We haven't cut it yet, let alone put it up and decorate it. And what about our time for shopping? In other years, my mother gave me a dime and let me buy a gift for Father while she worked in the store, and then Father gave me a dime to buy Mother a gift when he was on duty.

But with Mother's passing, I had no dime to buy him a gift, and at any rate, if I did, he would see because he was always in the store, which would spoil the surprise. And what about my gifts? Had he already done his shopping and hidden the parcels in the house?

Eleven o'clock rolls around, and still he keeps on. A quarter past, half past, a quarter 'til. I lean against the counter and lay my head down. I can keep my eyes open no longer, and I must have slept in that position, because the next thing I know his rough hand is on my shoulder waking me.

"Come, child, it's five 'til midnight, and I won't work on the Lord's birthday for anybody."

I nod, and he wraps my coat around my shoulders, picks me up, and nestles me against his shoulder as he carries me back up to the house. Leaving me in my day clothes, he settles me in bed and blows out the light.

It is the first physical contact I remember from my father since my mother's death, and I wish I could stay in his arms forever.

It is his only Christmas gift to me.

When I rise the next morning, there is no tree, no packages waiting to be opened. Irena rises from her room, and we sit at the kitchen table and prepare our Christmas dinner. Father is gone to church, she says, and then he is going to Mr. Royal's for dinner.

We eat alone in the kitchen that afternoon, and I am reminded all over again that my father's love was only for my mother. Which was his second clay foot. And when she was gone, the legs were cut out from under him. And I come to grips with one certain truth: my father's love died with my mother, and I doubt he even knows.

Chapter 4

The winter passes slowly, and the maid and I spend a lot of time together yet alone. This is the first time I understand there is a difference between being alone and being lonely. Mother and I could spend an entire afternoon in the same room and never speak, and yet I felt as connected to her as if I were tied to her apron strings.

With Father, the feeling is quite the opposite. I eat at the same table, sleep under the same roof, and occasionally I help out in the shop, and yet we are as alone as if we were on different planets.

Sometimes I sneak from my bed and climb upstairs to the attic where my father has stored my mother's clothes and personal items. I open the trunks carefully so the hinges don't squeak, and pick up articles as familiar to me as my own dresses. Her old blue cotton shift that she wore when she cleaned the house. The black satin she wore to the New Year's Eve ball the last year she was alive. The pale pink silk she wore to Mr. Penney's wedding the summer before she died.

On this particular night, I hold the silk in front of me and stare into the old mirror propped against the wall. In the dim light, I squint, trying to alter my vision so I can see something of my mother. But I am flat and angular in all the places she was curvy, and I am plain and dull where she was so beautiful.

No wonder my father wants nothing to do with me. At first I thought perhaps his indifference was because I reminded him too much of my mother, but now I see the opposite is true: I don't look or act anything like her, and so how could he love such an ugly duckling?

I sink my face into the material and inhale my mother's scent—lily of the valley eau de toilette, the fresh scent of Ivory soap. I remember her as she left the house that last afternoon, a bandeau of peach blossoms highlighting the lighter parts of her chestnut hair, which had been pulled into a French twist on the back of her head.

And Father, so dashing in his grey summer suit, a handkerchief matching my mother's dress peeking from his jacket pocket. She'd made sure to stitch the piece for him when she sewed her outfit.

Tonight I can bear the memories no more, and I drop the dress into its trunk and close the lid, hardly caring whether anyone hears me. Perhaps, deep down, I want Father to climb the ladder, to stick his head into my hiding place, and invite me into his embrace. And I would run to him, dive into his arms, and never leave there, certain of his deep affection for me.

But that doesn't happen.

Instead, I wander to the small window in the peak of the house facing the harbour, and stare out into the dark night. A full moon casts a ribbon of light on the ice, and the boats at dry dock for the winter line the beach like observers at a hockey game. A shadow passes over the moon, and I look up, expecting to see a cloud.

Instead, a cigar-shaped object with wings roars past.

My tongue sticks in my mouth, and my mouth dries so I cannot form a sound. My breathing becomes shallow. I cannot fathom what I am seeing. Surely the end of the world has come, and I don't want to be alone.

I stumble across the uneven planking to the ladder. In my haste, I miss the top two steps, and for one horrible moment, I hang by the edge as my legs flail for purchase. My bare toes grasp the wooden step, and I cling to the spindly uprights, willing my heart to cease its thundering.

When finally I can draw a decent breath, I scoot to the floor and race down the hall to my father's room. I pause long enough to knock once then shove the door open so hard it bangs on the dresser.

My father sits bolt upright in his bed, blinking in the dark. "What is it? Is the house afire?"

I stand beside the bed, the cover bunched in my fists. "Father, the world is ending."

I am close to hysteria, but I know he will not abide my blubbering, so I bite the inside of my cheek to keep the tears at bay.

He throws back the covers, snatching the only solid thing that is keeping me sane, and swings his legs to the side of bed and into his slippers. "What are you babbling about, child?"

I draw a deep breath to steady my voice. "The world is ending. There is something out there covering the moon."

He takes me by the hand, the gentlest touch I've felt from him in months, and together we cross the room to the window. He pulls back the curtain and stares out. From this room, we cannot see the moon, and there is nothing moving outside. He cups my face between his hands. "What did you see?"

"Something big flying in the sky. Big enough to block out the moon, just like in the Bible."

He releases my face and straightens. "Get your slippers and housecoat on, and we'll go see."

He believes me! I'm not certain whether that fact surprises me more than his desire to go outside at that hour of the morning, and I stand rooted to the spot. The clock downstairs chimes, and I count the gongs: one, two, three, four, five. Almost time to get up, and here I am, rousing my father. And here he is, suggesting we go outside to confirm what I saw.

I race for my bedroom, struggle into my housecoat—why is it that when you're in a hurry, the sleeves never seem to cooperate—and frantically search for my slippers. I never leave them in the same place twice, so I waste several minutes looking under the bed, in the closet, and on the dresser, until I find them beneath a pile of books. I slip my feet into the suede mules and meet my father in the hallway.

We descend the stairs, and I wonder if he will pick up his gun as we pass the front room, but no, he heads directly for the door. Once again the moonlight is bright, and the stained glass panels in the door and front porch cast a rainbow of colours on the floor. He unlocks the door and we step outside on the verandah.

Still I am afraid, and I grip his hand. To our left, several neighbors stroll down Captain Frank's Lane toward Water Street and the harbour. The wind whips around the corner, and I am chilled to the bone. If the world is not coming to an end, I will feel particularly foolish and regret my haste in not also pulling on a sweater. And shoes instead of my house slippers.

We walk down the garden path, beneath the spreading branches of the now-bare maple tree, and he opens the gate leading to the street. The store is dark, its windows lit from the front by the streetlight, the counter and shelves in shadow. My father nods to Mr. and Mrs. Antle as they pass, but they are too caught up in their own whispered conversation to speak to us.

Straight down the lane, past Mr. Parsons' house, past the fish sheds, and we join about twenty others on the chandlery wharf. Several boys I recognize from school jostle, threatening to push each other onto the ice. A mother whispers a loud reprimand, and they stop. My father joins a group of men clustered at the end of the wharf. I am still glued to his leg. Somehow this strange world of twilight is almost as scary as seeing the moon blotted out of the sky.

I stare into the heavens. The moon is as normal as can be, and I chastise myself for my foolishness. What had I been thinking? Nothing could be big enough to completely cover the moon. Overhead, the stars twinkle against the black backdrop of space, and I wonder about the verse where God said He knows the name of each star. I don't know enough names for each one to be different.

My father squeezes my hand, and I look up at him. He swings me up into his arms for a moment and holds me at eye level. "No fear, child. The world is not ending. An airship has come to visit."

He sets me down, and although my feet are on the ground, I am floating. He picked me up, something he hadn't done for many years. Dear God, let an airship—whatever that is—come to visit every day!

He takes my hand again and we walk back up the lane. I think we're going home, but instead, we turn left and head down Water Street. I skip to keep up with his long strides, and the brisk air burns my lungs as we walk. All around us, it feels as though we are part of a party, a celebration. More people join us from the houses along the way, and they, too, seem infused with a queer drunkenness. Laughter, loud talk, bragging boys, simpering girls clutching their housecoats to their throats as the boys sneak a peek.

At the public wharf, we turn toward the ocean, and I look up for the first time. About a hundred feet out in the harbour, a huge bird races toward the surface then plops to the ground. Chips of ice and shovels-full of snow fly in all directions, and I am certain the beast will devour us as it slows and turns in our direction. Several of the men in our group jump from the wharf to the ice and run, slipping and sliding, toward the beast.

Something in me wants to scream at them to stop, afraid the thing will devour them before we can take action. But before the words can form in my muddled brain, a door opens and several figures appear. Dark objects that look like canvas sacks, but I imagine are eggs or young of some sort, drop to the ice. Our men grab an object in each hand and head toward shore, while several figures jump from the beast onto the ice and follow. As the first of our men draw near, I hear the words "mail" and "weather", and the crowd around me murmurs in approval.

Tom Doolan from down around the beach mumbles something, and I concentrate to decipher his words. I fear he has forgotten to put in his teeth before running down to see the goings-on, and I'm not certain at first I understand what he's saying. Hair slip? Art shop? No, that makes no sense. I ask him to repeat himself, and he stares at me, his eyebrows resembling drunken caterpillars. "Airship, I said, Miss Laura. Clean out your h'ears."

An airship. Not a giant bird or a marauding enemy. And not the end of the world, to be sure. My father stares at the activity around him, perhaps wishing he were one of the men with a sack, instead of merely standing on the wharf tethered to me, and for an instant, I consider releasing his hand to allow him to venture forth. But the moment passes, and he stands beside me.

Deep inside I am glad he doesn't leave me.

The people from the airship are still merely black forms because of the distance and the lack of illumination, and I wonder if flying high in the air causes people to turn black. I'd seen a black man once, in St. John's. His skin was so dark he was nearly blue, and I remember wondering at the time why God would make skin that colour when white seemed a perfectly good shade.

One of our men hands his sacks off to the postmaster, and the other men with bags follow his lead. Receiving mail in the dead of winter, when the roads and trains are closed because of the snow, is an exciting time in Carbonear. Sometimes we are truly cut off from civilization for days on end.

One of the men from the airship wears a leather helmet and a set of eyepieces which now rest on top of his head. It must be cold up in the sky, as he also wears a leather jacket and a scarf looped around his neck several times.

Another of our men helps someone onto the beach, and as they draw closer, I see this visitor is a woman. She wears a fancy hat, and for a moment

I wonder if she is from another planet. My heart races all over again, and I'm certain the people around me can hear the pounding.

When nobody mentions the racket I hear in my head, I turn my attention back to the people crossing the ice toward us. The first have reached the shore, and they step over the rocks lining the beach. One man slips and falls, and a foreign language leaves his mouth. Several of the women in our group gasp, and one covers her daughter's ears. The man stands, brushes off his hands and the knees of his pants, and laughs.

I release the breath I'd been holding. What manner of people are these, who speak such strange words? I let go my father's hand and edge forward, pushing my way between the people lining the edge of the wharf.

Another man and a woman reach the shore, and I catch snatches of their words. Something about airsickness, wind currents, and quaint folks. I understand the words, but I don't know what they mean the way they're using them. I've heard of sea sickness, summer sickness, and the influenza. I look around me. The people from Carbonear are just *people*—they aren't quaint. They're just regular.

By the time everyone is off the airship, the town's population has increased by five. After much discussion regarding the weather, their intended route, and their plans for leaving again, the people from the airship ask where they can get a hot bath and a hotel room. If they expect a hot bath, they might as well get back in their flying beast and head for St. John's. And they certainly won't all fit in Abbott's Hotel down near the train tracks. Old Man Abbott only has three rooms, and those are currently filled. At least, that's what Tom Doolan said. He should know. He works there as a bellboy and room cleaner.

My father gets the crowd's attention, and they fall silent as he prepares to speak. One thing I'll say about my father, he chooses his words with care, and that makes people listen to him. There are several men in town more powerful, more influential, than my father, but none can hold a candle to him when it comes to oration.

"Ladies and gentlemen visitors, welcome to our humble town."

Humble? Carbonear is anything but humble, even in the Biblical sense. Mind you, we were never so prideful as to consider competing with St. John's as the capital of Newfoundland. Unlike Harbour Grace, which still holds to its pretensions.

"Thank you for gracing us with your presence. We are anxious to get to know you and to learn more about this wonderful vehicle you arrived in." Father gestures to the airship, and a ripple of approval runs through the crowd. "Perhaps we can billet you in our homes for the time you are here. In that way, you can learn more about us, and we can learn about you. An exchange of ideas, as it were."

He sounds just like the prime minister in one of my storybooks who welcomes men from another planet to Earth. I am so proud of him at this moment.

The small knot of newcomers whisper among themselves, and amidst a great deal of head shaking and pointing back to the harbour, they come to a decision. The man wearing the leather jacket and eye goggles steps forward. He glances from one to another of us as if gauging our potential reaction to the words he is about to speak.

Apparently satisfied we will not mob him or shoot him on the spot, he speaks to everyone, but addresses my father. "Thank you for your kind invitation, people of—" He looks around as if hoping to see a sign with the town name inscribed.

My father whispers in a loud stage voice, "Carbonear."

The speaker ducks his head then resumes. "Carbonear, but we must press on. Our itinerary precludes us from staying. We are due in St. John's at two o'clock, and if we are late, they will worry."

Well, that's all right then, isn't it? Expected in St. John's is as good a reason to escape our clutches as any. St. John's expects—and generally gets—the best of everything. The best doctors, topnotch teachers, quality hospitals and schools, and, of course, airships.

My father catches the captain's eye. "Sir, perhaps you could stay until sunrise? For safety's sake."

The captain nods, his smile slipping away in the twilight. "This airship we travel in is very safe. It must be, since the Royal Post wouldn't entrust the delivery of its mail otherwise."

What he said makes sense. Whatever will be next? Flying mail across the ocean? The wonders of air travel! I push closer. Perhaps he will see me and offer a ride in his magical airship. All hard feelings toward the visitors disappear on the freshening breeze.

Mr. Abbott from the hotel—oh Lord, did he hear my thoughts about his establishment a moment ago?—asks, "Ain't you 'fraid to go up in that t'ing?"

I grit my teeth at his common language, and pray the visitors don't paint us all with the same brush regarding our education and culture.

The captain raises an eyebrow. "Afraid, sir?" He gestures to the airship, stark against the surrounding ice and snow, like a mountain rising from the ocean. "No. We are as safe as you are sitting in your parlor. Soon airships will cross the ocean and fly around the world. It's the beginning of an exciting time for air travel."

I think so, too, and press in, dying to be invited for a ride. But my father puts a heavy hand on my shoulder and encourages me to step back. I comply even though I don't want to.

The visitors file back to their beast, and our men follow with several sacks of mail headed for St. John's. A fan on the nose of the creature spins like mad, and I jump at the roar of the engine. A part on the tail that looks like a rudder on a boat moves up and down, and they head toward the open ocean, gathering speed until they lift from the ice on silent wings, higher and higher, before proceeding forth in a more or less southeasterly direction.

Two days later, my father reads in the St. John's Evening Telegram of the landing of the airship at Quidi Vidi Lake in St. John's, and the great commotion caused by the traffic jam as folks in their wagons and new-fangled automobiles lined the roads, trying to catch a glimpse of this eighth wonder of the world. Apparently, several cows in Holyrood ran amuck during the early morning hours as the airship flew over, and in Portugal Cove, one farmer's hens stopped laying and hadn't resumed.

But the cover story in the paper that same day was the crash of the *Roma*, another kind of airship, in the United States. He reads the story about the semi-rigid dirigible owned by the United States Army aloud to me over dinner that evening, an intimacy we haven't shared since before my mother died. Many people died in that crash, and any resentment I might feel over the snubbing by our visitors vanishes in a flash.

As I say my prayers that night, I thank God that He protected our visitors. Oh, yes, and I thank Him that the world didn't end.

Chapter 5

When I have a cold or a sore throat, I keep my complaints to myself. First of all, my school chums tell me that when they go to the doctor, they always get a needle. And I don't like shots. Secondly, my mother went to the doctor with a pain in her stomach, and she ended up dead.

So I avoid doctors and hospitals.

I manage to get through the mumps and the measles without the doctor being called in. The maid sat up a good many nights with me and shooed away monsters with her hanky when they threatened to chase me around my room. One particular night, I recall she sat at the foot of my bed and waved that small square of cotton edged with tatting around like she held Goliath's sword in her hand.

"Away with you, monsters." Her face, almost as pale as the handkerchief, seemed to glow in the dim light of the room. "Are they gone?"

I risked another glance at the corner where I'd last seen them. Another dragon-looking creature ran across my vision. I shook my head and pointed. "No. It's over there. And it's chasing me and Poppa."

She waved the hanky again and again until I couldn't see the monster any longer, and I settled down in my bed. She pulled the cover up to my chin and waited until my eyes closed.

But today is different. This morning I awaken with a pain in my throat that feels like a knife cutting into my being. Irena comes into the room and opens the curtain, expecting me to jump out of bed and dress for school. I groan and turn over, burying my head beneath the covers. She sets my cup of milky tea on the bedside table and tugs at the quilt.

"Rise and shine, sleepyhead miss." Her voice, like the trilling of a bird, hurts my ears. "It's off to school for you."

I shake my head and bury deeper.

She tugs the harder, and manages to pull the cover from me. I turn my face toward her, my eyes slits, and she gasps.

"My word, Laura, what happened to you?"

I point to my throat and shake my head again.

"Can't talk?"

I shrug.

"Sore throat?"

I nod.

"I'll call your father."

I shake my head vehemently, and the room spins. I grab the coverlet and sink into the bed.

She lays a cool hand across my forehead, much as my mother used to do, and tears spring unbidden to my eyes. Since my mother passed, I get so little physical affection that even this one small act of kindness opens the floodgates of my heart, and I start to bawl like a hungry calf.

I am starved for love, and I am sick.

Much sicker than the simple act of judging my temperature can diagnose. Her eyebrows rise in alarm, and the small "o" her lips form tells me that my father will be summoned, and he, in all likelihood, will call for the doctor. No matter how much he doesn't care about me, no daughter of his will die in her bed for lack of a doctor. People might wonder if he didn't call for help because he couldn't afford it, and that would never do.

Irena bustles from the room, and I am left in blessed peace for a few minutes. I think about how much unlike my mother this woman is. And yet she fills a small hole in my heart, a tiny part of the huge chasm left by my mother's death. As I said, Irena bustles, whereas my mother never seemed hurried. Irena has the sharp twang of those born and raised in Twillingate, while my mother's cultivated tone soothed men, children, and savage beasts alike. Irena cooks well enough, in that we haven't starved to death in the past three years, but suffice to say our taste buds are never challenged. She's a fair to middling housekeeper, and she can sew on a button or raise a hem as well as anyone, but will never be the skilled seamstress my mother was.

When at first I worried that Father might marry her out of desperation to have a housekeeper for him and mother for me under the roof, I don't fear that event any longer. He keeps her on because she is useful and obedient, but she is not in his class, and no amount of trying on her part will make her so. And Father would never marry below his station. To do so could be detrimental to his standing in the community and to his reputation as a businessman.

A few minutes later, and my father's heavy tread on the stairs heralds his arrival. He pauses outside my door and knocks, a habit he adopted last year when I turned thirteen. He said that a young woman needs her privacy, and I was very glad to be afforded that privilege.

Today he is wearing his usual outfit of white shirt with sleeve protectors that run up to his elbows, grey pants, and his casual black boots. The hobnails click-clack on the floor as he comes to stand beside my bed. He perches on the edge as if afraid to touch me.

I smile up at him. While waiting for him, I'd thrown off the cover to cool off. Perhaps if he feels my forehead and sees I'm not hot, he'll think Irena overreacted and will dismiss me to spend the day in bed.

"Irena says you're under the weather."

I nod.

"Sore throat?"

We've gone through all this, Irena and I, but I nod again anyway.

I go one step further: I clear my throat softly, trying to dislodge the gob of whatever it is that is sitting on my vocal chords and prevents me from assuring my father that I am fine and just need to rest.

"Do you have a test today at school?"

Well, I hadn't thought of that one before. Imagine feigning sickness to avoid taking a test. I lick my dry lips and force out one word. "No."

His brow draws down, a sure indication of his displeasure. He nods and stands. "Good."

He turns to leave, and I am certain I've managed to convince him that I am well enough not to see the doctor, but not well enough to go to school today.

Nothing doing. "I'll call Doctor Antle. Perhaps he can check on you this morning."

I struggle to rise from the bed. "I'm f-f-fine. F-feel bet-better already."

Even to my own ears, my desperate attempt to belay the medico sounds feeble and barely intelligible.

Father pauses in the doorway and faces me. "You don't look fine, and perhaps whatever you have is contagious. Stop thinking about yourself and think of those around you."

With those stinging words of chastisement, he descends the stairs and returns to whatever he was doing, probably eating breakfast.

And I am left to await my fate.

My school chums had told me tales of Doctor Antle. An old man, his eyesight failing, who stuck with old-fashioned ideas about medicine, including the notion that if one needle did wonders, two would perform miracles. And he wasn't the least bit hesitant about shooting a person in the bum whether they were at home or in his office.

The doctor shows up about an hour later. He takes my temperature and checks my throat, hemming and hawing in the way doctors do. They must take a course on that skill in medical school. At any rate, he isn't happy with what he sees and makes his pronouncement as he tosses his tongue depressor into a trash basket beside my bed. I am glad to know he doesn't reuse those little wooden sticks. I shudder to think whose throat he'd last shoved it down and what germs the rough surface could hold.

"Tonsils."

And his one word diagnosis seals my fate.

I have a friend, Patty Malone, who had her tonsils out. She was in hospital for a week, and when she came out, she sounded like a boy. The surgeon had scraped her vocal chords by mistake, and the former soprano, who had aspirations toward a singing career, ended up an alto who couldn't reach past middle C to save her life.

And while I didn't want to sing for my supper, as it were, I had no desire to sound like I'd spent a hard weekend in a saloon or a speakeasy.

So I do the only thing I could. I shake my head.

He peers at me over his spectacles. "You doubt my diagnosis?"

I shrug.

He pushes his specs up the bridge of his nose. "Think maybe it's simply a cold or the influenza?"

I nod, my smile dazzling him, no doubt.

He shakes his head. "Not likely, but if you want to wait it out, see if you get better, that's fine with me. But I expect your father will call me in again in a couple of days, and he'll be none too happy paying my bill twice, I tell you."

He pats my shoulder. I hate when adults do that. Makes me feel like a cocker spaniel.

I wrestle with my choices. I can get over this tonsil thing on my own, Father won't have to take me to St. John's for surgery, and he'll be pleased he will save more than seventy-five cents if I don't really have tonsils. Or, I can agree with Doctor Antle, go to hospital, have an operation, and come out sounding like a strangled rooster.

But if I stick to my guns and Father ends up paying for two doctor visits, the old doc is correct: Father won't be pleased that my stubbornness cost him an additional seventy-five cents.

I tip my head in his direction, being careful not to make the room spin.

"You're wondering how certain I am?"

I nod and the room bounces in time. I grip the edge of the mattress.

"As sure as more than thirty years of practice can be."

I shrug.

Doctor Antle sighs, snaps his medical bag shut, and leaves the room. A couple of minutes later, Irena appears in the doorway.

"So, you've decided to take your chances, have you, miss?"

I nod.

"Your father won't be pleased."

There is no answer to this statement of fact. When Father calls for the doctor and pays good money for advice, he expects me to take that advice.

"I'll just go down to the shop and let him know. Maybe he'll take a moment at lunch to set you on the right track."

I lay down in bed, wanting to fall asleep and awaken all healed, but sleep will not come. Instead, I hear every sound Irena makes, from the closing of the front door as she heads to the shop, to her return. Then she sweeps the hallway downstairs, beats a few rugs in the back yard, and bustles about in the kitchen clearing up from breakfast and preparing the midday meal.

Every sound makes me jump, and rest is impossible. I start to imagine my father's anger, the doctor's smirk when I am forced to acquiesce, the terrifying journey to St. John's to the hospital, and awakening with the voice of a teenage boy.

I come to the conclusion that my mother was right: there is no rest for the wicked.

At noon, my father comes up the stairs, knocks, and sits on the bed with me. I force a smile, trying to show him how much better I'm feeling now that I've had some rest. He smiles at me. At least I think he's smiling. One side of his mouth turns up, at any rate.

"Now, now." He pats my hand beneath the cover. "Don't worry any more about this entire matter." He stands and stares out the window. "In fact, I think we should take the day tomorrow and do something together." He faces me. "How does that sound?"

How does that sound? Supposing I had both legs amputated, I would go with him. I nod.

"Good. That's settled. Tomorrow we'll go in town and visit Aunt Margaret and Uncle Reginald. Maybe we'll go to Sterlings' for lunch."

This was a grand idea, and I let him know how I feel. I launch myself from the bed and fling myself indecorously into his arms, hugging him so tight he expels a breath in a grunt. The effort tires me so much that I stagger back into bed and collapse upon the cover, but I will not let him see my exhaustion. I will not risk losing a day in St. John's, with my father.

A day anywhere with my father is something to be treasured.

The next day we climb aboard the train heading to St. John's and points in between. Father allows me to sit next to the window, and I enjoy the two-hour ride through the coastal communities of the Avalon Peninsula. I marvel at the changes in the towns since my last trip, the one Mother and I took the December before she died. Ever since I could remember, she and I rode the train into the city and did our Christmas shopping.

I haven't been on the train for over three years. I don't take my eyes off the scenes before me. Towns and villages spread out along the tracks.

Several new houses, a new train station in Avondale, and even a few automobiles trundle along the rutted roads. In this I agree with Father: the automobile will never catch on. Horses are much more useful, for plowing, pulling, and riding, and barns are more common than garages. Not to mention that gasoline is available in only a few select locations, whereas grass, hay, and grain are plentiful.

We arrive in the big city just before noon, and Father decides to stop at Sterling's then for lunch. I enter the store, and immediately I smell the food—sandwiches, coffee, fried potatoes, cabbage, and salt fish. We sit at one of the horseshoe-shaped counters, and Father hands me a menu, as if I am an adult.

I scan the items offered, selecting the special of the day: chicken salad sandwich, chips, and a glass of milk. My father chooses a ham sandwich and a cup of coffee. I feel so mature as I sit on the stool, resisting the urge to spin around as a small boy at the next station is doing. I am glad I am feeling well enough to take this trip, although I'm not certain I will be able to eat much. I haven't eaten at all for two days. My throat is still so raw I hesitate to swallow. But I will not let my father know that.

The waitress sets our plates before us, and I groan with pleasure at the presentation of the food. The sandwich looks big enough for two, and indeed, the last time I was here with my mother, we shared this exact same dish. I force a bite into my mouth.

Chewing is relatively painless, but once I try to swallow, my throat protests. Taking small sips of milk, I wash down the food a little at a time, trying not to show my discomfort. At one point, I catch my father watching me from the corner of his eye. I pop a chip into my mouth and smile.

"Enjoying your lunch, maid?"

I nod, my mouth still full of food, relishing the sound of the endearment. He offers affection so seldom I savour each morsel, whether it comes in the form of words, a touch, or, infrequently, a gift, such as this day with him.

Eating our lunch takes nearly an hour, and I am unable to finish my meal. A moment of disapproval flashes across his face as he clenches his jaw and works his mouth as if to speak, but he remains silent. We choose to have the waitress wrap the remaining food in waxed paper, and my father tucks the packet into his coat pocket.

We browse the aisles of the Arcade Store and ride the inclined stairway to the second floor. I don't stop to view any of the goods on this floor, but turn and immediately ride the stairway back to the first floor. My father follows, a bemused smile on his mouth, then waits for me at the bottom while I repeat my ride several more times.

As we leave the store, the cool March breeze catches the brim of Father's hat, and he drops my hand to keep his bowler firmly planted. I keep walking, and a moment later, he catches up with me. He pulls his watch from his pocket.

"Where are we going next, Poppa?"

I detect an irritation at my question, so I don't pester him further. We walk a block or so further before he finds what he is looking for: a streetcar. I am so excited. Of course, I've ridden in a streetcar before. Once. The leather seat is smooth and cool to the touch, and itchy woolen blankets are available to put over our knees. Father slides in beside me and leans forward to speak to the driver, letting him know where we want to get off.

I settle back in the seat and look out the window at the people and buildings below us. I feel so high up and special. Won't Ivy be jealous when I get home and tell her about my adventures today. I bet she's never ridden in a streetcar. As we turn a corner, several boys jump back out of the street to avoid being run over, and I wave at them, pretending I'm a princess in my royal carriage, feeling sorry for all the poor people who must walk. We go west along Water Street, then turn north on Springdale Street. This part of the city is familiar to me, as I have traveled with my mother to visit Poppa's brother and wife several times. However, instead of veering to the right to go to Pennywell Road, we turn left on Lemarchant Road.

I am confused, and I turn to my father. Surely we've gotten on the wrong streetcar. But my father is deaf to my questions and my tugging on his sleeve, and he stares resolutely out the window, not meeting my gaze.

The food in my stomach roils as I consider what lies in the direction we are heading. The only businesses I can think of are Newfoundland Margarine Company, Brookfield Ice Cream, and the Salvation Army Grace Maternity Hospital.

And I am fairly certain we are not going in search of margarine or ice cream.

Sure enough, the streetcar pulls up in front of the hospital. Did my father notice my discomfort when eating? He wasn't fooled that my throat was better.

I tug on his sleeve and whisper, my voice hoarse from whatever infection rages through me. "Poppa, I'm sorry for not eating my lunch. I can eat now. I'll eat every bite, I promise."

He continues to ignore me, then he alights but I remain frozen in my seat. I will not get out! I will not! He can't make me! At least, that's what my voice screams to me, even as my mind tells me I must do what he says. What choice do I have?

He stands on the sidewalk and reaches for my hand to assist me down. My knees shake as I stand there, and another gust of wind comes around the corner, threatening to blow me away. I wish it would. Perhaps then I would float off to a better place.

Father continues to hold my hand. Perhaps he is afraid I will bolt like a frightened kitten, and he will be forced to chase me down, making a scene or drawing attention, an anathema to him and to all in our class. At least, according to him. We walk in through the hospital doors.

The smells of disinfectant, cleaner, and something else faintly like a dirty mop assails me. I feel much as I did the night the airship landed, as if perhaps the world is about to end, and only my Poppa can thwart the plans of the enemy. For surely, the enemy, whoever he is, must be behind this dastardly plan of deception.

My father walks down a long hallway, and for an instant I wonder if this is the same way he walked with my mother on the day she came to the hospital. I square my shoulders and try to match him step for step, as I'm certain my mother would have done. We stop outside a door marked "Admissions", and a woman in a uniform greets us.

"Good afternoon, Mr. Cameron. We've been expecting you." She glances at me then gestures to her office. "Come in, and we'll get everything straightened out."

She's been expecting me? Then we weren't here because I didn't eat my lunch. He'd made plans to bring me here. All along he knew that his promise of a day together in the city was a ruse to get me to come along with him.

I will never trust him again.

Chapter 6

The woman, Nurse Adams according to her nametag, completes the forms and slides them across the desk for my father to sign. He scribbles his name in several places then returns the papers to her. All the while this is going on, I stand in the corner, glowering at the pair of them as they discuss arrangements for my stay.

When they are done, my father stands and crosses the room to where I hunch then bends to meet my eyes.

"Laura, be a brave girl and do what Nurse Adams tells you. I will come back for you. If you do as they say, you should come home in a week."

I can't believe what he's saying. I've never been away from home for more than a day or two, and even then, I was always with my parents. "You-you're leaving me?" I glance around the room. "Here? With her?"

He straightens. "Nurse Adams, and, indeed, all the staff here, are most experienced. You will do exactly what they tell you." He bends low again. "Or you will answer to me. Do you understand?"

I nod, unable to form any other response. He straightens again, nods to the nurse, and exits the room. I sidle toward the doorway so I can see him for as long as possible. He exits the door then takes a right and is gone from my sight.

Nurse Adams touches my shoulder, and I shrug off the touch. She gestures down the hallway in the opposite direction my father took.

"The elevators are over here. You're going to the fifth floor. Won't that be exciting to ride in an elevator?"

I turn my most stern look on her. What does she think I am, a bayman who has never seen an elevator or a multi-storey building? She returns the look, and I can read her mind: Behave yourself or you'll answer to *me*, first, then your father. I don't doubt her unspoken warning.

She escorts me to the elevator, and we ride in silence to the fifth floor. She checks in at the nurse's station, and I hang back, hoping she might forget I'm there. But she doesn't, and soon I am ensconced in the bed nearest the window of an eight-bed ward. The other patients in the room range from a girl of about nine to an old woman, older even than Grandmother Abbott. And that's old.

Nurse Adams waits while I undress and change into a nightshirt she provides, then issues several instructions.

"The bathroom is over there. You can't leave the room. You can't have anything else to eat or drink tonight, because you're going into surgery first thing in the morning."

Surgery? I thought I was here to get some medicine so I could get well. Tears blur my vision, and I bite my lower lip to keep from crying.

Her stern expression softens. "You didn't know you were having your tonsils taken out?"

I shake my head.

"Shall I stay with you until you fall asleep?"

"Y-yes."

I climb into bed, and she pulls the heavy sheets over me.

"Are you scared?"

I nod.

"Why?"

"My m-mother died here three ye-years ago."

Now it's Nurse Adams' turn to cry, and she turns her head and sniffles into a hanky she pulls from a pocket. I wait until she regains control, because I'm afraid that we both might lose our heads.

When she turns to me again, she smiles. "This surgery is quite simple, and once you are well, you won't get a sore throat again. Won't that be grand?"

I nod, because in truth, I had been having more sore throats lately, each one worse than the previous. Then again, can I trust what she is saying? "Will it hurt?"

"The surgery? No. You'll be asleep. When you wake up, your throat will feel a little sore, but we'll give you ice cream, and flavored gelatin, and crushed ice, and in a day or two, you'll be all better. You should be able to go home in about five to seven days."

To be honest, all I hear is ice cream, gelatin, and crushed ice. I'd only had homemade ice cream before, made in the hand-cranked ice cream maker on a hot summer's day. Gelatin was reserved for crushed pineapple or shredded carrot salads served at church cold plate dinners, and crushed ice was unheard of.

Later I wished I'd listened more carefully, because when I wake up near noon the next day, I'm certain they've left a hot coal in my throat. I can't talk or swallow, not even the ice cream or ice chips they tempt me with. I toss and turn in a fever for the next three days before I'm able to sit up in bed.

When I first try to eat the promised ice cream, the taste is heavenly, and I almost moan in pleasure. But as soon as I swallow, it comes back up again. I cannot decide which is more painful: the swallowing or the retching.

The next day, Aunt Helen and Uncle William visit, but I barely remember them being there. They leave a small posy of daisies and a note saying they'll come back in a few days. Nurse Adams comes to visit a few days later, telling me my father called to inquire after my progress, and she assures him I'm following all the doctor's orders and am doing well.

Doing well? I feel as if all my sins have caught up with me and I am in hell. I am sore from my head to my toes, I still can't keep anything down, and, obeying the doctor, I haven't tried to talk yet. Something about straining the vocal chords. All I can think is they don't want me to know I sound like a boy.

Somewhere along the line, I contract an infection which sets me back two weeks as the doctors struggle to find the cause and the medicine to cure me. Everything they give me makes me sicker, and I cannot eat. Even drinking is a chore, and I lose weight. The nightgown hangs on me like an oversized suit on a scarecrow, and my hair is matted to my head, the result of alternating chills and sweats.

After three weeks, I open my eyes and am finally able to focus on the woman across the way from me. She is cooing over a small baby wrapped in a pink blanket, and for a moment I am jealous: she just went through labour, while I went through tonsil surgery and infection. I nod in her direction and scoot up in the bed.

Somewhere down the hallway I hear a rattle of dishes, and a woman appears in the door with a tray of food which she sets before the new mother. Next she places a tray of food at the other six beds in the room, then turns to leave.

I call to her, surprised my voice even works. "What about me?"

She shakes her head. "Nothing for you today, Miss Cameron. Maybe tomorrow."

Maybe tomorrow? I've been here for three weeks with little to nothing passing my lips, and she wants me to wait until tomorrow? I call to her again, using my most commanding voice, learned from my mother. "No, today. I'm hungry."

A familiar face appears in the doorway. Nurse Adams. "Not causing an upset are you, Miss Cameron?"

"No. I am hungry and I want something to eat."

She smiles. "Wonderful, We'll see to that immediately."

Having friends in high places always helps.

Chapter 7

I had seen some great changes in my father after my mother died. He has taken to spending less time with me and more time in the shop or in his study. Irena stays on, more out of pity for me, I suspect, than because of her desire to spend her best years as housemaid and nanny to a teenager. Because my father is not around much, he doesn't require her to be ship-shape in her housekeeping duties, and he seems most relieved that she is there to supervise me.

Not being much older than my fourteen years, she doesn't discipline me much. In fact, a great deal of our time is spent covering for each other. She takes many afternoons off, when in fact Wednesday after lunch through to tea time is her official leave day. I know she is stepping out with the butcher's assistant, and likely has high hopes they would marry and she would rise a half-notch on the social ladder of Carbonear. Unbeknownst to her, he is also stepping out with the postmaster's assistant, likely with the same goal of marrying above himself in mind.

During my growing-up years, the British influence is still very strong, particularly in our town. In other areas of Newfoundland the Irish, Scottish, or French comprise a larger percentage of the population, and so those towns and villages tend to adopt the attitudes and habits of those cultures. But in Carbonear, although we deny there is a class system, we understand that beneath the surface niceties, some people are simply better than others, and for no other reason than who "their people" were.

In fact, entire communities are considered better than others, and Carbonear is one of the best. Our town was the first permanent settlement in the area, and unlike most of the other towns, families settled here, started businesses, and flourished. I suppose Harbour Grace runs a close second. Bay Roberts is more Irish, and therefore more Catholic, so definitely not of our class. Further away, Brigus and Cupids are smaller communities that we like to pass through, or attend their garden party, but we would never choose to live there.

And then there is Heart's Content. A small town across the barrens from Carbonear that is populated by fishermen and shipbuilders. Few businessmen, fewer shops, and mostly men, at least in the early years. Nowadays, I wonder why anybody chooses to live there. Unlike the quaint name, the town itself is not quaint, looking for all the world as if it wants to fall down around itself.

Why, then, is Father, all of a sudden, taking Sunday afternoons to drive over to Heart's Content as soon as the last mouthful of food from his dinner is down? I asked Irena last week, and she clamped her lips together and shook her head, indicating she isn't going to tell me.

So at Sunday dinner today, I venture to ask my father. "Poppa, can we go for a drive after dinner?"

He shakes his head and concentrates on cutting his roast beef, his nose pinched at the bloody offering on his plate. Despite the fact that Irena knows he likes his meat well-done, and I like mine rare, she has managed to reverse our servings. I try to wash my too-much-done meat down with water, while Father pushes his to one side of the plate and shovels some potato and carrots into his mouth.

"Why not, Poppa? We haven't gone for a drive in months."

Journeys in the car were reserved for emergency trips to the doctor or jaunts on Sundays after church and dinner. Other than those two purposes, Father used the horse and wagon or the horse and buggy, preferring to keep the automobile for "special".

"I am going elsewhere and you cannot come along."

"Elsewhere? And why can't I go?"

He sets his fork and knife on his plate and stands. "Because I said so. Now stay here and help Irena, and behave yourself."

With that, he strides from the dining room, and a moment later I hear the front door shut. I cannot believe he won't tell me where he's going.

I turn to Irena, who is hovering in the doorway. "Do you know where he's going?"

"He didn't tell me."

I detect she is avoiding answering my question. "But you know. Where?"

"If he wants you to know, he will tell you himself."

I pull out the big guns. "If you don't tell me, I'll tell him where you go in the afternoons when you're being paid to be here."

Her face drains of colour and she wrings her hands together. "Please don't tell him. I'll lose my position."

"Well?"

"He's going to Heart's Content."

"Heart's Content? Whatever is he going there for?"

"I can't say, miss."

I adopt a growl in my voice that my mother used when she wanted me to know she was serious. "Irena."

"I believe he is courting a woman, miss."

Courting a woman? That always leads to marriage. He doesn't need a wife. He has me and Irena. We do everything around the house a wife would do. He can't possibly think that marriage will improve his position in the community. Widowers are held in high regard. Widowers with children are saints. And a widower with a teenage daughter has wings and a halo already.

"Why does he need to court a woman?"

Irena smiles, one of those knowing smiles I've always hated, implying she knows something that I couldn't possibly understand.

I cross the room and grab her by the shoulders. "Tell me!"

Her smile flees, and for a moment I think she may faint. But she regains her composure and steps beyond my grip. "He doesn't discuss his personal life with me, miss, but I believe he might be lonely."

Lonely? I hadn't considered that perhaps Poppa might want companionship. He doesn't spend much time with me or Irena, but that is his own choice. He works every weekday in the shop with townspeople coming and going all day. Sundays are spent in church in the morning then dinner with me. Sunday afternoons we often had someone come to visit. He went to St. John's on a regular basis to visit his brothers and their families. How could he be lonely?

Then I thought back to shortly after my mother died, how alone I felt at the time. My one confidante was gone, and none of my friends, who still had their mothers, knew how I suffered. My father was morose and distant, and every time I looked at Irena's somber face, I wanted to cry.

Somehow I hadn't understood that perhaps my father suffered many of the same feelings of abandonment, anger, and emptiness that I had felt, and to some degree, still did.

"Well, I don't want him to marry."

She pushes past me to clear the dining room table of the remains of dinner. "I don't think you have much say in the matter, miss."

Well, then, if he doesn't confide in me about his business, I guess what is sauce for the goose will be sauce for the gander. He can live his own life, and I'll live mine. I have nothing to say about his getting married again, so he will have no say in my affairs.

He's going to be gone until tea, and Irena will likely shuttle away as soon as the dishes are done, so I make plans to spend time with friends of my own. This chasm between my father and me has widened over the years, but never so much or so quickly as on that Sunday afternoon in October of 1927.

While he was off to Heart's Content to court this unknown woman, I slip out the back door and head for my best friend's house. Beulah Clarke lives about six doors down Water Street, in a ramshackle house that has seen better days. My father isn't keen on our friendship, but if I have no say in his life, well—

Beulah's father is a fisherman on an ocean-going boat that goes to the Grand Banks for months at a time, leaving her mother and Beulah and her six brothers to fend for themselves. He is out at sea now, due back in a couple of weeks.

Beulah is always game for fun. Her mother is sickly and depends on Beulah to fix meals and keep house, and her brothers are useless for things around the house. So when I show up at her door, she calls to her mother that she's going out for a walk, grabs her sweater and a kerchief for her hair, and we race down the garden path before someone calls her back.

We stroll down Water Street, chatting about events at school the previous week, until we exhaust the topic. The wind comes up, and Beulah tucks stray strands of reddish-blonde hair beneath her kerchief. I hadn't stopped to pick up a hat, so my hair blows into my eyes, and I tuck the length down inside my sweater.

We wander down around Crocker's Cove beach and sit on the edge of a dory pulled up on the rocks. Overhead, the seagulls swoop and soar, squawking and complaining about whatever it is they talk to each other about. The tide is out, but the wind has the water dancing with whitecaps, and a saying of my mother's comes to mind: I'm glad I'm not out in an open boat today.

A couple of local boys stroll along the beach toward us, and when they catch sight of us, they angle away from the water in a beeline for where we are sitting. Beulah nudges me in the ribs, and I shush her, trying to appear nonchalant and disinterested. Every girl knows that a boy isn't interested in a girl who chases them. Even I know that, despite the fact my main contact with boys up to this point has been playing Post Office at a party.

As the boys near, I recognize them as Ted Philpott and Norman White. Both are a year ahead of us in school. Ted is the taller of the two, but he has red hair and freckles—distinctly Irish. Norman is round and soft where Ted is angular and sinewy, but Norman has brown hair and brown eyes—much more British in heritage.

I glance at Beulah. Her lips are slightly open, and her nostrils flare as the two approach. I think how silly she looks, but I wonder where she learned that expression. All of a sudden, she seems much more experienced and I feel like a child in her presence.

Ted and Norman pause about ten feet away, and Norman nudges a rock with the toe of his boot. Their hands are shoved in their pockets, and they don't look at us directly, but they mutter under their breath. Ted laughs at something Norman says, then slies a glance at Beulah. The boys nod to each other, then close the distance to where we sit.

Rather than have them tower over me, I stand, and Beulah follows. Ted leans over and whispers something in her ear. She nods then links her arm through his, and they head toward a small shack about fifty feet away. There is no door on the shack, and I know there isn't much in there to see. I'd been in there a year or so ago looking for a pail to catch capelin, and the shack was empty of everything except some trash and a musty old blanket in a corner. For the life of me, I couldn't figure why a blanket would be in this place, but I was too embarrassed to ask Beulah at the time.

Norman is staring at me when I pull my gaze from Beulah and Ted. "Do you want to wait for the shack?"

I don't know what he's talking about, but I don't want to let him know. "No."

He smiles. Well, actually, the expression is more of a leer. He extends his hand to me, and I allow him to wrap his meaty fisherman's-son's hand around mine. I don't have any idea where we're going or what Beulah and Ted are up to, but I follow because I don't want to be left alone.

Norman leads me to a pile of lobster pots that looks like a haphazard stack, but in actuality are assembled to provide the maximum shelter and minimum visibility. We snake in around the pots to a small area just big enough for six or eight people to stand. Here, too, is an old blanket, although this one is definitely the worse for wear since it is more out in the elements.

He sits and gestures for me to follow, which I do. There isn't much else to do in here beside sit. He continues to hold my hand, then pulls me closer and hangs his arm over my shoulder. I am starved for physical attention, and I nestle my face against his side. He plays with my hair, then slips my sweater from my shoulder. I am chilled and I rub my arms, so he pulls me closer and closer then presses me down on my back.

I don't resist, because I see now what his goal is: he wants to kiss me. And I want to kiss him. He closes his eyes and leans closer, and I close my eyes. This is the first time I've been kissed by a boy when I haven't been in a closet at a party. There is something delicious about the risk of discovery, kissing a boy in a shelter of lobster pots on a beach in broad daylight, and I press in harder.

When his tongue touches my closed lips, I don't resist him. His hands roam over my body, igniting feelings I've never felt before, never even heard about, never dreamt could happen. My father has been remiss in educating me of the things that happen between men and women, so the only details I know are from observing horses and dogs, or from whispered rumors amongst my girlfriends.

I don't know why, but I want what he wants, and I let him have his way. There is much pleasure and some pain involved, and when it's done, I don't know what to say or do. I pull my bloomers on and adjust my dress down over my knees, and he fastens the front of his britches. Then we lay on our backs and stare at the sky, as I try to figure out what just happened and what we're supposed to do next.

He turns on his side and runs a finger down my cheek. "I've always liked you, Laura."

I haven't always liked him. In fact, I hardly knew he existed, but I play along. "I like you, too, Norman."

"Perhaps we can do this again?"

I don't want to play too interested in him, despite the intimate act we've just completed. "Perhaps."

Beulah calls to me, and we stand and exit our temporary shelter. She runs across the beach and flings herself into my arms. I think how close I feel to her as we share this secret about our actions of the past minutes. What stories we can share. I want to know every detail of her time in the shack, comparing her experience with mine. What a joy to have a friend to share this most important moment with.

Tears streak her face, and her hair looks like she hasn't brushed it since last week. A small tear in the neckline of her dress allows a peak at the white skin beneath. She glances back at Ted as he stalks toward us, and turns to me, her eyes wide with fear.

"Let's get out of here, Laura."

I nod.

Norman runs to Ted, and the two hold a heated conversation. Norman makes a gesture where he holds a forefinger horizontal and makes a circle with the forefinger and thumb of the other hand, then slides the circle over the straight finger.

The Physics of Love

I get a sinking feeling in my stomach as I realize what he is telling Ted. Ted laughs, claps him on the back, and the two saunter away, laughing. Beulah stares at them, horror written all over her face, then turns to me.

"Is he telling the truth?"

I don't want to answer until I know what happened between her and Ted. "What happened? Why are you crying?"

"He tried to have his carnal way with me, and when I resisted, he tried to force his way on me."

Carnal? Force? "So you didn't allow him?"

She gasps and steps away from me. "No! Did you allow Norman to—to—you know."

It is only Norman's word against mine. I can protect my virtue, if that's the thing to do. "Of course not. He's so common. I have no interest in him. We just sat and talked."

We commiserate as we walk back up Water Street toward our homes. Beulah stops at the water tank to wash her face and straighten her hair, and she covers the tear in her dress with her sweater.

"I'll stitch that up in my room later. I'll keep my sweater on for now. Nobody will know the difference."

Nobody will know. Except I know that I have crossed a line, one that I know my father would not approve, and I fear there is no going back. I suspect the boys will believe Norman, and the girls will side with me. At least, I hope the girls will.

As for my father, I now have a better understanding of what loneliness means for an adult. Because I have been thrust into the adult world by this one base act. And for an instant, I wish my time back. I would have made a different decision.

But time does not reverse, and decisions once made change everything from then on.

After my experience on the beach with Norman, my friendship with

Beulah seems to cool. I cannot look her in the eye because I'm certain she will know the truth. Instead, I spend more time with the popular girls from school, the ones who sneak out at night, who don't go to classes, the ones that the boys seek out.

And I've had many boys seeking me. Even though I've managed to avoid Norman and Ted, the others are drawn to me like flies to honey. At first I try to convince myself that it's because I am blossoming into a beautiful woman, but deep down I know it's because I give them something many of the less popular girls won't.

Chapter 8

When my father tells me at dinner one evening in November that he needs to talk to me about something serious, I am certain he's found out about me. I draw a deep breath and nod, resigned to the lecture I am sure to get about sin and the dangers of fornication with different boys, not to mention how huge a disappointment I am to him, and how my behaviour endangers his standing in the community.

In truth, I've been expecting this moment ever since the night on the beach nearly a month ago. I fold my hands in my lap so he won't see how much they shake, and I press my shoulder blades against the wooden back of the dining room chair. I've never found these chairs comfortable, even though my mother adored the decorative curlicue work. I sometimes imagine taking a plane to them and shaving down the rises and making the back more level.

He waits until Irena has the plates in her hands. "Thank you, Irena, we won't need you any more tonight."

I glance around at the remaining dishes on the table and sigh. This is really important if he's willing to leave the clearing away until the morning. Perhaps I'll be sent to a boarding school. Or a reform school. I've heard that's where they send incorrigibles, and I suppose I'm as incorrigible as anyone.

And so I wait.

He clears his throat, and without once glancing in my direction, says what he came to say, "I have decided to get married. In St. John's. Next Wednesday, on the twenty-third. Since that's a school night, you won't be attending. Your stepmother and I will return that evening, and we will start our lives as a family immediately."

Married? I knew he was courting, of course. And that I would have no say in the decision, as Irena said. But never in my wildest dreams had I thought I would first meet her after the wedding. Unless, of course, I already knew her.

"Poppa, who will you marry?" Oh please, God, let it be John Barnes's daughter, a comely woman much sought after, with plenty of class and a good education. Or Tom Parsons's niece, the one whose parents died and he was her guardian. She has a lovely singing voice and makes wonderful fudge for the garden parties.

"Miss Annie Foote."

Surely I'd heard wrong. Why, she wasn't lovely or educated, at least not in my opinion. I'd met her a couple of times at the shop, her and her dotty cousins, giggling behind the bolts of material. She could sew, that was for sure, and judging by the amount of wool and yarn she purchased, she could knit as well.

But she definitely wasn't marriage quality. Not for my father. What did he see in her?

As if reading my mind, he leaned across the table. "Now, look here, child. I know this is a shock. But Annie is a good woman. She has a soft spot in her heart for you, and she will look after us very well. She isn't a businesswoman, but we can hire that task out. As for keeping house, cooking, sewing, all the things we need a woman about the house for, she is first class."

I want to scream that he isn't to use Annie Foote and first class in the same sentence. She is not of our class. He is marrying beneath himself, and he knows it. I can tell by the look on his face, the fact he hasn't once looked me in the eye. I must let him know how I feel, and I force the words past the lump in my throat, "Why, Poppa? Don't Irena and I take care of you and the house? I'll stay home after school every day so you don't have to get married."

He slaps the table. "Laura, you are old enough not to blubber so. A wife isn't merely a servant. She is also a companion, a confidante, and a helpmate to me. You are at an age where you need a woman's touch if you are to take your position in life. I fear for you, child. You are running wild, and I can do nothing to stop you. You are too old to spank, and I am at a loss as to how to control you." He stands. "Have no fear. Nothing will change between us, child."

Well, that was something to look forward to. More of the same as we'd had for the past six years. Perhaps his getting married would be for the better. If I was going to be alone, I might as well be alone amongst three as amongst two.

"I feel there is nothing for it but for me to marry. I must think of you, child."

So now it's my fault he's getting married? "Poppa, I'll behave myself. I'll listen to you. I promise. Please, Poppa, don't bring that woman into this house."

He shakes his head. "My decision is made, and my troth is pledged. You must make the best of it."

Make the best of it? I've been making the best of it ever since my mother died. I've learned to live without affection of any kind. I've taken a step of seeking out some form of love, only to find myself trapped in a revolving door of boys wanting the only thing I can give them that belongs to me—my body. I've learned to lie and deceive to explain my whereabouts, and I've turned my back on the only true friend I ever had. Beulah hasn't spoken to me for several weeks, ever since I snubbed her at school. And while I try to convince myself I don't need her friendship, I know I am lying again, except this time to myself.

I drag myself up the stairs to my room and collapse on my bed. The tears flow freely as I consider the predicament I find myself in. I have lost my father and gained a stepmother I don't need and don't want. I have lost my self-respect and gained a sordid succession of relationships in the shack, in the lobster pot enclosure, and even in the back of Joe Miller's father's barn.

I don't see how my life could possibly get any worse.

But it does.

The next week my father brings home his new bride. I come down the stairs the morning of the twenty-fourth and find Irena bringing breakfast dishes into the dining room and setting them on the sideboard.

"Why are we eating in here? We always eat breakfast in the kitchen."

"Your father specifically instructed me to serve in here from now on. All meals."

"I hope he isn't trying to impress her. A roof over her head and three meals a day will do that."

"What's that you are mumbling under your breath, child?"

I turn at my father's voice, heat rising to my cheeks at being overhead uttering an uncharitable remark. Gossip and meanness are two traits my father abhors.

"I was just telling Irena how blessed we are to have a roof over our heads and three meals a day, Poppa."

Irena's eyes narrow at my glib lie, but she keeps herself to herself and returns to the kitchen.

"Indeed." He turns and ushers a woman who is shorter than my five foot three but heavier than my ninety-five pounds into the room. "Laura, this is your stepmother. Annie, what would you prefer Laura call you?"

The woman stares at me a long moment then lays a hand on his arm. "Why don't you ask her what she'd prefer to call me?"

If she is trying to buy her way into my good graces, the price will be higher than that, let me tell you. However, she does move one notch higher in my opinion. How do I answer her to deflect the question? Her blue eyes bore into me, pulling an answer from deep within like a hook on a drag line.

There is no way out of this. "Can we start with Aunt Annie?"

She drops her gaze and her mouth turns down in disapproval.

I look to my father for his assent, but he has eyes only for her. I am losing him but am powerless to take back the words or change their impact.

Instead of answering, my father escorts her to the end of the table, and he takes his seat at the opposite end. I sit at my usual space to his right, and we eat our breakfast without conversation. The only words spoken relate to requests for a particular dish.

When Irena returns for the empty plates, my father rouses from his stupor. "Laura, you may be excused."

I don't want to be excused. I want another sausage and a piece of toast, but his tone brooks no argument. I mumble to nobody in particular, "Excuse me."

Then I stand and leave the room, but I halt outside the door and listen. Already they are in conversation about the coming day, about how she would like to talk to Irena to arrange taking over most of the household duties, about the times my father will work in the shop, about the grocery budget, and the housing budget, and her allowance, and all the myriad important things a husband and wife discuss over breakfast.

The only thing they don't mention is me.

Which should have been a clue to me about not only my relationship with my step-mother, but my new relationship with my father. Because as much as he might want to argue, and as much as I might wish to believe, his marriage did change things.

Chapter 9

The year after my father remarried, I am sent into the Capital to do my final year of high school. I don't know for certain, but I think there were several reasons for this decision. I have no part in the discussion, but I hear Aunt Annie and my father talking late into the night for several months.

So when they come to me in June of 1928 and tell me what is going to happen, I'm not surprised they have made a decision, although I am surprised at what the decision is.

I will spend a year in St. John's, living with Uncle William. Not a suggestion. A command. Much like the rest of my relationship with my father, I was given no choice in the matter.

At least, that's what they think.

Truth is, I will make many choices in the coming year. Not all of them good. In fact, I suspect that when I look back on my life in my later years, I will wish I had done some things differently. But right now, I didn't care. I determine to be young and carefree, experiencing a first moving away from my home and family, stretching my wings to grow.

Instead, I continue the headlong race from my father, from my mother's death, and from the life I find myself in.

I arrive in the Capital a week before school begins. My father and Aunt Annie drive me into town, and drop me at Uncle William's house, and they extract a promise from me that I will return to Carbonear every weekend and holiday. Knowing how the roads are in winter, they understand I may not come home as often as they anticipate. Arrangements have also been made with another of my father's brothers, Uncle Reginald, that I can stay there on the weekends if I don't get back home.

Truth is, I already plan to stay in St. John's as much as possible.

By the time school starts the following Monday, I am sick to death of where I'm living. The kids drive me crazy, crawling all over everything, and I can't seem to find a private space to call my own. As bad as I thought life was in Carbonear, this is worse.

Uncle William is ill again and not working, so his wife, Aunt Helen, is taking in laundry and ironing to make ends meet "until he gets back on his feet". I share a room with their oldest daughter, and she has no concept of what that means. She barges in without pausing, and a closed door means nothing to her. I promise myself I will never share my bedroom again—except with a husband.

But for now, I am the new one in the neighborhood. The family treats me as if I don't belong here, which is fine with me, because I don't. The only good thing is that Uncle William's wife is so busy with working, the children, and keeping the house, that she pays no attention to me. And Uncle William is ill enough that he thinks only of himself. Not that I blame him. I suspect it's part of his survival mechanism.

Because in many ways, I am like Uncle William. We have a gypsy's heart, a wanderlust that makes us want to visit other places and meet other people. Because he is married and has children, I think Uncle William survives by changing jobs as often as he can. Otherwise, he would go mad.

Perhaps that gypsy nature explains why I struggle to find peace in any one place or any one relationship for too long. I feel I am constantly seeking whatever is around the next corner, on the next street, in the next stranger I meet. I have never been intimidated by people I don't know, and I am always looking forward to the next adventure.

At any rate, the overall lack of supervision in the household is to my benefit. Uncle Reginald is much more strict, more like my father. There is no way I will stay there on the weekends, not when I can have full run of the house at Uncle William's.

So school starts, and everybody in my class knows everybody else. Except for two other girls and myself, these kids have been together since kindergarten. And it shows. On the second day, at recess and lunch, the three of us new girls sit by ourselves while the others take turns staring and whispering and giggling together.

Except we don't really sit together in the sense that we talk with each other. Instead, we sit at a table, close enough to touch, but not meeting each other's gaze, not talking to each other.

The second day isn't much better, except by now I've managed to suss out the relationships between the other kids in the class. I see which ones are teacher's pet, which ones are going steady, and which ones are hanging onto the outside fringe. One of the girls is dating a boy on a local hockey team, which gives her an edge up on the other girls.

I want to be her.

Or rather, I want her hockey player.

So every time the boy shows up to meet his girl, I make certain to walk past, flicking the tail of my skirt to show some knee, tossing him a smile, running my tongue over my lips. I've seen the way the women in the movies catch their man, and I am a good student. I've even tried to flare my nose like Beulah does, something she picked up in a movie magazine, no doubt.

Within a week, he nods slowly in my direction and casts his eyes to the parking lot. I know what he's saying. "Meet me near the cars." I give a tiny nod and saunter off in the direction of the teacher's lot.

He's older than me by about two years, and he's one of the most desirable boys I've seen. When he comes to meet me, we walk side by side, innocently enough, as if we'd just met by accident. Once we're off school property, he grabs my hand and we run down the street, along a path through the park, and collapse on a bench hidden behind some lilac bushes.

He tells me his name, but I really don't care about the formalities. My goal is to steal this boy from the girl in my class, and I set out to use my best assets and superior social skills to do just that.

In truth, my best assets lie in the fact that I know what this boy wants, and I know Anna is not giving it to him. Before we've sat there five minutes, I already know he's in his second year at Memorial College, studying accounting. I almost yawn. He wants to go into business with his father, who runs a wholesale company.

And before we've been there ten minutes, he has one hand on my knee beneath my skirt and the other is draped over my shoulder on its way to groping my breast. He is so obvious he is tiresome. I've been there before, with boys who knew a lot more than he'll ever know.

I shift over on the bench closer to him, and lean in, my eyes closed and lips slightly open. As our lips touch, I open my eyes and catch the look of surprise—raised eyebrows, widening irises. But he presses in, his tongue probing mine.

He's mine.

We spend about an hour there, ending up on the ground behind the bench, his scratchy woolen sweater beneath my head. Later, as he zips his pants and I straighten my skirt and blouse, he grins at me like a kid with a new puppy, and I wonder if this was his first tumble with a girl. Oh well, everybody has to have a first time, and he's lucky his was with me. I know what I'm doing by now.

We make plans to meet again the next day, same time, same place, and we part ways. As I walk past the school, I check around to see if his girl is still at the school. She isn't. Too bad. I would have liked to give her *the look* to let her know my secret. Thinking about my liaison that afternoon is the only thing that keeps me sane at Uncle William's that night. Supper is sparse because money is scarce. The first of the month means most of the money goes to pay the rent, and there isn't much left over until the end of the week. Beans and bread fill a stomach but don't offer much joy in the eating.

My clandestine affair goes on for several weeks. Then suddenly, my boy-now-a-man doesn't come by to see his girl. Or me. I hang around school until suppertime, and when he doesn't show up, I go to Uncle William's, consoling myself that he won't be able to stay away. Maybe he was sick today. Or had something else he had to do. He'll be back.

But he doesn't come the next day or the next.

Then I sense a change in the other kids in the class. Although they had never opened up and befriended me, at least they spoke to me occasionally. Now they ignore me again. Pointedly. Whenever I approach, they stop talking and turn away from me. And my hockey player's girl avoids me completely. She changes seats in class so she is sitting as far from me as possible.

I know the signs. She's figured out what her boy has been doing after school.

So I do what I've always done in this situation. I march up to her, holding my books close to my chest and ask her if her boyfriend is feeling okay because I haven't seen him in a few days.

She lifts one eyebrow as her mouth pinches. "And you won't be seeing him again."

I return her frown, pretending concern. "Did you break up? He wasn't good enough for you, you know."

"Really? But he was good enough for you?"

She'd walked right into that one. I shake my head. "No, he wasn't, really. But desperate times calls for desperate measures. Sometimes you just have to take what you can get."

Tears fill her eyes. "We were going to be married when I graduated."

Silly girl. "No, you weren't. You would tire of him long before that."

"Tire of him?"

"Yes. He wasn't very bright, and he would never make much of himself."

She wheels around and practically runs from me. Of course, what I already knew about him was that the likelihood of them ever marrying was zero once he'd had a taste of what she was holding back. Not that I gave much thought to their future together. And I surely wasn't thinking we'd end up a couple.

I have my sights sets higher than a local hockey player.

As I go through the rest of the school year, I find that the boys are eager to explore what I offer, and, as I did with Carbonear, I work my way through the boys who are dating the girls in my class, and the boys who aren't.

I guess in some ways my gypsy nature extends to more than merely miles and locations.

I tire quickly of one and move on to the next. The girls hate me, but the boys practically line up to sign my dance card, so to speak. I am never alone, always invited to whatever party is going on, constantly sought out after school and on the weekends.

For this reason, I stay at Uncle William's and never with my father's other brother. I am able to sneak out during the night to go to a rendezvous, and I can come home at all hours and never face a reprimand or discipline. In fact, I look for reasons to not go to Carbonear for the weekends. I tell my father I am babysitting, or looking for a job, or in charge of any number of school functions, or helping some poor gawky girl in my class to attain some social graces. Occasionally I say I am involved in a church event. All of these excuses satisfy my father.

But not his wife.

One of the few times I do go home, she asks me how school is going. As if she's really interested, which I know she isn't. I've only been home for three hours, and already I'm looking for an excuse to go out. Somewhere. Not with friends, for I've burned all those bridges. None of the girls from Carbonear want to be seen with me, and I've already tired of the boys.

"School is going fine, Aunt Annie." I return to the fashion magazine I am reading.

"Have you made many friends?" She is determined to poke her nose into my business.

"Yes. I'm very popular."

She sniffs and continues polishing the silver serving piece she's working on. "You're in there to go to school and to learn, not to be popular."

"I believe Father would say something different."

She sets the silver tray on the table. "Your father's good money is not to be wasted on fast living and loose morals."

What a nerve she has, speaking to me in that manner. "My father's money is already being wasted on more useless pursuits."

She stares across the table at me. "What are you implying?"

"Nothing."

"Don't make sniping comments and not be willing to explain yourself."

I lay the magazine on the table. "Then I'll say it. You spend a lot of time going around, gossiping with the other women in this town. You tear people apart, make judgments about situations you know nothing about, and don't give people a chance." I snatch up my magazine and head for the door. Before I leave, I turn and toss her *the look* as I pause in the doorway. "And, if it weren't for you, I wouldn't have to leave the only home I've ever known and live in St. John's for a year. Whatever happens, I'll blame you for it."

I march up the stairs to my room, slamming the door for good measure.

I don't know what went on between my father and his wife, because I'm certain she told him, word for word, what was said between us. At any rate, he rarely asked me to come home for the weekends again, and only visited me once or twice for the rest of the school year when he came into the city.

He didn't attend my graduation the following year, although he did gift me with a typewriter I wanted. I had no plans for further training beyond high school, feeling very much at loose ends. I desperately want my father to want me, to ask me to work beside him in the shop, to come into business with him.

But he doesn't. When he wants unpaid labour, he is quick to tell me he needs me.

But that's not the kind of need I'm looking for.

I fear I will never get the recognition or relationship with my father that I want. And based on my revolving relationships with the boys of our town and my high school, I doubt I will ever have the kind of relationship I long for with a man.

More than ever, I miss my mother. Surely she could advise me in the ways of men and women. Perhaps reassure me that true love and mutual respect was possible in a marriage. Explain the process of winning a man's heart and his loyalty.

But that opportunity is forever gone, and my father's wife will never fill the hole in my heart and my learning.

Chapter 10

In 1930, my father and I spend a week or so together in St. John's. It's our first days away from Carbonear, away from his wife. We stay the week at Uncle Reginald's house, cramped in with their children, but I don't mind.

I am with my father.

Two weeks before this, he'd received a notice that he was being called as a witness in a court case in the Capital, which sent a flurry of excitement in the household over dinner the evening he disclosed the matter.

He set his newspaper aside. "I have to go to St. John's next week."

Aunt Annie smiled. "Good. I've been wanting to go downtown to the London, New York, and Paris. They have some—"

He shook his head. "No. I must go alone. I don't know how long I'll be gone. Edward Barnes is suing the Carbonear Water Company again, and I must testify."

Her smile dropped. "He wasn't satisfied with the decision last month?"

"Apparently not."

"What will you say?"

He shrugged. "I don't know what questions I'll be asked."

"Why does he want you?"

He picked up his paper again. "I don't know."

I leaned across the table and laid a hand on his arm. "Father, can I go with you?"

He removed his spectacles and looked first at me and then at Aunt Annie. "I don't know, Laura. I think the entire matter will be boring."

"I have been thinking of taking a court stenographer's course, and it would be a good opportunity to see how the thing works."

I hadn't really, but thought a possible career direction might strengthen my request.

Aunt Annie nodded. "Yes, Henry, that's a good idea."

Father's brow came down, and he stared at me a long moment as if trying to decide whether I was telling the truth. He'd never been able to figure that out in the past, and wasn't likely to do so now. He put his spectacles back on. "Very well. But only if you stay out of trouble until then."

On Wednesday, April 23rd of 1930, my father and I take the train into St. John's. I feel as though I am going on a journey around the world. I am so glad to be rid of Carbonear, even if only for a few days. We chat together on our ride, almost like the old days when I was but a child, before my mother died.

Before my world changed forever.

All too soon we are in the Capital, and Uncle Reginald picks us up at the station. His wife, Aunt Margaret, smothers us with her good-naturedness and bustling, and I wonder if my father has snuck his Annie into her place.

I hate this already, and wonder why I wanted to come.

But I know the answer: to get away from *her*.

We arrive at court the next day, and I absorb all the goings-on so my father doesn't suspect my true motives. My father greets Mr. Barnes and spends some time with his attorney while I sit in the courtroom and watch people come and go. Just before eleven o'clock, my father slides into the chair next to me.

The bailiff stands and announces the case, and we all rise to our feet. In the front of the courtroom, near the judge's bench, a woman types on a machine that looks like a miniature typewriter. The stenographer. I'd best watch her as I listen, or else Father will wonder what I'm up to.

The judge comes in, and the next hour is spent asking questions of the special jury called to hear the case, nine in total. Civil cases are treated differently than criminal cases, apparently.

First, the lawyers go into a long spiel about why we are here today, and I smile to myself. They have no idea why I am here. Then Mr. Barnes is called to the stand, and manages to stumble through the questions asked by his attorney and the attorney for the Carbonear Water Company.

Of course, I'd heard most of this before. Poor Mr. Barnes's basement had flooded the previous December, and no matter how many times he went down to the Carbonear Water Company office, or how many letters he sent them, he got the same response: they weren't going to do anything until the spring.

Which didn't satisfy him, and I must say, I didn't blame him. He'd lost his winter load of coal, not to mention the vegetables stored in his cold cellar, and the furniture and whatever else was down in his basement.

And he'd paid a couple of men to dig out the water main in the street, which is where he thought the water was coming from, and still he couldn't get anybody from the water company to take a look at it. Apparently he'd had the same problem two years before which was caused by a break in the main water line, and he thought the same thing had happened again.

So he'd sued the company, and at the first trial in March, the jury had returned a verdict against him, so he hadn't gotten his basement fixed or the money for his losses.

Around twelve-thirty, the judge raps a gavel on the desk and announces we are in recess until two-thirty.

At school, recess was a mid-morning break where you had the opportunity to stretch your legs, get a snack, use the lavatory, and perhaps go outside in good weather. And it lasts about fifteen minutes.

But in court, recess was what they call the lunch break. Father and I join Mr. Baldwin, Mr. Fitzgerald, and another man from Carbonear I don't recognize, and we go to a local café to eat. I feel so grown up with these men as they discuss everything but the case, since the judge had warned them not to talk about anything they might testify about. Which was a little unfair, I think, since I know we are all busting to talk about that very thing. Not to mention the vagueness of the instruction. How are we to know what they might be called to testify about when they didn't really know why they were here at all?

We eat sandwiches and sip coffee until a few minutes after two, then return to the courtroom. Father and I sit in the same seats. Someone had taken a picture of Mr. Barnes standing in the hole at the bottom of his garden, next to the street, to show the amount of water. That hole made a mess of the street down there for quite a while, and when the water company wouldn't make the repairs and fill in the hole, Mr. Barnes did it himself, and he didn't take much care with it. Now there is a huge hump of dirt just before you come to the post office.

At any rate, we sit through the entire afternoon, and still my father isn't called to testify. Judging by the way he shuffles his feet and nods off occasionally, he is frustrated and bored with the entire process, and to be honest, I am also having a difficult time keeping my eyes open. The stenographer's job looks to be the most boring of all. At least the bailiff and the court clerk are taking notes in books and stamping exhibits while she tap-taps on her little machine. I don't know how she keeps up with all the talking.

At five o'clock, the judge calls a dinner recess until seven o'clock. Father must have seen me yawning, because instead of going out to eat dinner, he takes me back to Uncle Reginald's in a taxi. I want to stay with him, to avoid Aunt Margaret's fussing, but he is not to be dissuaded.

"Out on the streets of St. John's at all hours is no place for a respectable young woman."

Little does he know that I'm not as respectable as he thinks, but I don't argue. "Yes, Father."

"And there's no telling what time I might get back."

Uncle Reginald waves him off. "The door will be on the latch, Henry. We'll keep an eye on her."

I have no doubt he would be as good as his word. Any hopes I had of sneaking off for the evening with some of my old pals are dashed to the ground. Father leaves around six-thirty to return to court, muttering about tying up people's good time with little to no thought that they had businesses to run and families to raise.

I note that he puts his business before his family.

Staying with Uncle Reginald is like living in a convent. No radio other than the news at six and ten, nothing in the house to read other than the newspaper, the Bible, and some old books from the previous century. Of course, there is always work, and Aunt Margaret never hesitates to offer to teach me to darn socks or turn cuffs.

Thankfully, I have a headache.

Or so I say.

And I retire early.

A little after eleven my father returns, and I hear him talking with Uncle Reginald for a few minutes before retiring in the room down the hall from mine. The next morning he knocks on my door and tells me to prepare to return to Carbonear.

I don't want to go back yet. "Father, can't we stay one more day?"

He is adamant. "No. Annie will be missing us, and we've wasted enough time on this fool matter."

"What did you testify about?"

He faces me. "I waited around all day to have one fool question asked: what did you know about Edward Barnes's troubles with the Carbonear Water Company?"

I perch on the end of my bed. "What did you say?"

"The truth. All I knew was he had water in his basement and thought it was coming from the main. Then his attorney asked me if he'd had water in his basement two years before that came from the main, and I said yes. That's all there was to it. Fool waste of time."

"Perhaps a day downtown will take your mind off this."

"I've spent enough time here. I want to go home. If you argue any more, you will not come into town with me again. Do as you're told."

I know my father is as good as his word. Few things in life could be depended on as much as God and my father.

And sometimes I'm not certain who I fear the most.

Chapter 11

The summer before I turned nineteen I had to face up to two truths: I was never going to get ahead in Carbonear, and if I didn't leave this town I was going to end up either dead or in jail.

Those two statements might seem angst-laden, spoken by a gifted young woman trapped by circumstances in a small town.

And that assessment would be partially true.

The other side of the coin, however, is that I was born too soon.

Born and raised in a time when women had few aspirations beyond marriage and family, I had little to no interest in either. Perhaps my emotionless upbringing since my mother's death contributed in part to my predicament, but I truly believe that this overall lack of empathy runs in my family.

On my father's side, he had several men who had no desire to settle down and marry. Or at least, no desire to settle down. In particular, Uncle Reginald was a wanderer, as was Uncle William. And on my mother's side, her father used to go away in his little boat all the time. People thought he was peculiar but accepted it as his way of living. I think he just got fed up with all the melodrama around him what with his wife and the children, and he just needed to get away.

If I had been a man, I could have gone to sea, spent months away from Carbonear, and looked forward to returning. But I was not a man and therefore my options were more limited. When I was younger, I joked to my father that perhaps my mother was chased by a gypsy, but the look he gave me was so dark and angry I never mentioned the topic again, not even in jest.

And so I settle in to make the best of my life. I work in the shop with my father and am never paid a dime for the work. I once asked him and he said I was investing in my inheritance.

If this shop is what I can expect to receive, I'll die a poor, old maid, for I see nothing here to attract a man worth marrying.

In between working, I spend as much time as is expected in church. Thankfully, my father is not strict about Sunday attendance. If the weather is poor, or he feels poorly, or Aunt Annie's back is acting up, we don't go, and he doesn't expect me to go alone. That would never do, to show him up by being there by myself.

Sometimes if I know he isn't going to the Sunday evening service, I'll say I'm going but go out with my friends instead. In some ways, I feel like the prodigal son's brother, the one who stays home and works hard, but never has any fun. I might have an inheritance, but by the time my father quits this world, I'll be too old and frail to enjoy it.

Not to mention that if I marry, the shop will legally belong to my husband, and I'll have little to no say in the matter.

I see my friends get married and settle into a way of life that's been here for two hundred years or more. Buy or build or rent a little house, the man goes off to sea or works in one of the companies in town, and the woman keeps house and waits to get with child. The few old maids around town are tolerated and supported by their families, earning their pocket money by taking in sewing, doing laundry, or watching other people's children.

We have a couple of spinsters in our family, so we are no different than others, and Aunt Annie brought several more in through marriage. They come to tea a couple of times a month, to dinner once or twice a year, and always manage to finagle an invitation to a week in the summer or a week over Christmas. They seem older than their years, but that may be an act they put on so not much is expected of them. In most cases, they are silly women without a grain of sense who no man would want in charge of his household or his children.

Perhaps I'm destined to join their rolls.

I like men, perhaps too much, but I suspect if I give them everything they want too soon, they won't want me anymore. But I'm even more afraid if I don't give them what they want, they will quickly lose interest and move on to the next girl who will. I can't talk about this dilemma with anybody, because to do so would be to admit that I've lain with most of the boys in my graduating class, as well as the one ahead of me and the one behind me. Even the boys who didn't stay in school are on my list. There are probably about twenty boys I've walked out with, in one way or another. I thought I would find love, or even just affection, but I've learned that the situation is giving me a bad name amongst the girls, and brings about lewd hand gestures and snickers from the boys.

And the sad thing is, I don't know what to do about it. I seem to be perpetually in a bed of my own making.

One I have no way out of.

I'm not particularly enjoying being with these boys, but I don't know what else to do, and I have nobody to steer me in the right direction.

It only seems natural, then, that I should get tangled up with a group of girls and boys who are termed "a bad lot", at least by the more upright and well-behaved in our town. Truth is, we are bored out of our heads with nothing to do. Most of the bad boys in Carbonear are sons of businessmen, and thus have no requirement to work, their fathers providing all the spending money they need.

As for the girls, well, most of them are in the same situation I am in—detached parents, or, in some cases, no parents at all. Three of the girls in my group live in foster-type situations, and I know at least one of them is being regularly used by the foster father.

No wonder she ends up in our group.

This secret club of ours, made up of about ten or twelve regulars with too much time and money on our hands, meet down at the beach late at night. This means I have to sneak out of the house, but I soon figure out which stair riser squeaks and to use the back door.

On this particular May night, I race down the street, late for my assignation because my father chose tonight to stay up late and catch up the shop books. The clock at the United Church down the street gongs eleven-thirty as I run past darkened houses and shops. In one yard, a dog barks a couple of times, but when I pass from his view, he quiets again.

On the beach, everyone else is already there with a plan of action for the evening. They had previously drank four bottles of homemade beer between them, and are working on the fifth as I step over the boulders set up as a break and clatter through the beach rocks to where they lounge on a couple of overturned dories. I slip between Deborah and Tom, and take a huge swallow of the warm ale before passing the bottle on.

I catch snatches of conversation but not enough to know what is planned, so when the bottle comes back around to me, I hold it aloft, a signal for everyone to stop talking. "What are we doing tonight?"

Tom thumps the underside of the boat we sit against. "We're going to make these two ocean-worthy and sail off to China."

The rest of the group laughs.

I hold the bottle up again. "Seriously, what are we going to do?"

Deborah grabs for the beer. "Drink up or pass it on. We've got work to do."

I swallow and hand her the bottle. "What work?"

One of the other boys, Junior, claps Tom on the back. "He spoke right, he did. We're going to fix these boats up and sail off."

That idea appeals to the wanderer in me. "I'm in."

Tom leans in close to me and leers in my face. His breath smells of beer and cigarettes and something else—poor dental hygiene, perhaps. "Good, because otherwise we'd have to kill you."

For a split second, I take him seriously, and I wonder what I've gotten myself into. Then the others laugh, and I join in. But I am still a little scared, wondering what part of his words were in jest, and what part may have been a veiled threat.

Junior swipes a hand across his mouth. "The plan is we go get the caulking and varnish and stuff we need, come back here, fix the boats, and sail away."

Sounds like a good plan, except when I look at the boats, I think they might take more than a little caulk and varnish. The others sound like they are all in, so there is no way I am going to throw water on their plans.

Tom and Junior grab my hands and pull me to my feet.

"You're going to be our helper," Tom announces, and together the three of us trot down toward Water Street.

Junior wants to sing at the top of his lungs as we pass his house on Harbour Rock Hill, but Tom and I shush him. If we're found out now, we'll not get another chance tonight, and honestly, sailing away appeals to me.

As I struggle to keep up with the two boys, whose legs are longer than mine, and who are wearing pants, not a skirt as I am, I think about the newspaper headlines if we accomplish our goal: Pied Piper lures town's brightest and best away.

Not that the others are exactly Carbonear's brightest and best, but I can dream.

Outside Johnson and Sons on Water Street, we pause. Tom runs around the back of the building and returns a couple of minutes later.

"No sign of the watchman."

We keep our voices to a whisper, but even so, the sound is amplified by the utter silence around us and the stout clapboard walls of the warehouse.

We huddle together near the only lamp outside the business to plan our next step.

Junior nods to Tom. "You go get the varnish, and I'll go around the other side and get the caulking."

That plan leaves me standing beneath the streetlight.

"What about me?"

Tom plants a wet kiss on my mouth. I haven't allowed him to so much as hold my hand before because he is so far down the social ladder in Carbonear that he isn't even fit to hold the ladder. But he's treated me nice tonight, held my hand, and he does kiss nice. I smile at him, and he grins back.

Junior interrupts our romantic moment. "Laura, you keep a lookout for the watchman."

That made sense. "What if I see him?"

"Figure out some way to keep him busy."

"How?"

He waggles his eyebrows at me. "Use your imagination."

If he's thinking what I think he's thinking…

"Junior Penney, he's an old man, with a wife and a family. Why, he must be every bit of forty."

Tom slaps my bum, and it stings. "I hope when I'm his age, I've still got what it takes."

I rub the spot, wondering what I thought I saw in him just a few moments before.

And the two disappear into the shadows surrounding the building. I pull my sweater close around me as the minutes tick past. Out in the harbour, the fog buoy sounds its presence, a haunting tone that always raises the hair on the back of my neck. At one point, I think I hear footsteps, but nobody appears.

The church clock gongs midnight, and then I detect a funny smell, like burning shoe leather mixed with kerosene. I turn around, trying to locate its origin, when I hear a voice shouting something I can't quite make out.

The sound of running footsteps comes around the corner of the building, and the old watchman comes into view. "Fire! Fire!" he calls as he bumbles past, arms flailing, face white in the dark.

I wait another couple of heartbeats, screaming in my head for Tom and Junior to appear, but when they don't, I decide to run to the beach. As I do, people stream out of their homes in various states of undress and half-dress, and I think how strange I must look, running away as they run toward.

When I get back to the beach, Junior and Tom are already there. I stalk toward them, fists clenched. "I could have been caught. Why did you leave me?"

Junior pops open a bucket of boat caulk. "We thought you were busy entertaining the night watchman."

"I told you—"

He waves me off. "I know. He's too old for you."

Deborah calls out from the next boat. "We didn't think anybody was too old for you, Laura. Or too young. Or too fat or too thin. You've had them all."

I look around at the people I'd thought were my friends, speechless at the way they are treating me.

And I realize what a fool I've been.

I'm the one the watchman saw on the street when the fire started.

I'm the one people saw running away from the fire.

I see Tom and hurry to him. He likes me. I can reason with him.

"You've got to tell them what happened."

He looks at me as if I have two heads. "Can I help it if I dropped my cigarette in the paint room? It was an accident. But nobody saw *me*. They saw *you*."

I glance toward town. The sky is orange and yellow with the flames. I run toward my home, praying Father—and yes, even Aunt Annie—are safe. Johnson and Sons is invisible behind the wall of flames and smoke, and the fire has jumped to the north side of the street. Within minutes, the fire brigade is on scene, but they cannot hold back the fire.

I watch, helpless, as houses and sheds and businesses are devoured as if by a huge fire-breathing dragon. My father runs past me, pausing only long enough to stare at me for a moment as if surprised to see me here. Then he orders me home to help Aunt Annie protect the house, and he disappears into the smoke.

I return home and find her in the kitchen, bustling about. When she's worried, she bustles. She glances up from the table where she's kneading biscuits.

"There you are. Help me make biscuits and tea. The men will be hungry before long."

Her words and her thought process touch me at my deepest core. In her mind, there are few things that a cup of tea and a biscuit cannot cure.

How I wish my life were as easily repaired as that.

Where earlier tonight I thought I had a dozen of the greatest friends a girl could have, I find myself alone.

And not only alone.

I'm the one without a friend in the world to back me up.

Chapter 12

Not five weeks later, our town is rocked by another fire. The rebuilding has barely begun, the rubble hasn't been sorted through yet to salvage whatever can be saved, when four houses and the barrel making shop burn to the ground.

The difference is that this time, I am not at the center of the activity. The previous fire burned the bridges between my gang of friends and me. I've seen them around town, of course, but haven't spoken with them. The investigation into the fire from May didn't arrive at any conclusion about the cause, and people are so relieved the entire town didn't go up that they are willing to move on.

It does seem to me that while there was a tension between people at first, that has since evolved into a general air of willingness to help a neighbor in need or a family in want. Folks are so happy to have what they have that they are more open to sharing.

Of course, the group of my former acquaintances—why did I ever think of them as friends?—never did sail away. In fact, they abandoned their work on the boats after only a couple of hours and slunk away to steal more beer and pair off for the night. The boats sit on the beach with a few holes patched with suspiciously new-looking caulking and paint, and I don't understand why the Constabulary hasn't realized who was behind the fire.

The local officers came to the house to ask me questions, since the watchman and some other folks remembered seeing me in the area. After years of making up stories for my own benefit—Aunt Annie calls this lying—I was sufficiently believable to set their minds at ease that my being there was because I'd smelled smoke from my bedroom window and had gone down to investigate. Whether the Constable wondered how I'd managed to get dressed before venturing out and still be there just seconds after the fire started, he never asked about that.

I don't think he wanted Henry Cameron's daughter to be a suspect in a suspicious fire any more than I did.

At any rate, this second fire began just before noon today, and I am working in the shop with Father, so I'm not a suspect. I don't know if Junior and Tom and Deborah and their group were involved, but I wouldn't be surprised. They'd had a row with Eloil Penney up on Harbour Rock Hill when he'd thrown them out of his barn one night. Chased them away with a pitchfork is how I heard it. Father thought they'd gotten what they deserved, but secretly I worried.

I was glad they'd waited until now before starting another fire, because the hoses from the Carbonear fire brigade had been destroyed in the previous fire, and had only just been replaced a couple of weeks ago. Father had attended a big meeting of the town council to discuss who was going to pay for the hoses. Seemed that the fire captain was being blamed, something about not enough supervision of the men or some such thing, but he rejected that and said the hoses were old and used up.

The superintendent of the St. John's fire brigade, which had come out and helped save the town in May, graciously replaced the hoses and said the town could pay for their purchase as they could. I don't know how much all that cost, but I know that Father has given money to a fund set up for that purpose.

As for this fire, the Carbonear brigade learned the hard way last time that calling for help to Harbour Grace is a waste of breath, since they use a different size hose coupling and aren't able to assist. Once again, St. John's comes to our aid, which I know is a bitter pill for our town to swallow, what with the ongoing rivalry between us.

Harbour Rock Hill isn't near us, so we are never in danger, but the smoke blotted out the sun for a while as a strong westerly wind kept the fires going. The flankers jumped from house to house and even across the road. I feel badly for the people who lost everything material in their lives and must now start over again. Already Aunt Annie is going through our blankets and sheets and towels and dishes to see what can be given to the church to distribute to those affected.

That is one thing about the people of Newfoundland in general, and of Carbonear in particular: they don't have much but they'll never see you go hungry or naked. After the last fire, so much clothing was donated they had to put out a general appeal to stop donating. Father said there was a story in the Bible similar to that, so we must be doing a good thing.

Although I wasn't involved in this fire, I can't see clear to doing enough to wash my conscience clean for the first fire. I've volunteered at the Harbour Rock Hill, I've given away my best shoes and dresses, I've even gone to the burned-out houses and helped people dig through the rubble for anything they could save. And still I feel responsible.

There was an ad in the newspaper a week or so ago asking for information into the cause of the fires. A person could respond to a post office box without saying who they were. Several times I sat in my room, pen poised over paper, to tell what I knew, and each time, I tore my beginning into shreds and burned them in the grate.

I know I should say what I know, but I cannot bear the thought of disappointing my father and proving to Aunt Annie that she was correct about me all along.

Maybe I'm nothing at all like my father.

Maybe he isn't even my father.

He definitely doesn't seem to like me.

Maybe I'm adopted.

Chapter 13

As I leave the house this Thursday afternoon in May, 1933, I am sick to death of death.

Two of my father's contemporaries are dead; one is buried, the other funeral will happen in two days. Regular as clockwork, buried on the third day. I asked my father about that this morning, and he said he believes the custom dates back to the Bible and that Jesus rose on the third day. I don't understand what sense that makes.

At any rate, my father and Aunt Annie are down to J.B. Parsons's house—or rather his widow's house since he's dead—along with half of Carbonear, I suspect. They'll talk about the dearly departed and eat up some of the food the church women brought over the last few days. I beg off, and Father and his wife seem just as happy to go by themselves.

Lately, that's how it's been around the house. Just the two of them, talking and whispering together. When I walk into a room, conversation stops, and they both bustle about as if caught with their hand in the cookie jar.

Seems like the only time my father wants to talk to me is to sit me down and give me one of his morality lectures. As careful as I've been to keep my goings-on secret, he's gotten wind that I've become more and more popular with the boys around town. He has just called me into the front room, where he sits for a long time as if chewing over his words. Finally, he sighs with a sound like the wind through a cave, and hangs his head.

For the moment, my heart pangs with an ache akin to sympathy. Or love. But as soon as he raises his head, any soft feelings I might have had fled. I fix my gaze on a flower in the rug beneath my feet, adopt a look of abject apology, and endure his sermon. Why he never became a preacher is beyond me. He certainly knows enough Bible verses, because this time he rehearsed every passage that even remotely touched on the subject of fornication and adultery.

On that point, I raise my head to let him know I don't abide with interfering with other people's marriages, but his stormy look silences me, and I lose my train of thought. So I keep quiet as he reminds me, yet again, of what a disappointment I am to our family, how wagging tongues are always looking for something to latch on to, and what chances I am taking of "getting in the family way", as he puts it.

I sneak a glance at him as he says that, and have to struggle to keep from smiling at his flame-red cheeks. I'd forgotten that my father is, for all his holiness, a married man, and would know of such things. Not to forget the wild oats he'd sown in Labrador. And he knew all about getting a girl with child. At least, according to Mother.

I nod in the appropriate places, and when he finishes, he slumps in his chair and mops his forehead with his handkerchief. After about five minutes of silence, where I make sure to look as if I am thinking over his words, he stands.

"I'm glad we've had this chat, child. I hope we never have to discuss this matter again."

If it was up to me, we'd have never brought up the topic to begin with, but I suppose parents will be parents. Particularly parents with a veneer of righteousness they struggle to maintain.

"We won't have to talk about this again, Poppa."

That seems to satisfy him, and he nods then leaves the room. I'm certain he relayed the entire conversation, word for word, to Aunt Annie, and between them, they would dissect his words and my reaction, and find me wanting.

But I don't care, because Carbonear is not where I plan to spend the rest of my life. Before my father remarried, I imagined myself as the lady of the house and that someday I would inherit the shop and show the rest of the town what an independent woman of means could accomplish.

But that's all changed with Aunt Annie coming into the picture. My father's attention is solely on her and what she wants. If she wants another dollar in her household allowance, she shall have it. If I want a dollar to go to the movies, I must earn it. Well, I won't be treated like a common servant or a shop clerk. I won't.

And so I seek ways to spite my father as often as I can, even if he never learns of my deeds. I exploit any opportunity to go behind his back, to take what I know he doesn't want me to have, to divulge a family confidence. Just last week I heard my father and his wife arguing over whether new drapes were needed in the front room. Not a knock-down-drag-it-out kind of fight, really, but by the time I whispered in the ear of several of my friends, and they in turn to their parents, the minister was knocking at the door asking if they needed a intercessor.

Word gets around quickly in small towns.

I'll never forget the look on my father's face as I smirk at him across the dinner table, where we are sitting when the reverend comes to visit. Aunt Annie is mortified and almost chokes on her food. My father's only comment when he returns to the table is that little jugs have big ears, and the Cameron family is supposed to set the example and be above gossip.

Well, it's not gossip if it's true, is it?

So today, I head down toward Water Street. I hear that some of the older boys who are attending Memorial College in St. John's are home for a long weekend, and I hope I might get a ride in one of their cars. My father has warned me away from them, which makes my deception so much more delicious.

Down the street, I hear the roar of several engines, and I quicken my step. Marilyn Butt calls to me from the porch of her family's house, and I slow to wait for her. She joins me on the road, and we walk together, chattering about boys and cars.

She pulls her sweater closer around her neck as a breeze from the harbour freshens around. "I heard Samson Baldwin is back for the weekend."

I know who she's talking about, of course, but pretend not to be interested. "Really?"

"Yes. He's studying engineering at the college, you know."

"Really? Where do they get their money for such fanciness?"

"Oh, Laura, you know the Baldwins. They always have money for what they want."

I chuckle. "One of the benefits of being a businessman, I suppose."

She sighs. "I wish my father was in business."

Her father *is* in business. The business of being on the dole. Marilyn's family is dirt poor. And dirt, according to my father. She has thirteen brothers and sisters. My world, how would I ever keep all those faces and names straight? But I don't say what I'm thinking. I don't have many friends who are girls, and while Marilyn isn't exactly a confidante, she is someone I talk with, someone I can go to a movie with.

Someone I can walk down the street with so I don't look quite so—desperate.

We round the final corner and find the source of the engine noises and the loud laughter. A group of boys—no, men—clusters around a car that looks like it's seen better days. A piece of baling wire holds on the front fender, a front headlamp hangs slightly askew, and the grill is pushed in, giving the appearance of a drunken sailor on wheels.

One of the boys—men—straightens and stares boldly at me. I know he's staring at me because Marilyn is plain as dirt and almost as flat. Me, I have curves in all the right places. I toss my head, copying the motion I've seen actresses in the motion pictures adopt to convey their interest while feigning disinterest, and he smiles.

I know who he is. Samson Baldwin. Of the Baldwin family that my father hates. I don't know why. I've never heard anything bad about them. Well, nothing any worse than some of Father's best friends and most upstanding citizens have done. I'm sure his family has their share of skeletons in the closet, but whose doesn't? For certain, he has nothing worse than our circle of friends, including two cousins of the same gender who share a house, and a close personal friend of my father's who has never married but lives in a house with a widow. And they travel together and go about as a couple, despite the fact she claims to be his housekeeper.

Samson pulls a greasy rag from his back pocket and scrubs his hands as he walks toward me. I survey him from top to bottom, then return to focus on those eyes that are as blue as the Delftware plates in my father's shop. He appraises me too, his gaze pausing a moment too long on my chest. I refuse to break the connection between us, except I find myself drowning in his eyes.

I turn my attention to Marilyn as he draws near. "Marilyn, would you introduce us?"

She stammers a moment before retrieving any good habits she might have learned from me. "Th-this is Samson Baldwin. Samson, my friend Laura Cameron."

I offer my hand in the most forward gesture I've seen in a magazine, and he grasps the tips of my fingers, turns my hand palm down, and brushes the back of my hand with his lips. The touch feels like hot coals, and I resist the urge to snatch my hand away. Instead, I smile down at him as he bends in this servitude position.

I appreciate when people acknowledge my position in this town.

After too short a moment, he straightens and holds out an arm for me to accept. I do. I almost giggle at the thought. I do. I would, if he asked me. Marriage to Samson Baldwin would upset my father to no degree, not to mention would free me from the expected responsibility of working for my keep or marrying a fisherman or a clerk at Royal's. Just because that job was good enough for my father doesn't mean it's good enough for me, and in fact, would feel like a step down at this point in my life.

So Samson and I saunter back toward his car. I take every opportunity to bat my eyelashes at him, to accidentally bump up against him or require him to support me as I almost stumble on the uneven ground. Marilyn is long forgotten, and I suppose she must have joined another group of the boys and girls. I don't know, and I don't care.

Samson pauses in front of his car. "She's a beauty, isn't she?"

I'd never heard an automobile referred to as a female before, so I think he is talking about one of the girls in the group. Although I'd known the man a total of five minutes at this point, jealousy courses through me, and I grip his arm the tighter and remain silent.

He steps forward and runs a hand along the lines of the hood. "I spent two hours this morning waxing and polishing her."

Relief at not being in competition for his attention makes my knees sag, and to cover my stupidity, I lean against the side of the car. He hurries forward and puts his arms around my waist. I close my eyes, thinking he's going to kiss me right here, in front of everybody.

Instead, he lifts me gently away from the car. "Careful. I don't want you to smudge the paint."

I can see I'm going to have my work cut out for me if I must always think of his vehicle's safety. I smile at him and blink a couple of times. "Silly me."

I've never considered myself silly at any time, so this just goes to show how much I'm slathering on the act for Samson. The less interested in me he seems, the more I want him. He has turned the game around. Where usually I'm the one fighting off the attentions of the town boys, now I am chasing this man like a dog on the scent. My tongue is practically lolling, and I suspect I look like an idiot, but I don't care.

I must have him.

I will have him.

And then I will have the one thing I've always wanted. No, make that two.

I will have a man to love me.

And I will have a man my father hates.

Samson and I spend the rest of the afternoon with the other boys and girls. Around teatime, the suggestion is made that we all go for a ride. A couple of the boys have their vehicles there, and we pile into the automobiles and trundle down Water Street toward Freshwater, tooting the horns and waving to folks as we pass. In some ways, I feel we are in a parade of sorts.

I sit next to Samson, of course, in the front seat of his car, and on my right another couple squish against us. I think there are about six in the back seat, girls sitting on boys' laps, and once again, I am jealous. I would much rather be back there with Samson, sitting on his lap. I could press my bosom into his face when we hit a pothole, or squirm in anticipation. I know the boys like that. I'm sure Samson would, too.

But here I sit, out in the open, because he is driving his 1933 Ford Coupe Convertible, with the top down to make certain as many people as possible can see us. And I am proud to be seen with him.

Out past my father's shop we go, but the shades are drawn and the door closed because Father and Aunt Annie are at the Parsons's house. The streets are fairly quiet, perhaps because of the recent funeral and death. We pass the funeral home and go on towards Freshwater, down past the beach and up the hill. The hard-packed dirt road sends a plume of dust behind us like the tail of a kite against the sky.

We pass the shops in Freshwater, and still we sail along. I think we actually get up past twenty-five miles an hour on the straightaway stretch through that small hamlet. At one point, a dog runs out of an alley and races alongside us for a few feet, barking and wagging its tail, but we soon leave the animal standing in the middle of the road.

At the far end of Freshwater is a path that leads down to a beach, and Samson pulls in and we all pile out. He grabs my hand and holds me back as the rest pair off and seek out more privacy amongst the rocks and nooks and crannies.

He pulls me against him, and I smell the fresh air and the faint smell of Lifebuoy soap on his skin. I know he wants to kiss me, so I tip my face toward him and close my eyes. He steps forward, and so I step back, until I feel the car against me, keeping me from going any further. Before I know it, he has opened the back door of the car and presses me down on the seat, and I don't resist.

Samson is the first *man* I've been with, and I fully expect something different, something more important than the liaisons I've had with the Carbonear and St. John's boys. I am certain there must be something more than the quick encounters I've had in places that leave me feeling dirty and cheap.

The soft leather seat beneath me cushions us, and already I feel that this is better in some way I cannot explain. He kisses me all over my face and neck, then unbuttons my blouse. Well, this is a first. I've never removed my clothes in front of anyone before, let alone a man. The times with the boys resulted in bloomers being pulled to one side, out of the way. Never this.

I try to slow my breathing as my heart threatens to explode. For a man to take the time to remove my clothing must mean he loves me. I seek out his mouth with mine, wanting the assurance of his kisses and his words that I am more than the town lay. He touches my lips with his tongue, and I open my lips a little, tasting his tongue in my mouth. Another first.

Next he removes my undergarments and roams his hands and mouth all over me. I've never felt so alive before. He is straddling me, and I feel his manhood pressing into me. He straightens and shrugs out of his shirt, then unbuckles his pants and slips them off.

I have never actually seen a man even partially naked before. All the other boys have been a series of grunting and endurance in some tawdry shack or dory or doorway, with no interest on their part as to whether I am enjoying this act as much as they.

But Samson is different.

He takes his time with me, as if this were my first time, and although I am screaming on the inside to get on with it, I am glad I don't voice my desire. We spend some time preparing, and in the preparation, I discover the experience is intensified.

Afterwards, we dress again then lay there, pressed together by our spent passion and sweat. He rolls onto his side and cups me like spoons in a drawer against him, then lights a cigarette. I don't smoke, but I enjoy the shared intimacy of the moment, inhaling the smoke he wafts through his nostrils onto the evening breeze.

He plays with my hair, a feeling I quite enjoy, and I nestle back against him, content in the moment to be *his* girl.

"I go back to college tomorrow."

No. I don't want to hear this. "But you'll be back soon?"

He shakes his head. "Got a job in Halifax for the summer work term, and when I finish that, I'll start back at college right away."

"But you'll be home for weekends?"

He sits up and pulls me up next to him, his arm laying easily over my shoulder, as if created to be there. "Listen, Laura, this was fun. You're a lot of fun. I knew you would be when I saw you on the street today. But I have a fiancé in St. John's. We're getting married at Christmas, so I have to spend my time with her."

No. I don't want to share him. "Samson, I can give you everything that other woman can give you. I'll inherit my father's business someday—"

He interrupts me with a laugh. "If I wanted to stay in Carbonear, my father already owns the biggest business around here. Much bigger than your father's little shop."

His words cut me to the core, and I want to rush to my father's defense. But his soft lips silence me in another kiss. He pulls back and stares at me. "I want out of Carbonear."

I nod and grip his hand. "Me, too. We can go together."

He twists the end of my hair between his fingers, and my pulse quickens once more.

He will come around to my way of thinking. I am certain of it.

Then he shakes his head. "No, Laura, it wouldn't work. She's from a good family, and I until I get married, I can get what I want from any woman I choose."

"I'm from a good family."

"Sure. The best there is in Carbonear. But you're a big fish in a small pond, Laura. I want to be a big fish in a big pond. Besides, your father would never let me darken your door."

"My father doesn't run my life."

"So long as you are unmarried, he does. No matter what you do behind his back."

This is so unfair. I push him away and scoot over the seat and out the other door. "But what we just did, it was—it was—"

He buttons his sweater against the chill. "It was no different than what you've done with a dozen or more boys before me. And likely you'll do with a dozen or more after me."

I feel as if he's seen right through me, into those dark and dusty corners of my soul that I keep hidden from everybody. And that scares me a little, because if he can see, who else can as well? As much as I long for love and affection, I'm not certain I want the other side of the intimacy coin, to not have any secrets from another person.

Father once told me that he married again because he wanted someone to share his most innermost thoughts and dreams with.

If this is what he was talking about, I don't want any part of it.

To open myself to this kind of emotion is to offer up my heart on a silver platter.

And I will never do that again.

Not after today.

It hurts too much.

Donna Schlachter

Chapter 14

By the time July rolls around, I haven't seen hide nor hair of Samson Baldwin, and I've suffered from the worst case of the influenza ever. For the past two months, every morning, I've been sick to my stomach. I'd lost weight and had dark circles beneath my eyes. Aunt Annie watches over me, fussing at me like a mother hen. And, as usual, I resist her ministrations.

Truth is, I don't want to like her. I am old enough to know that my simply treating her badly won't send her away, but the little girl inside me wants that fallacy to be true.

But it doesn't work. In fact, the more I languish, the more she hovers over me. And the more she hovers, the more I hold her at a very long arm's length.

And then comes the middle of July, and Aunt Annie's younger sister has her first child. Frank Young is born on a glorious day. I hadn't paid much attention to the fact that Aunt Florence was about to deliver, but I know Aunt Annie had. She's been knitting up a storm for the previous six months, ever since the formal announcement was made to the family. I puzzle over such a to-do surrounding one of the most natural happenings since creation.

At any rate, I keep my distance from her side of the family, and don't really consider them family at all. Family by marriage is family in name only. It's not like we're actually related. But a couple of days after the sixteenth, we trundle into St. John's to greet the child and extend our congratulations to the proud parents.

Florence is still in the hospital, recuperating from a difficult birth, by her account. We gather around her bed like pigs at a trough, except instead of food, we feast on the baby in her arms. Her husband Morris sits in a chair nearby, a bewildered expression on his face. He simply stares at each person in turn, then his wife and babe.

Florence regales us with horror stories of the birth, including the fourteen hours of labor, the lack of regard by the medical staff, and the fact that the baby started in the breach position. Once she's told that tale at least twice, she passes the child around for each of us to hold and exclaim over. I take one look at its wrinkled red face, think it the most ugly child I'd ever seen, and pass it along to my father to cuddle against his chest. The baby smells of sour milk and a soiled diaper, and I cannot understand why people make such a fuss over such disgusting creatures.

When next I tune in to the conversation, Florence is comparing pregnancy stories with the other women gathered around the bed. Seems she had something called "morning sickness". For the first three months of her pregnancy, she thought she had influenza and finally went to the doctor for a cure. She was ever so glad to be assured she was hale and healthy and pregnant, and would wake up one morning and discover the symptoms gone.

As I listen, my stomach roils, and not at what she is saying.

Instead, her words create in me a concern that perhaps I don't have a common viral infection.

Perhaps I have a very common pregnancy.

I listen more closely to their discussion of other symptoms:

moodiness, lethargy, tenderness, and missed monthlies. Although my monthly visitor has never been regular, of late I've had several months of nothing. And the other indicators, which up to this point I'd attributed to the influenza, now carries with them a double innuendo.

My father's words have come true, and I find myself in the family way.

The question now wasn't how or why, but what next? If my previous behaviour had triggered the innumerable lectures and sermons on morality from my father, I could only envision what the revelation of my pregnancy outside marriage and no hope of wedding the father would engender.

Because I'd recently had word that Samson was beyond my grasp. Their engagement had been announced in all the newspapers. He would marry the woman who wouldn't give him before the wedding what I had, and no doubt, I was a distant memory to him. One of a succession of women not to be mentioned in polite society. One of those the wife knows about but pretends doesn't exist.

Such a wicked double-standard. Samson was simply sowing his wild oats, as my father had done. But for the girl involved, a life-changing and shameful outcome.

Which gives me the answer I seek. Just as the girl in Labrador had sought out another man to marry her when my father left her alone, so would I.

Like father, like daughter.

So, when the invitation comes inviting me to spend a couple of weeks in Grand Falls with a girl I went to school with, I see a way out of my predicament. Carol married a man from Botwood who worked as a clerk in a bank in Grand Falls, and she sounds like she is a bit lonely, so I make arrangements to go visit her.

And Albert Jamieson is in Grand Falls.

I'd dated Albert when he lived in Carbonear, before he'd graduated high school and gone off to work in the paper mill. He'd been a couple or three years ahead of me in school, and at the time, seemed like a good way to pass a summer.

However, I'd soon discovered him to be particularly jealous of my flirtation with other boys.

And unlike Samson, he wouldn't give me what I wanted.

When I broach the subject with Father, he is hesitant. I suspect the reason he doesn't want me to go has less to do with missing me than that he doesn't want to let me out of his sight. However, I convince him that while I know what a hardship my absence will create for him in the shop, Carol needs me, and it is my Christian duty to do what I can to help an old friend.

He ultimately acquiesces, agreeing we each need to make sacrifices for the good of others. In some ways I know my father better than he knows himself, and I understand his desire to be seen as a good man, eager to assist others in their time of need.

When he breaks the news to Aunt Annie at dinner, I believe I see a look of gratitude pass between them, and I almost change my mind on the instant. I know she will be happy to see the back of me, and I am hesitant to grant her wish. However, I need to get out of town and seek an opportunity to rectify my predicament.

Letters go back and forth between Carol and me, and we finally agree on the first week of November. I would prefer to go earlier, but she is on holiday in September, and her mother is visiting in October, so November is my first opportunity.

I encourage her to line up several dinners during my visit, including eligible bachelors from the town, hinting at my desire to be as happily married as she sounds. I mention Albert's name, reminding her of our past friendship. She seems excited to accommodate my wishes, and I look forward to solving my dilemma.

The weeks go past quickly as every day seems filled to the hilt with details and activities in preparation for my leave-taking. Carol assures me she and her husband are happy to host me for as long as I want to stay, so I make no firm plans to return to Carbonear and my father's house. With any good providence, I will not come back.

I am booked on the nine o'clock train. Because it is a workday, my father does not see me off. Instead, I walk to the station, a valise in each hand. Somehow I manage to cram in several gowns as well as four day dresses. I wear my best wool coat and an everyday hat. Buried deep in the bottom are my best heels and the little jewelry I own, mostly my mother's. The day is cool but sunny, but as we travel west, the sky clouds over. While at first the change in weather concerns me, I decide not to adopt its darkening attitude. Instead, I stare out the window of the second-class car I ride in and silently bid adieu to each change of scene.

I stay on the train in St. John's. I don't have money to buy anything, and I cannot afford to miss the train. To return to Carbonear now will be like admitting defeat, and that I will not do. I watch people scurry along the platform, bidding their good-byes to loved ones, and wish, for a moment, I had someone waving me off.

But no, the more important thing is that I have someone to meet me at my destination. Carol and her husband Jonas have promised to be there, welcoming me into their new home, and that will suffice for now.

Apparently I nod off, because a jolt of the train wakes me as we round the last bend into Grand Falls. I've never seen this town before, but for some reason, I had visions of a smaller version of St. John's. Instead what I find is a train station out in the middle of nowhere, with the town about a mile away.

The buildings in the distance seem little more than wooden shacks awaiting a strong wind to blow them over and put them out of their misery. The only bright spot is Carol and a thin man beside her, who I take to be her husband.

As soon as the train pulls to a stop, Carol is scanning the windows. When she spies me, she jumps up and down like a schoolgirl, and my heart lifts in hopes of a good outcome to my adventure. Her husband Jonas seems the right gentleman, and awaits me at the step, extending a hand to grasp mine and assist me to the platform. The conductor passes him my suitcases, and Carol's husband hands him a couple of coins for his trouble.

Carol grabs me by the shoulders and pulls me in for a hug. I am caught a little off guard, since she and I were never bosom buddies, but I embrace her nonetheless. She appraises me up and down, and chucks my cheek as if she were my Great-Aunt Beatrice. "You have grown up so much in the last couple of years, Laura."

"As have you, Carol. Imagine, the married woman and all." I glance at Jonas. "No little ones on the way?"

Carol grips my hand and leads me toward an older sedan. "Not yet. We're having too much fun trying, aren't we, Jonas?"

Jonas's face has turned a remarkable shade of crimson. I shouldn't wonder Carol is so forward in speaking of private matters. She was raised in a family of twelve, and they lived in three rooms at the top of Woodpecker Hill. There's no telling what she saw and heard before she left home. At least, that's what my mother used to say of the family.

As we ride to Carol's house, I think of my mother, and wonder what she would say now. Although, I suspect had she lived, I would not be in this situation.

We arrive, and I am beat. All I want to do is to curl up in my bed and sleep for a week.

But Carol will have none of that. "You said you were excited to meet all the right people in Grand Falls, and so we have been invited to a party tonight hosted by the mill manager. I made sure Albert was included. You have time for a quick lie-down, then we'll go out. There will be food and spirits, and I hear a local dinner band has been hired for the evening. You must go."

Despite my exhaustion, I agree. If my plan is to work, I must mingle with Grand Falls society as soon as possible.

An hour later, we head out. Already the sun has gone down and the night has closed in, and being a stranger in this place, I have no idea where we are going. The streets are dark with few lamps, and the road rutted, although Jonas does his best to avoid the worst ones.

Although I doubt that anything good will come of this venture of mine, within fifteen minutes we pull up outside a stately brick house. Every window is lit, and the three chimneys spew out smoke. We wait our turn, as there are a number of automobiles ahead of us, each one carrying partygoers.

When our turn comes, a liveried valet opens the back door and assists we ladies out, while another trots around to the driver's side then slides in and drives off once we alight. I am amazed at how quickly the vehicles are moved along, while we do not feel rushed in the least. A red carpet lines the walkway, and a distinguished-looking butler greets us at the door.

I am wearing my second-best gown, and as soon as I enter the foyer, I wish I'd chosen my best. The ladies inside are gowned in sequins and lace galore, with daring off-the-shoulder styles designed to show off their best features. Tiaras and diamond bandeaus are the norm, and I check my reflection in a conveniently placed wall mirror before entering the main party room.

At once, the host and his wife, a diminutive blonde in a red gown designed for her, as is obvious by the tailored fit, welcomes me. Despite my attire, she loops her arm in mine and proceeds to introduce me to everybody in the room. My head fairly swims with names and faces, not to mention promises of dances from almost every man.

When I feel that I can take no more, I sidle into the next room, which is much more subdued. The furniture in this room has been gathered into conversational groups of three or four, and every seat is occupied. An oak bar has been set up against an outer wall, and I wander over.

The bartender looks up from slicing limes. "What can I get you,

Miss?"

I tug at the white gloves that insist on slipping down and try to look as sophisticated as possible. I am here to make an impression, and I must not fail. I can't think of the name of a drink that will accomplish that particular goal. "Perhaps a martini?"

A man stands beside me. "You don't sound as if you're sure of yourself."

I face him. "Where I come from, gentlemen don't accuse of lady of being unsure."

He stands about six inches taller than me, and so gives the impression of looking down his nose at me. "Perhaps I'm no gentleman."

I don't need to impress a man who wouldn't consider himself genteel. I've had enough of that type. They like to take what you'll offer and leave you high and dry, a fact I was reminded of when I put on my gown earlier. I had to lie on the bed to get the zipper done. "A martini, please."

The bartender nods and adds ingredients to a stainless steel shaker. The man next to me shrugs and leaves.

I don't miss him in the least.

The bartender slides the stemmed glass filled with a cranberry-coloured liquid toward me. "I thought you might prefer a Cosmopolitan."

I sip. "You're right. I do."

Feeling wise and sophisticated beyond my years and experience, I lean against the bar and survey the room. Since the music started up as I entered the room, most of the couples are in the other room. I enjoy the sensation as the alcohol goes down smooth and sweet. At a touch on my elbow I turn, prepared to rebuff the cad from a few minutes before.

But it is not he.

Instead, a dashing and mature man faces me. His suit is a little older than my three-year-old dress, but the red pocket hankie brightens the charcoal gray wool and matches his tie perfectly. His dark hair and perfectly groomed mustache speak of attention to detail, while the soft skin of the hand he extends to me speaks of office work.

Albert.

And not the weedly young boy who left Carbonear three years ago with grand dreams of managing the mill.

No, he has grown up quite nicely, thank you very much.

Already I am interested. He has turned into a man of quality.

He bows at the waist then meets my gaze. "We haven't been formally introduced, but I can wait no longer. I am Albert Johnson. And you are—" He pauses and surveys me from head to foot and back again. Unlike the boys in Carbonear, he doesn't pause on my chest, but meets my eyes fully. "Laura. Laura Cameron." He bows again. "Forgive my lapse of memory. You've grown up."

I accept his hand and enjoy the feel of his in mine. I set my drink on the bar and pat his arm. "As have you, Albert." I glance around the room to break the intensity of his stare. "Carol and Jonas Garland said they knew you were on the guest list."

He offers his arm, and I accept. We walk into the other room, and he pulls me into his arms as the band plays a waltz. We move around the dance floor as if we'd practiced together for years, and now I know how Cinderella felt when the prince asked her to dance.

Albert and I are inseparable for the rest of that evening. He tells me of his position as purchasing officer for the pulp and paper mill, and we share stories about our common friends. He hasn't been in touch with anyone from Carbonear, for which I am eternally thankful, and the only people I know in Grand Falls are Jonas and Carol. He shares with me his desire to marry soon, feeling he is secure in his position and reaching an age where marriage might be beyond his grasp.

I assure him I, too, wish a marriage where together we can work to achieve our greatest dreams. In an off-handed remark, he mentions his engagement to a woman several years prior, which he broke off once he learned she had been married before. His statement that he didn't want another man's cast-offs send a shiver of dread through me. He seems the perfect catch, but I must be careful not to cause him to question my purity.

Before we leave, he asks permission to court me. I accept, and I ride home with Carol and Jonas, although I feel I could have flown.

Finally, a respectable man has seen something in me that other men failed to see.

Now all I need do is convince him of my sincerity, and to urge him on to a quick marriage, so I can cover my secret.

Once he has fallen in love with me, I am certain he will forgive me my deception.

Chapter 15

How naïve we can be, to believe—no, perhaps hope—that if we can change our circumstances, we can change our lives. Albert Johnson is one of the most eligible bachelors in Grand Falls that season, and my friend Carol repeats many times how lucky I am that he'd set his cap for me.

At first, I consider his attention and absolute devotion to me an endearing charm. For the first time since before my mother died, I am the center of someone's life. I adore the fact that he expects to go out somewhere every evening after he finishes his work day. I appreciate that he attends church regularly, and expects the same of me. I bask in his compliments and lavish gifts.

While his proposal three weeks after our meeting comes as no surprise, I am dismayed when I learn he expects a longer engagement than I anticipated. Albert is a singularly moral man, and being older, understands the temptations of the flesh, although he adamantly denies having any experience with physical relations between men and women. Of course, I echo him, sensing that even acknowledging being kissed by a man not related to me will open a Pandora's box of questions I don't want to address.

I can't wait for him to marry me, not because I am so passionately in love with him, but because of the child growing within me. For by now, I know without question that I am pregnant. A quick marriage is not going to fool Albert into thinking we had conceived on our honeymoon, but I hope that once we are married, he will come to accept the child—and forgive me.

I need the marriage to happen before he becomes suspicious of my enlarging belly, and the only way I can think to bring this about is to tell him I have to return to Carbonear. I do this one evening after we dine and he has consumed several drinks. As my pregnancy progresses, I develop a distaste for alcohol, as well as several other foods. My refusal to drink does not please Albert, so I find myself feigning a cold or influenza several times to explain my situation.

On this evening, we sit in the living room of his apartment. We'd entertained a couple whose husband works under Albert at the mill. They were gone, and we now have the place to ourselves.

I start in on the next step of my plan. "Albert, I will soon wear out my welcome with Carol and Jonas."

He waves off my words. "Nonsense. They love you nearly as much as I do."

"But I cannot stay with them for the next year."

"You could get your own apartment."

"Yes, but then I'd need to get a job to support myself. And jobs are scarce."

"I could help you out."

I shake my head. "No, Albert. People will begin to talk, and I don't want our marriage tarnished with gossip."

He seems to consider my words a moment. "I don't want you to leave."

"Oh, I guess a year isn't so long. Perhaps I can save my money and come visit you again at Easter."

He stands and paces the room. "What? That's over three months away." He pauses near the window. "No, that will never do."

At last, I have him coming around to my way of thinking. I wait. Best to let him think the idea is his.

He comes to a conclusion. "Then we shall marry. Immediately."

I jump up and run into his arms, pressing myself against him. He kisses me then holds me close. I stand so that my bulging belly doesn't press into him so much as to be noticeable, and we remain in that position several minutes.

When at last he releases me, he smiles a lopsided grin. "I know what you're up to."

My dinner threatens to come back up, and I swallow hard. "You do?"

He runs a hand down my back and pats my bum. "You can't keep your hands off me."

I smile and drop my gaze.

He pulls me close again. "I, too, am looking forward to the consummation of our marriage."

Oh, God, if he only knew why I was marrying him. Am I being fair to him?

Am I being fair to myself?

By January, I can hide the pregnancy no longer. My belly has protruded more than would be normal had I become with child during my month-long marriage. To say Albert is livid would be an understatement, and now I see something else in his eyes. Disappointment? Disgust? While at first he is hesitant to leave me even to go to work, now he spends longer hours at the office, claiming an increased workload.

Every day is like walking on eggshells. Albert moves his belongings into the other bedroom, and in so many ways, I am no better off now than I was in Carbonear. What I thought would be my salvation has instead become a living hell for me. I put on a happy face to all of Albert's friends and associates, but inside I am dying.

By the middle of February, he gives me an ultimatum. At breakfast, he sets his coffee cup and newspaper aside and clears his throat in that irritating way he has of letting me know he's going to speak to me. "Laura, you must go talk to your father."

I set the crust of toast I am nibbling on my plate. "I cannot tell him."

"You mean he doesn't know?"

"No. Nobody knows."

"I don't believe you. How could you have married me knowing you were carrying another man's get?"

"I didn't know I was pregnant when I agreed to marry you."

The words ring hollow in my head, and I know they must sound the same to him.

Perhaps if I repeat them enough times, they will become true.

He stands and lays his open palms on the table. "You need to go to Carbonear and take care of this. Have the child. But do not come back here with it."

There. He's said the words. Now it's out in the open.

"Do you understand?"

I nod, not meeting his gaze. So much like my father's. Stern. Unmoving. "What will our friends say?"

"I'll tell them something. Family troubles. Homesickness. Woman troubles so you're going to a specialist in St. John's."

"Yes, that will do. Thank you, Albert."

Gratitude is not the emotion I feel, however.

Loss overwhelms me. Loss of face, loss of position, loss of reputation, although until now, what others thought of me never mattered. But here, in my new life, with new friends, their opinion of me is of high importance.

"When do you deliver?"

I shrug. "I'm not certain. I haven't seen a doctor."

He pounds the table, clattering the china and silver. "You must know when it happened."

Is he asking me or telling me?

I have wracked my brain about that particular detail. My last monthly visitor was in late April, which means Samson Baldwin—the cad—would be the father. I was so certain I could win him back that I hadn't coupled with any boy after him. And by the time I learned of his formal engagement in September, I was so ill I couldn't even think of sex.

I count off on my fingers. "I guess the child will come in March."

He glances at my belly, which I cannot hide beneath my dressing gown. I wrap my hands around my distended abdomen, and a flutter from within startles me. I snatch my hands away. For the first time, this child has become real to me. And now I have a decision I must make.

Albert continues, talking through his plans as if I have no say in them. "You will not be seen in public in that—" He points a finger in my direction. "In that condition. I will tell people you are unwell."

"If you do that, they may think I am pregnant with your child."

"Better for them to think that than to know the truth." He turns his back on me. "You will go to St. John's in March and have the child. Our friends and associates will be told you are having health problems. Let them think you miscarried. And when you come back—" He faces me again. "If you come back, you come back alone. We will observe a short mourning attitude then you will become pregnant again, and we will put this behind us."

He speaks as if the child within me is nothing more than an overcooked dinner or an overspent budget. Most of my friends have had discussions with their husbands about their cooking abilities or propensity to spend too much money that culminated in much the same words and tone.

Except the child has kicked within my womb. And no matter which path I choose, it will never truly be "behind us".

Always this child will be between us.

Chapter 16

I ride the train from Grand Falls to St. John's around the middle of March, and I stay with Uncle William and his family in the Capital. I tell them the barest of details, just enough to garner their sympathy and their secrecy.

Then today, on the twenty-second, I awake early in the morning with pains I cannot describe other than to say I feel as if a dull saw is cutting me in two. I try to stay calm and quiet, because Uncle William abhors noise and fuss, but my cries waken his wife, who instantly recognizes I am in labor.

She drags Uncle William out of bed and convinces him to drive me to the Grace Maternity Hospital, where I am ushered into a delivery room and bring forth my firstborn son four hours later. Pain and stark terror bathe the trip to the hospital, and the entire birthing experience is swathed in a haze of morphine, unfocused faces, and the uncontrollable desire to be rid of this child.

I name the boy-child Richard in honor of the Cameron family tradition of having one so named in every generation. I give him the middle name of Gilbert, from my mother's side of the Abbott family. On the birth certificate, I leave the father's name blank, since Samson Baldwin will not be his father, and I use my maiden name, as the child will never be a Jamieson.

Albert already made that perfectly clear.

I am shuttled off to the charity ward, where poor or unmarried mothers are kept. I think it an odd place to recuperate, since I am neither poor nor unmarried, but I suppose that is the best the hospital can do in the matter. At any rate, I spend my three days there, refusing to nurse the child, refusing to hold him or look at him. I do not want to become attached to this infant, because I have made up my mind: I will return to Grand Falls, alone, and attempt to live by Albert's rules and make the best of the hard bed I've made for myself.

A week later, and I am on the train, carrying a newborn infant from St. John's to Carbonear. I can think of nothing else to do with it.

No, not it.

Him.

I board the train mid-afternoon after spending last night at Uncle William's. I see the pity and the pain in his eyes as he helps me board, the child in a carrying bassinet. I set Richard at my feet and allow the motion of the train to lull him to sleep. I cannot abide his crying. My breasts ache with milk when he cries, but I know if I suckle him the once, I will change my mind, and I cannot do that.

I arrive around teatime and get off the train. I haven't told anyone I'm coming or what I plan to do, because I don't want them to try to convince me to do otherwise. With my hat pulled low over my face, I walk the mile or so from the station to Samson Baldwin's father's home. I know he isn't home from work yet, but I march up the walkway and knock on the door.

One of Samson's sisters answers the door, and her mouth opens in surprise when she sees me. "Laura, what a surprise. Come in, come in."

I pick up the bassinet and hand it to her. "Here, this belongs to Samson."

She takes the bundle without comment, simply looking from the still-sleeping baby and back to me. Before she can say anything, I turn and walk back down the walkway toward the station.

Already my arms are crying at the emptiness, and tears run down my cheeks. But there is no turning back.

I sit on the hard wooden bench and wait for the train to return to St. John's. I've planned my actions carefully, taking the last train out of Carbonear that evening. I will connect in Whitbourne to the train heading west. My suitcase waits for me in the baggage room there, and by morning, I will be home.

The train pulls forward, and I board again, sitting in the same seat I'd ridden here. I settle against the seat, close my eyes, and ask for forgiveness.

From God.

From the child.

When we pull into Whitbourne, I gather my purse and gloves, and step down from the car. At the head of the train, on the platform, I see a knot of men gathered, heads together and arms gesticulating. I turn into the depot to avoid them, not wanting to become entangled in their discussion. I have a train to catch in a few minutes.

At the door, I cast another glance in their direction, and one turns and looks straight at me.

Sergeant Bussey. Of the Newfoundland Constabulary, Carbonear detachment. And he's standing near a marked police car. I can see his intentions in his expression as he glances from me to the train and then to the station. He intends to stop me and take me back to my father.

I pause, uncertain whether my eyes deceive me. He grabs the arm of another man, and the two come toward me, and I recognize another man from the Constabulary. I break into a run and dash along the platform, trying to get lost in the crowd, but before I can, I feel a hard hand on my shoulder. I try to shake off his hand, but he has latched onto me.

"Laura. Stop." The constable pulls me back toward the waiting car, and again I try to pull away. "If you don't come with me peaceably, I'll have to arrest you."

I look down my nose at him, a gesture I learned from my mother. "Arrest me? What right—"

"At your father's request, Miss. Please come without making a scene."

The people on the platform stare, and I want to sink through the boards and into the ground. My mother's words come back to haunt me, from a day when I was about three or four, and I'd gone with her to the shop. I wanted a candy drop, and when she wouldn't give me one, I dropped to the floor and flailed about, screaming at the top of my lungs.

When I opened my eyes, my father was looking down at me, fists on his hips. He yanked me up by the collar, turned me around, and swatted my bum over and over again with such force that I felt it through to my innards. I was so surprised I stopped my tantrum. My mother grabbed my hand and pulled me from the shop and up the walk to the house. When we got back to the house, she stood me in the corner for an hour or more. At least, it seemed that long. I hiccupped for most of that time, trying to control my sobs. I'd never seen my father look at me with such anger in his eyes.

I've often felt he might have killed me had my mother not intervened.

And then to see her tear-filled eyes as she told me I would never humiliate her like that again, because she would never take me out in public without my father. And she never did.

All of those lost precious moments with her, all over a candy drop that I could have gotten from my father's store anytime.

As I stand here now, the chill March wind blowing down the neck of my coat, I think of the depth of her humiliation, and I know exactly how she felt. I am again speechless.

Sergeant Bussey directs me toward the police car, boldly emblazoned with the Newfoundland Constabulary insignia, and I slip into the back seat. He slides in next to me, the constable in the driver's seat starts the engine, and we begin the trek back to Carbonear. The sergeant, a family man with daughters of his own, stares straight ahead, his mouth a grim line.

Once or twice, I try to speak, but he waves me silent. Perhaps he is afraid my words might stick to him and contaminate his girls, so they could end up in my predicament. Maybe he is afraid he will believe me and let me go on my way, thus risking my father's wrath. Whatever the reason, we travel the two hours back to Carbonear without a word passing between us. We pull up to my father's house, and I alight. I glance up Water Street, toward the train station, but the burly sergeant shakes his head.

The front door opens and my father descends the steps. Down the garden path he comes, his mouth grim, and he grabs me by the arm. I resist, but he is stronger than I, and, after all, he is my father. He has every right to command my movements. Father speaks to the sergeant, and the car pulls off into the night.

We are left standing there in the chill evening air. I wish at that moment for the earth to open up and swallow me. But that is yet another prayer never answered. I glance at the house. All the windows are dark except the front room. Father and I enter the house and he pushes me into the front room. The bassinet is on the floor near the fire, and the baby is asleep, his tiny lips moving in sucking motions.

An ache build inside me.

My father sinks into a chair, and I sit across from him, my back to the child as much as possible in that room. Everything in this room is familiar to me, articles that have been there since I was a child. The table and the glass lamp that rests on it. The chairs arranged around the fireplace. The painting on the wall. Even the settee and the rug beneath my feet.

The only things that are strange are the baby and my father.

"Well, Laura, you've got yourself into a situation here."

An understatement, to be sure. "One I was trying to get myself out of."

"Mr. Baldwin brought the child here. Said you dropped it off at his house and said it was Samson's."

I square my shoulders. "It is."

"Well, Samson has no use for the child. And apparently, neither do you."

"Albert said I was to come back alone."

He leaned closer. "And what do you think Samson and his bride-to-be are going to do with a wee babe?"

I look away. I will not let him see the tears building up and threatening to spill over. "I don't know."

"Laura, you've always been a disappointment to me. To Annie and me."

Well, that was no surprise, that I was a disappointment to *her*.

"To your mother before her, God rest her soul."

I whirl to face him. "Mother said that?"

He nodded. "We spent many evenings discussing how to get you back on the right track before she died. Even at a young age, she saw you were trouble."

The tears come. I cannot believe my mother—my confidante, the one I thought knew me, the real me—would speak of me that way. I want to scream at the unfairness of it all, but I cannot speak past the lump in my throat that threatens to suffocate me.

He continues. "I'm so glad she didn't live to see this. But I think she can see. Looking down from heaven. And her heart is broken all over again."

Knowing I'd caused my mother pain during her life and now more pain during her heavenly reward, if there is such a thing, is more than I can bear. I fall to my knees on the floor, the rug scratchy beneath me, and sob.

"Well, child, you might as well sit up. We need to figure out what to do, and crying won't get the job done."

Using my handkerchief, I blow my nose in a most unladylike manner, then sit and wait, because I'm certain of one thing: my father doesn't need—and doesn't want—my input. He already has the situation summed up and the outcome decided.

"Laura, I fear you're going to come to a bad end, and I can see that I am partly to blame. Letting you run wild all the time, being so busy with the shop and my other responsibilities. I was ill-equipped to raise a daughter, and I hoped when I married Annie that things would change. But you were so angry with me, you wouldn't give her a chance. I think the only thing to do is to send you on your way, and hope the good Lord gets ahold of you before it's too late."

In the bassinet, the child whimpers. In some deep recess of my mind, I want to pick him up. Perhaps we can comfort each other. But I know that will make what I must do only the more difficult. After a few minutes, he settles down again, and I let out a pent-in breath.

"You can stay the night in your old room, but you must be gone on the first train in the morning. There is no question of your staying in Carbonear. Go back to Albert and make the best of it."

I know there is no best of it, no good outcome for me or anybody else concerned. "What of the child?"

"I think it best if he's raised in a family with children. Mrs. Baldwin is ready to have one of her own, so they don't want another. William will take him in. He has several small ones already."

I nod. Uncle William's houseful of children and his itinerant income will mean the child will have few options, but I know my father won't see him in want. The baby could do worse.

Father stands, and although we are mere feet from each other, I feel a widening chasm between us. "Annie will tend to the child tonight. Good night."

He picks up the bassinet and trudges up the stairs, each footstep sounding like a man twice his age.

I follow and pause in the doorway of my room then glance toward my father's and Aunt Annie's room. The baby mewls then is silent. I envision Aunt Annie holding him, his hair and eyes dark against the pale blanket wrapped around him. How ironic that there are two women in this house: one who desperately wants a child, and one who wants to run as far as possible from this particular child.

I am gone before they rise in the morning, and I sit for an hour waiting for the train that will return me to St. John's and then to another train that will take me back to Albert and Grand Falls.

Despite having a plan, I feel like I have no direction.

Chapter 17

Lately it seems as if all I do is ride trains to places where I don't really want to go. Although, I don't think I can say where I truly want to be. Not in Carbonear with my father, Aunt Annie, and a child I'm not prepared to raise.

And not in Grand Falls with a man I'm not prepared to love.

I have no doubt what Albert's reaction will be when I arrive. One brow will raise in a controlled expression of surprise, and one side of his mouth will turn down in disapproval. I sent a telegram from the St. John's station to let him know when I will arrive, but I doubt he will be there to meet me.

No, he will have me haul my bedraggled self to our house to make a point. He doesn't chase after me any longer. I will now have to work to ingratiate myself into his good graces. And one of my first duties will be to get with child again.

Exhausted from the past several weeks, still recovering from Richard's birth and my father's rejection, I am in no state to get pregnant right away. But if I don't—oh, dear God, please let me get pregnant the first time with him, so I don't have to endure that again.

How ironic if I never conceive with Albert. What a living hell, to spend the rest of my life laying with a man whose only reason to have a child will be to put his brand on me.

I arrive in Grand Falls around four o'clock, and sure enough, Albert is not there. I hail a taxi and get home a half hour later. I sink into a chair just inside the door and cry. I don't even know for certain what I'm crying about. My emotions are ragged, and I hurt all over. The train ride has jostled every bone and sinew and ligament out of place, and if I never ride another train, it will be too soon.

The five o'clock whistle at the mill sounds, and I am still in the chair. I hurry to my bedroom and change my clothes, wash my face, and go to the kitchen to prepare dinner. Albert will expect that of me, and I must do as he expects if I am ever to get through this time. He walks through the door at a quarter past five and greets me as if I'd never left, with a light peck on the cheek before disappearing into his bedroom to hang up his suit jacket and to slip out of his work shoes and into his mules.

Dinner is tortuous, with the only conversation on his part about what is happening at the mill. I want to scream at him, to tell him what happened. I want to tell him I delivered a boy. A son.

No. Never a son.

I remain silent. As I stand to take the plates to the kitchen to begin the clearing-up, he stops me with a gesture. I sit again.

"You're looking well."

I don't feel well, but I say nothing.

"We will remain in separate rooms. You will not come to my bed, but you will always be ready and available for me. Once you are pregnant with *my* child, you will be permitted more freedom in your day-to-day activities. Until then, you will go out in public only with me. Do you understand?"

A tear slips down my cheek. I nod, not meeting his gaze.

He stands. "Good. I'm glad we talked that out."

I am soon pregnant. I know because of the return of the violent morning sickness within a couple of months of my return, and a subsequent visit to the doctor confirms I am three months along. Albert is as good as his word, and he grants me permission to leave the house occasionally, so long as he knows where I am going. I am glad to be carrying his child because of the freedom I receive in exchange. Housekeeper, baby-carrier, occasional social companion—there is much to be said for knowing one's place.

And I make my place in Grand Falls. Until I begin to show, I carry on much the same as I did in Carbonear, except now I am not trying to show up my father with my poor choices in friends.

Now I seek to embarrass my husband, to show him how I feel about him, by hanging around with the men in his social group, acting as if I am not married. He tries to treat me as a servant, or worse, as property, and I will not abide that. Albert has as much control over me as my father had.

Which wasn't much.

Nine months later, I deliver a healthy baby girl. Not the boy Albert hoped for, but a child was our deal. Not a son. And I feel about as much empathy for this child as I did for my firstborn.

And while I might think he is my secret, mine and Albert's, I know I am fooling myself. All of Carbonear and half of Grand Falls knows the truth, down to even who the father is. But I don't care.

Aunt Annie gave the child to Uncle William, but within six months, he was back in Carbonear, being raised by my father and his wife as their own. I am amazed when I visit at how much he has grown. And after Edna is born, I find myself holding her to Richard's standard. Did she walk at the same age? Is she as verbal as Richard was at that age?

I mourn the loss of his growing-up years, of that special bond between a mother and her son. I know that at some point he will marry, and I will not be the mother of the groom. He will have children, and I will not be their grandmother. Perhaps I will live long enough to see his grandchildren.

And what of Samson? He has missed even more, because he will likely never meet our son, never know the pride a father feels for this son.

And so I must focus on Edna, give her all the love and attention and emotional strength I cannot give Richard. Because I suppose a woman's firstborn will always be her first.

I guess my father was correct.

I am *unredeemable*.

Book 2—Momentum
Richard's Story

mo·men·tum

[moh-men-tuh m]
noun, plural mo·men·ta [moh-men-tuh] Show IPA , mo·men·tums.
1.

force or speed of <u>movement</u>; impetus, as of a physical <u>object</u> or course of events: The car gained momentum going downhill. Her career lost momentum after two unsuccessful films.
2.

Also called **linear momentum**. Mechanics . a quantity expressing the motion of a body or system, equal to the product of the mass of a body and its velocity, and for a system equal to the vector sum of the products of mass and velocity of each particle in the system.

"You are unwanted."

No matter how many times I've felt that, I know the truth.

At a tender age, I had a deep-set sense of not belonging. While I have no specific memory of any moment where I understood the reality of my situation, apart from when my cousin Max told me, the truth hung over my head like a cloud.

Until I learned the truth about *that* day.

Richard

Chapter 1
November 1949

"Sure, you know Laura is your mother, not your sister, right?"

If you'd told me the man in the moon was my father, I couldn't have been more surprised. I was about twelve at the time, and my cousin, Maxwell, and I were hanging around the beach, killing time until tea.

"Go away, Max, you're cracked. What makes you think that?"

"Saw some stuff my father had. Stuff your father gave him to hold onto."

"Such as?"

"There's your birth certificate. And some letters from Laura after she married Jamieson."

I pondered his words a long moment as I stared out to sea. If what he said was true, that would sure answer a lot of questions I had always put down to fanciful imaginings. Such as the time I caught Laura watching me across the room, a funny look in her eyes, like she was going to cry. "Who is my father?"

He shrugged. "Don't know."

"Who do folks think is my father?"

"Some says it's Sam Baldwin."

That explained the time I was mistaken for a Baldwin down at the post office.

I'd wondered why there was such a spread of years between Laura and me. Or why I didn't have younger siblings. Mom and Dad were married long enough to have a passel of kids. That's what folks did. I knew Laura's mother was my father's first wife. Although Louise Abbott Cameron's name was never mentioned in our house, that wasn't a secret.

But apparently my parentage was.

Or at least Laura and my folks were hoping it was.

Because if what Max said was true, that meant my father and mother were actually my grandparents.

But Laura—my mother?

Never in a thousand years would I think that. I couldn't think of any woman I knew who had less of a mothering way about her. Even the way she treated my cousin—half-sister?—Edna always seemed cold and indifferent.

My first reaction was to go to my mother and ask her. If anybody would tell me the truth, I believed she would. As I mulled that over, though, I knew that of all the people involved, she would be the one most hurt by this revelation.

I tossed a rock out into the water. "What else do you know?"

He clapped me on the shoulder. "Rats, Richard, I thought you knew. But then, the way you acted around Laura when she came to visit last week, all goofy and stuff. And chasing Edna around. I thought that was just weird."

Nothing weird about chasing a cousin through the house.

Except she wasn't my cousin.

I kicked at a string of seaweed that clung to my shoe, and the purple-green mass landed in the shallow water. The incoming tide picked up the stuff and tried to land it back on the gravelly beach. I poked it with a stick, and a small crab scuttled away to hide amongst the larger rocks.

All around me looked the same. My cousin was the same, with his sun-bleached hair and wide-open smile. And why shouldn't he look happy? He'd known he was adopted since he was old enough to understand what that meant.

And what about me? Was I even adopted? Or was I foisted on my parents—no, my grandparents? An abandoned foundling left on their doorstep, perhaps?

I had to know the story.

And I had to know who else knew the truth.

I suppose if I was to go back to the beginning, that would truly be a time before I could actually remember, but it seems as if that is the place to start. Not the beginning of time, for sure, and not the beginning of my life, because everyone begins at the same place, don't they? Everybody is conceived in more or less the same way, the coming together of a man and a woman. Everybody is born in more or less the same way.

No, my story really began sometime after that point. And so I set out to discover that story. In fact, I embraced it, because this fact made me somehow different than most people I knew. The only adopted person I knew was Maxwell, and the details of his coming into my uncle's family were fairly mundane. His birth parents were destitute, like many people in Newfoundland during those years, and they couldn't keep him. They struggled to feed and clothe their other children, and so they did what so many other families did during that time—they looked for a family better off than their own to take the child in, to give him a better opportunity than they could offer.

And Uncle Reginald and his wife were just such a family. They already had one child and plenty of room and love for another. At the time, if they struggled with another mouth to feed, nobody noticed, because everybody was the same. At least, everybody in our family and our circle of friends.

Maxwell flourished with his new family and, as far as I knew, never resented his adopted status. He was proud to be a Cameron.

But I was always a Cameron. Or I thought I was. And now I knew I was more than that. Or perhaps less, in some way.

I needed to fully understand how I came to be who and where I was.

So I began asking questions, and this is the story I was told.

My father, Henry Cameron, realized fairly early on after Laura brought me back to Carbonear at less than a week old and left me with the Baldwins, that he couldn't—and really didn't want—to take on the raising of a child. My mother, Annie Foote Cameron, no doubt felt otherwise, but had no success in convincing him differently.

So a few weeks after I arrived, I was returned to St. John's and placed in the care of my uncle. Uncle William Cameron, my father's younger brother, was a different man. Unlike my father, he was unlikely to settle into a job and stick with it. He had moved several times during his married life, and was as often without a job as with one, but somehow he always managed to survive. His children might not have been the best-dressed on the street, but in those days, that wasn't important.

Their intention was to raise me as their own, a common practice at the time. They took care of me as best they could, given their limited resources. And I'm not talking about just money and food.

Uncle William's health prevented him from working very much, and as they already had children of their own clamoring for love and attention, I was the last to receive any additional affection, or so I was told. Uncle William, when he worked, labored long hours and didn't have much of anything left over once he came home. Aunt Helen also worked long hours, even though she didn't have a job outside the house. Cooking, cleaning, laundry, keeping the house, and tending to the children was a full-time job.

When my mother Annie came into St. John's, which she did approximately once a month, she came to visit me, and would bring stories back to my father Henry about my progress. She was never satisfied with how they cared for me and thought she could do a better job. She was forty-two years old, and my father was fifty-two.

Still, her heart broke each time she saw me. I was part of the family, but spent much of my day in a crib by myself. The way I would clasp onto her neck when she visited and cry when she was leaving wore her down.

In September, when I was about six months old, she came into St. John's to visit her sister and me. When she arrived, Aunt Helen had been going through a particularly bad day. Uncle William was ill, and no amount of doctors or medicines was making him well. He'd been out of work for a couple of weeks, and with no money coming in, I was on the bottom of her list of concerns. Not that she neglected or abused me in any way—she gave me what was left in the bottom of her bucket of love, and by this time, that wasn't much.

My mother did her best to clean me up, but couldn't find any clean clothes or bedding. She replaced my dirty diaper with the last clean one, and set the soiled nappie to soak in a pail.

At least, that's how she always told the story.

And then she returned to Carbonear on a mission.

At dinner that night, my mother asked my father if he would go with her next week to help hang some curtains and put up the rods for my aunt.

Whether my father saw through her ploy or not, he went into St. John's the next week. Usually they traveled by train, but on this trip, my father drove his car, a 1929 Nash sedan.

When they came to Uncle William's house, my mother led him to the room where I was kept. The curtains were still closed, even though the time was around noon. My father was stunned at the stale smell of a shut-up room and the smell of my dirty diaper. My nappie hadn't been changed yet that day.

I reached for my mother when I saw her.

Despite how disgusting I must have been, she picked me up, cuddled, cooed with me, and then handed me over to my father.

His heart broke. He sobbed and grabbed me. I guess my blue eyes won him over. No matter the Camerons all have brown eyes. No matter I looked as much like my birth father as I did my birth mother, Henry Cameron did the only thing he could do.

He opened his heart—and his home—and called me Son.

I was wanted.

Chapter 2

To say I was the perfect son would be a disservice to all those children much better behaved. Truth was, I was a handful. Never malicious, but like most children, I had no notion of the potential outcome of my actions, and I had a strong belief in my immortality. I figure I wore out several pairs of guardian angels throughout my childhood.

If you'd asked my mother, she'd have said, "He's both ends of a bad boy."

I suppose I didn't get myself into any worse trouble than the rest of the boys I hung around with. I was never punished for something I didn't do, but often punished for what I did that was wrong. My father was fair in his discipline—he never thrashed me unless he was pure certain I'd been involved. I learned early not to lie, and even earlier, I learned not to get caught.

As you can imagine, one of the biggest fears in those days was of drowning, being as how we lived on an island, next to a harbour. Strange how few people knew how to swim, and fewer yet bothered with any kind of safety equipment or flotation devices. There wasn't much of that stuff going around in those days.

At any rate, in the spring, the ice would blow down from up north, and the prevailing winds would shove it into Carbonear harbour. Depending on the temperatures and the amount of fog, the ice would last several weeks, or it might last just a few days.

Around about when I was thirteen or fourteen, we had a long, cold winter, and the harbour filled with ice. The pressure from the smaller floes and the wind and waves kind of packed the ice into larger sheets called pack ice. Four or five of us boys got on a piece of pack ice up near the old post office and thought we could ride it down the harbour and hop off once we got to Henry Johnson's wharf.

We had a grand old time, pushing and shoving each other, threatening to topple the other off the edge. At one point we got a couple on opposite sides and jumped up and down, setting the pan rocking, but when one of the boys slipped and nearly fell in, we straightened out. Getting dunked in the salt water in April could be a death sentence, since none of us could swim, and we didn't have a rope or anything to fish us out of the water.

Once we'd done fooling around, we hunkered down on the ice, feeling the cold up through our boots. We didn't have any oars to help move us along and give us some direction, and the westerly wind picked up and started to blow us out to the open ocean. Let me tell you, that was a moment of panic when we saw we were going to miss the wharf, miss the headland, what we call the Southside, and likely we'd go on out to sea. And this might sound strange, but worse than going out to sea was we might come up against Carbonear Island.

And I say that's worse because we would have ended up on the inside shore of Carbonear Island, from which there was no way to get up on the island. The only place to land is on the southeast end, because the rest is sheer rock. I don't know what would have happened, but from talking to the lighthouse keeper, Richard Earle, he said there was a landline telephone at the lighthouse, one of those old wind-up kinds. The lighthouse was never locked, he said, and so you could always get the telephone operator in Carbonear. Whether that was right, I don't know, and how we'd have gotten there, I don't know either. Not from that side we couldn't.

At any rate, we figured out that one or two of us had to stand up on the ice pan and act like a sail. Too many, and the wind would just buffet us around and around in circles until either the ice gave out beneath us or we went so far out we just froze to death.

As we rounded the point, we changed position and let the wind blow us toward Harbour Rock Hill, down near where the funeral home is. We had all we could do to get in there, and we got our feet wet getting ashore because the pan of ice that could float five or six guys was deep enough it wouldn't come right in on the beach. It would bring up on the first shelf going out. So we caught on the shelf and when we got in the water, we were most of us up to our crotch in salt water. Cold.

I was glad I'd decided to go out with the other guys, because once I had gone out by myself. Now, that time, I'd gotten in all right, but this time, I don't think I could have managed it by myself. The time I'd gone by myself, the weather had been more foggy, so the ice had melted into smaller pans, and we couldn't find a pan big enough to float the lot of us. Three or four had been out there at the time, and one by one we brought up on the shore, or at the wharf. I'd never really thought about being blown out to sea.

In this case, the piece of ice we were on was about as big as a good-sized kitchen, about twenty by twenty. You needed a big enough one so it would hold you up, and you always had in your mind that if a piece broke off, you needed enough left to stand on. Sometimes you could be standing on a piece, and if there was a fracture deep inside the ice, all of a sudden the piece you were standing on could break off, and what you thought was safe could now be minimally so.

At any rate, we never talked of our adventures to the adults, since we'd been threatened with a thrashing if we were caught on the ice pans. So we were never caught. But after this particular experience, I thought twice about going pan-hopping again. Not to say I never did it, but I made sure I had an oar or a long stick or something to use as a rudder, and I always checked to be sure the wind wasn't westerly.

I might have been both ends of a bad boy, but I wasn't stupid.

Living so close to the water, there were plenty of drownings, of course. Some happened out at sea, some in the harbour, and some off the wharf. Seemed like every time a ship came back from the Grand Banks or the seal fishery, at least one body was wrapped in canvas on deck. Those were hard times, and it was a hard life, for the men and the women. A wife never knew if her man was going to come back or not.

I was only about four years old when we had two drownings within a month, and so I only know what I've been told. First was Graham Udell. He was in Labrador fishing, and by all accounts, he was a strapping young fellow of about thirty-five years of age with a beautiful wife and four children in Carbonear. A great big wave caught their boat sideways, and he was washed overboard. News didn't travel so fast back then, and so it wasn't for about a month before his wife heard the news. Apparently when they sent the minister down to tell her, she laughed at him. Said it couldn't be possible because she'd dreamt about him just the night before. In those days, folks put great store in dreams. However, she believed he was dead when the ship he was on, the *Lavenia*, sailed into harbour a few days later, and there was his body, wrapped in black canvas on the deck.

The next fellow was Ernest Ash. His drowning was even more tragic, if that were possible. He was out for a walk late at night, after having a couple of drinks at the local public house. Maybe he had more than a few, but the proprietor wouldn't admit to more than a few because the law frowned on sending customers out into the night drunk as skunks. At any rate, out he went, and the fog being low to the ground, the police believe perhaps he went out to the head of the public wharf to relieve himself of those ales, and either slipped or overextended his reach, and toppled into the water. Being late, nobody heard his cries for help, if indeed he survived the fall. His body was found two days later after his wife reported him missing.

Living in Newfoundland in those days was hard work no matter what time of year. In the spring, the men would go sealing. That was a dangerous and dirty job, with not a lot of pay in return. Still, the thrill of seeing a part of the world a man had never seen was a big part of why so many would sign up to go. That, and I think some men just like to get away from civilization once in a while.

In the summer, there was the Grand Banks fishing, another excuse to be gone for months at a time. In good years, a man could work for three months and earn enough to stay home the other nine, but in lean years, when the Russians and the Spanish and the French got to the good fishing grounds ahead of the boats, a man and his family nearly starved, living off credit and promising to pay as soon as they could. Of course, shopkeepers knew that unless the man went to work somewhere else, they wouldn't see any money until the next spring.

And sometimes a man would get so desperate he would go to work in the woods in the winter, when the trees were so frozen that your ax bounced off like hitting a metal pole, and the dangers included falling trees, blunt axes, frostbite, and falling through the ice and drowning. Still, a man might also come home with enough money to tide the family over until spring, when he could start all over again.

I was lucky. My father was an established businessman. Almost everybody shopped for one thing or another at my father's shop. He charged a fair price and provided a necessary service. The closest grocery and dry goods store would have been in Harbour Grace, and even the Freshwater stores didn't boast as good a selection of goods as my father's shop.

Even the people he hated the most—and there was a long and varied list for a long and varied list of actual or perceived reasons—shopped at Henry Cameron's. I know one of them was Hayward Baldwin, my birth father's father. I never knew why my father hated him so much, but he did, and Hayward Baldwin knew it. I suspect Baldwin had to swallow a huge wad of pride to come into the shop, but my father served him well enough. And he never said a bad word to him, even though he never cracked a smile, either.

My father had his moral code he lived by and that he expected others to live by as well. I didn't always understand his reasons, but I respected him enough to try to stay on his right side. I failed at times, but I never had him tell me he was disappointed in me or any of the choices I'd made.

I sometimes heard him and Mom talking at night, and I'd hear my name and Laura's mentioned, and I knew they were comparing us.

Laura never measured up.

Chapter 3

Up to the point of my discovering about my parentage, I'd enjoyed what I would term a fairly normal upbringing. I knew my cousin Maxwell had a completely different set of life experiences, but he was being raised in the Capital. Some of our common escapades occurred when he came to Carbonear to visit. Add to that the fact that he was being raised in a family, while I was an only child.

My father worked long hours six days a week in the shop, and as I grew up, I was expected to help out when needed, and not only in the shop, but around the house as well. During that time, I discovered my mechanical aptitude and my fascination with electricity, and my parents put those interests to use whenever possible.

My mother enjoyed her status as wife, mother, homemaker, as well as her affiliations with the church and her social peers. She seemed always busy around the house, and although we often had "a girl" who either lived in or lived out come "to do" for us, my mother was always the boss of the house. She was a good cook and baker, loved to sit around and enjoy a cup of tea, and knit tirelessly for the church sale of works or whoever was having a baby at the moment.

Although many might think my father was nothing but a shopkeeper in a small town, he was far more than that. In many ways, he was a self-taught man. As the son of a fisherman, he'd decided early on that the fishing life wasn't for him, so he did well in school and got a job with a local fish merchant, Royal's.

He started out as a clerk in the Carbonear office, and worked his way up to a kind of purchasing manager. For several summers, Royal's sent him to northern Newfoundland and also to Labrador to oversee their operations. When he returned to Carbonear, he worked all the harder, and was promoted there as well. All the while he was learning the trade of retail and wholesale business, accounting, cash flow, inventory control, and managing employees.

When he began his shop in 1911, he was still working for Royal's. As he told me in later years, they wanted to be sure they could make a go of it in the shop, so his first wife Louise worked the shop while he kept his day job. He helped out on weekends and nights, and after several years, the shop was doing well enough he quit with Royal's and went full time in the shop.

Apart from the shop, he had many other interests. I remember him being a bit of a husbandman to some ducks, in that he would set a broody hen on some duck eggs as well as her own eggs. His goal was to hatch out more ducks, since he preferred duck to chicken.

He classified his first attempts as failures because of the low hatch rate. One thing he didn't know at the time was that duck eggs need to be wet down every day. The duck hen accomplishes this by going to the water every day and coming back with her feathers wet. However, hens don't do that.

He tried setting the eggs in different places, thinking perhaps a cold draft might be impeding the hatching. In fact, he had to make notes to himself to remind himself where he'd put the nests, since sometimes they were in out-of-the-way places that couldn't be seen.

One day he went out to check on a nest, and a foul smell met him. His heart sank because he knew something had died. The hen was pacing and pecking around the nest, but when he sat her on it, she wouldn't have anything to do with the two chicks and three ducklings that had hatched. When he investigated further, he discovered that four of the eggs had spoiled. This sometimes happens when the duckling inside starts to develop and then died or if the eggs were not fertilized.

Concerned for the health of the hen and the young occupants of the nest, he removed the spoiled eggs and investigated further by taking the eggs outdoors and opening them. Sure enough, the eggs had never developed, meaning they weren't fertilized. Old Cecil wasn't doing his job, apparently.

My father wasn't accustomed to failing, and so he read up on everything he could find about ducks and the differences with chickens, until he lit upon this tidbit of information. He would go out to the eggs every day and sprinkle water on them. His hatch rate did improve, but he never had as good a rate as he did with the chickens.

I don't think he'd really thought beyond getting the eggs to hatch and seeing if a hen could brood duck eggs as well as a duck could, because once the eggs hatched, that's when more trouble began. A hen knows how to peck, and it knows how to teach its chicks to peck. Unfortunately, ducks don't peck. And to see a hen and her chicks along with a couple of ducklings out in the yard, and the hen trying to teach the ducklings to peck, and they just can't do it, is a funny thing to watch. One hen nearly wore herself out, and my father had to take the ducklings and put them in with the other ducks, hoping they would teach the young ones what to do. They did, and all survived.

Another thing my father was involved in was dandelion. While most people consider it nothing more than a nuisance weed, in those days in Carbonear, dandelion was a delicacy. My father culled and cleaned a patch of dandelion in a small piece of property across the street from our house. He chose the larger leaves of the better plants, and made sure to pick out the plants that were less desirable.

Over a period of years, he produced dandelion plants with leaves as wide as your palm and a foot or longer. These leaves cooked up better and provided a more substantial portion than the smaller leaves. He took great pride in these plants, and to this day, there are some plants in that plot of ground with larger leaves than usual.

Perhaps my love of physics and chemistry came from my father. He was definitely a man ahead of his time, with his thoughts on breeding out the bad and breeding in the new. The thing was, as much alike as we might have seemed, we were often in a conflict that ran deep beneath the surface.

My mother was the peacekeeper in the family. She got along with most everybody, except Laura, and expected everyone to get along with her. My father didn't care what anybody thought about him, so long as it didn't affect their business relationship. That was one thing that was precious to him. I can't say as I saw anything toward me or my mother other than affection and care and concern. My father would always do what was right, but if he could do what was right and make a dollar, he would.

He didn't abide with lying, however, and so I learned early to check my words. One time, he got word that I'd been seen tearing around Carbonear in Tom Rowe' car. The problem was, Tom wasn't driving, I was. And I was only twelve at the time. Needless to say, I wasn't stupid enough to go past the shop, and so perhaps I hoped nobody would tell him.

What I should have remembered was that Henry Cameron's shop was the life hub of Carbonear, and even if a person didn't buy anything, they went in there on their way up or down Water Street. Within about ten minutes of my joyride, my father knew. So when I came sauntering into the shop later that day, he called me aside and told me in no uncertain terms I was not to tarnish the Cameron name again with my shenanigans.

Of course, there was no reason to ask him how he knew, because he would never tell me. He just knew, and that's what was important. But I'll not forget his words to me: don't let me see you doing that again, and don't let me hear of you doing that again.

I acknowledged his reprimand in the spirit it was delivered, and assured him he'd never see me or hear of me joyriding around town without a license. And he never did.

I always made sure to do my joyriding out in the country where the waggling tongues of Carbonear couldn't see me.

And we never had that discussion again.

I remember one Halloween night when I got caught up in the spirit of the times, no pun intended. In those days, the focus wasn't on getting candy. Instead, we would dress up and go around to the houses, and basically threaten the people that if they didn't give us some treat, they were going to get a trick.

Most everybody in town was more than willing to avoid the trick and give us a treat, be it a cookie, a song, or just invite us in from the cold for a cup of tea. But this one particular householder decided he wasn't having any of it. He'd turned out the lights, and so we thought he'd gone out for the evening.

We didn't have any particular trick in mind, but when we wandered out to his back yard, we saw this rickety old outhouse that looked like it was ready to fall over.

Greg Thoms ran over and pounded on the door. "Come out, you scaredy ghosts."

We thought that sounded like great fun, so we joined him. One of the boys had brought a rope with them. I don't know what he thought he was going to do with it, but we ended up wrapping one end around the outhouse with the intention of tipping the thing over. We thought we'd be doing the homeowner a favor, since just about everyone in Carbonear had an indoor toiled by this time.

We got on the opposite end of the rope and pulled.

What had looked spindly and unstable was, in fact, stout and upright. So we pulled all the harder.

I was in the middle of the line of boys, and there was much shouting and laughing going on, but still I thought I heard another sound. "Pull the harder, boys, before he comes out and finds us."

So we heaved for all we were worth, and finally the thing gave way. We ended up in a heap on the ground, laughing and congratulating ourselves on how smart we were.

Then I looked up, and Mr. Squibb was sitting on the seat, his pants down around his knees, bellowing at us as he tried to cover himself up.

I don't know who was more surprised—him or us.

At any rate, knowing we'd not only wrecked an outhouse that was still in use but we'd been found out, we scrambled to our feet and took off running.

Mr. Squibb shouted at us as we ran. "Greg Thoms, I know where you live. Tom Saunders, I know your father. I'm going to get my gun. I'll call the constable. Stuart Baldwin, you can't hide from me. I know you, too."

Now, Stuart Baldwin wasn't in our group. He was referring to me. I bore such a strong resemblance to my birth father's family that Mr. Squibb thought I was Hayward Baldwin's grandson.

That was the first time that happened to me, but I didn't care. Other times when people called me Stuart, I corrected them. But that time, my resemblance to the Baldwins saved me a severe thrashing, because Mr. Squibb was as good as his word. He called on the fathers of the boys he'd seen, and they were punished.

Not enough, apparently, since they never turned me in. And I heard that despite his protests that he was never there, Stuart Baldwin endured a similar discipline as my friends.

Didn't bother me one bit.

We didn't limit our practical jokes to Halloween. In fact, just five days later,

Guy Fawkes Day was created with young boys and scallywags in mind. Guy Fawkes was one of the plotters who tried to blow up the House of Lords in England hundreds of years before. Affectionately known as Bonfire Night, we celebrated by burning everything that wasn't nailed down.

On this particular night, we gang of five or six, including T.J. Royal, Matthew Parsons, and the other boys of our group, roamed Carbonear looking for an appropriate offering to sacrifice to the fire. We'd already torn off a few palings from the fences along the back road, and even managed to snag a wheelbarrow from Old Tom Larson's yard.

Rolling along Water Street, pushing a barrow, you might wonder why we weren't detained and the barrow returned to its rightful owner. However, most of the folks out and about that night were up to as much no good as we were. Several men ran past with a length of board, and a couple other teenagers trotted by with a tree that looked suspiciously like the spruce from in front of Johnson's Hotel.

When we came to the next house, I had a brilliant thought. "Hayward Ryan has a chicken coop in back of his house."

T.J. Royal thought this a grand idea. "How are we going to get it up to the fire?"

I pointed at the barrow. "No point bringing it there empty."

Matthew agreed, and we made the next turn up to where Hayward lived. He had a huge old dog that hung near the house, hiding out of sight behind a fence. A couple of times that old hound fooled me into thinking he was elsewhere, waiting until I came within about two feet of the property line. Then he launched himself onto his hind legs, front paws hanging over the fence, slathering and drooling all over himself, as he barked himself into a frenzy.

I hated that dog.

So we knew we had to be careful not to wake the beast or he'd alert Hayward of our presence. I figured the best way to do that was to send a decoy to keep him busy, so if Hayward looked out his window, he'd see why the dog was raising such a ruckus.

We'd need four or five stout boys to lift the chicken coop off its footing and onto the barrow, so we settled on the smallest of our bunch, Lloyd Royal. I warned him of the importance of his assignment, and reminded him to stay out of reach of that crazy hound. He said he understood, and off he went. Within a minute or so, the dog was barking and snarling and howling like his tail was on fire and someone was throwing gunpowder on him.

We went straight to work, because we didn't know how long we'd have before Duff came out and drove him away. The five of us surrounded the chicken coop, braced our hands against the sides, and rocked the structure back and forth a little at a time to loosen the boards from the fifty or so years of hen crap, dirt, and straw that had combined to form a kind of impromptu bird-poop-like cement.

After about ten minutes and a lot of mumbled cussing, the house shifted completely off its dirt foundation. We squat down and picked up the house. I don't think any of the others expected the wooden box to weigh as much as it did. I sure didn't, and I was ready to give it up for a bad lot at that point.

But T.J. Royal egged us on. "Come on, girls, we don't want to show up at the bonfire with nothin' but a barrow. The other boys will laugh us off the hill."

Strengthened by the truth of his words, we tried again, and managed to crab-walk the house, hens and all, to the barrow.

Except we had a problem. There was no bottom in the chicken coop to set on the bed of the wheelbarrow. We studied our predicament for a full minute as the sweat rolled off our brows and our fingers went numb where we held the bottom edge of the house.

Then I saw the solution. "Tip her over, boys. Put her roof down into the barrow."

To accomplish this maneuver meant we had to coordinate our efforts even more than we had previously.

I came up with the plan. "T.J., you and Matthew come up to the edge of the barrow."

They did as I said.

"Now, drop your end as low as you can without setting it on the ground."

T.J. and Matthew were built like two brick outhouses, and were the shortest and strongest of the lot, and still their eyes bulged with their effort.

"Okay, the rest of you lift your end up as high as you can so the house is standing on its side." I showed them what to do with my bit, and they did the same.

In the meantime, I've got one ear tuned into the hound from hell, who was still barking and braying at our friend. We still had some time, but not much, judging by the tired sound the old dog was making. He'd soon lose interest and come in search of new game, namely us. Or Hayward would tire of listening to the creature howl and would come out to investigate or shut him up.

"Okay, now, T.J. and Matthew, edge closer to the barrow. That's it. A little more." I kept one hand on the side of the house nearest me to keep it balanced. "Now, boys, tip her into the barrow."

The structure swayed on the lip of the wheelbarrow, perched like a crow on a pole, then toppled in with a crash and a groan. Another hen flew out the open bottom, squawking and fluttering feathers all over us.

The boys cheered, but I shushed them.

"Let's get going before we're found out."

We raced pell mell down Water Street toward Taylor's Bank where the fire was roaring. All along the way, a hen or two would fly out. One time, the old rooster, long past his prime, shot straight up and then landed on T.J. Royal's head, twisting its claws into his hair. T.J. lost his hold on the wheelbarrow handle, and if not for some quick thinking on my part, the whole load would have landed in the ditch.

We left T.J. back there fighting with the old cock, and continued on our way, laughing and congratulating ourselves for having brought the most dangerous and unique offering. We skidded to a stop and dumped the load on the ground. T.J., who had managed to extricate the rooster and lose only a couple tufts of hair in the process, ran forward and jumped onto the chicken coop, landing fairly in the middle of one side. The flimsy wood, perfect for housing hens, collapsed under this weight, and he fell to the ground amidst a flurry of old feathers, dank straw, and dust.

Sneezing, he stood, as we laughed at the way the feathers stuck to him, as if he'd been tarred and feathered. He brushed himself off, and we all dug in, tearing boards apart and tossing them into the fire. Once we got the chicken coop down to a more manageable size, we picked it up and threw it onto the fire.

We'd already checked to make certain there were no wayward hens huddled inside, but we were still surprised when the acrid stink of burnt chickens wafted off in the smoke.

Seems hen crap smells like chickens.

Go figure.

Chapter 4

I was about five years old when the war started. I don't remember much about the early years of the battle except my parents gathering around the radio and listening to the reports from England. When I was old enough to read, I looked up in the atlas where England was, and recall being fascinated at the distance between Newfoundland and so far across the ocean.

Every night in 1942 as we huddled in our chairs, blackout curtains making the rooms seem even darker, men with strange accents regaled us with tales of heroism and horror, of bravery and bravado. As the conflict continued, I found myself wanting to be those brave soldiers willing to fight and even die for something they believed in.

One night as a spokesperson for War Savings Bonds told us how we could help our country, I interrupted. "I don't want to fight the Germans by buying stupid old bonds. I want to fight them with guns."

I don't know how I thought I could possibly accomplish that feat, since I was only about seven and had seen a shotgun but once or twice in my life.

My father leaned back in his chair and chuckled. "Richard, my boy, we can all do our part. And we don't have to go overseas to do it."

I folded my arms across my chest and stuck out my bottom lip. "I don't see how I can help if I'm just sitting here, stuck in Carbonear. I need to be over there, helping our boys."

I'd heard people talking about our boys over there, and I desperately wanted to be one of them. I pictured other seven- and eight-year-old boys shooting at the enemy.

My mother set aside her knitting and opened her arms to me, and I dove into her ample bosom, glad to be held close to her. Her heart pounded like a cannon in my ear. "Richard, you are too young a boy to go over there. You have to wait until you're eighteen before you can fight."

I slid off her lap. "Eighteen! Why, that's—" I counted on my fingers. "More than ten years. The war will be over by that time."

My father stared into the fire, a strange, faraway look on his face, as if he wasn't really looking at the flames. "I hope so, Son. I hope so."

Well, that didn't really satisfy me. "Why did T.J.'s brother Wilson get to go?"

I'd watched Wilson and several other older boys from Carbonear climb on the train a couple of years ago. At the time, I didn't understand their words as they pulled away, vowing to fight every Kraut and send them back to Hitler. I thought Hitler was a place where Krauts—whatever they were—came from.

My mother wrapped her arms around me again. "He was old enough. And brave enough."

I pulled away from her and puffed out my chest. "I'm brave enough."

My father nodded. "Yes, I believe you are, Richard. But we need you here. Can you be brave enough to stay where you're needed?"

I thought about that for a while, and then I nodded. If my parents needed me, I could stay around a while longer and help them out. "What can I do?"

My father stood and drew me to his side. "Well, we need you to look after your mother."

I stepped away and looked up at him, ready to protest the unfairness. But his look quieted me.

"And you'll need to step in and fill Wilson's shoes in this town. You can help T.J. make sure his mother has all the firewood she needs because Wilson used to do that."

This sounded much more important, and I was ready for an important task.

"And I probably won't be able to hire as many young men to help me in the shop, or with roof repairs, or to haul firewood in for us, so we'll need you to lend a hand there."

"I'm ready, Dad."

He patted my shoulder. My father wasn't much at showing affection, and I rarely received much more than that. This time, though, his hand lay on my shoulder for a long while as we listened to the rest of the news. Even after he'd moved away from me, I felt the heat and the strength from his hand on my shoulder for a very long time.

Over the years, I'd heard people say that my father would give them the shirt off his back if they needed it, and I saw that generosity demonstrated first-hand during the war. Ration books were issued to families based on the number of people in the household. Being as there were three of us and a maid, we got three adult books and one child book for a year.

Ration books covered those things considered a luxury, such as butter, sugar, tea, and canned milk. The books had named stamps for these items, and stamps that were called spares. People would bring their ration books into the shop, and my father would keep them in the safe, since these were valuable, and we'd been warned to hide them. I heard some stories about people being robbed of their books and not being able to buy tea or sugar for months on end as they waded through the bureaucracy to get their books replaced.

At any rate, Dad knew that the folks who left their books with him would come back to him to shop for their groceries, so he didn't mind keeping them safe. When a family came in who didn't use butter—they bought Newfoundland butter, which was margarine—he might give their butter stamp to another family. Sometimes a relative came to stay with family in Carbonear, but their ration book hadn't caught up with them yet at their new address, and my father never hesitated to offer stamps from our books.

And we never went hungry.

See, the good thing about owning a grocery store is you have access to groceries. The process was fairly simple: he turned in the butter ration stamps to the wholesaler to buy more butter. He turned in the canned milk stamps to purchase more canned milk, and so on for the other items being rationed.

I saw women come to my father, tears in their eyes, and beg him for some tea. Not a package—simply enough for a single pot of tea. And he never sent them away empty-handed.

Despite my hopes that the war would continue long enough for me to be able to fight, the conflict drew to a close before I could take part in any way other than keeping the home fires burning, as the song said.

In March and April of 1945, we listened to the radio reports of increased fighting, of the thousands of men killed, of battles gone bad, of ships sank and planes shot down. Every week we'd read in the paper the names of the lost, and we'd search for our boys' names, glad when they didn't show up on that stark black ink on newsprint.

Of course, Mr. Churchill was a favorite of ours, as he rallied the troops and the people alike to hold fast and never give up. We forgot about talks of confederation, and we forgave our government for rationing those things that made life bearable.

Instead, we looked to the Kingman of England, to how he and his wife bravely stayed in London through the Blitz, even though they sent the princesses to Scotland to keep them safe. We cursed the Krauts when we heard about the sinking of the *Laconia* and the *Caribou* in 1942, not to mention the whalers and trawlers sunk in Europe and beyond beneath the torpedoes of the German navy.

And then came that day, May 8th, 1945. Victory over Europe Day. We awoke to horns blaring and guns firing in the streets of Carbonear. My father rushed outside to find out what was going on. When he couldn't make any sense of what people were saying, he ran back into the house, gathered my mother and me around the radio, and ignored the cold and drizzle outside as we clung to each other and to the excited voices of the announcer on the CBC telling us that the war was over.

My parents clapped, and I scowled.

I might have done my part for the war, but I wasn't one bit happy.

My only consolation was that the war going on with Japan might last long enough to fulfill my dreams of fighting with our boys.

My parents couldn't stop talking about the end of the fighting, of Wilson and our other boys coming home soon, of an end to ration books and blackout curtains and gasoline shortages. Of the chance to buy a new set of tires for the car. Perhaps the opportunity to look out over the ocean to the horizon and not envision a German U-boat patrolling off the shore.

Me, I was angry with the politicians who had managed to arrange the German surrender. I was a little bit upset with our boys for fighting a good enough war that it would end before I was able to take part. And I was mad that the Germans hadn't hung in there long enough for me to come and give them a good licking.

Still, I knew I could count on the Japanese.

Except just a few days shy of four months later, they, too, gave up.

For a twelve-year-old boy who desperately wanted to prove his bravery and his manhood, I was disappointed all over again.

Chapter 5

There was a spot of excitement early in the war when they started building a secret installation near the hydroelectric plant in Victoria. At first, the construction was all hush-hush. Nobody would tell us what was going on, and my father didn't like that one bit. We often took a drive on a Sunday afternoon down around the shore, stopping in at Clarke's store on the main highway for a soda or an ice cream, not to mention to hear the latest gossip and goings on.

On this particular day in late summer of 1940, we saw the road going out to the plant was more torn up than usual, and a chain link fence had been put up. We weren't certain whether they were trying to keep someone in or out. At any rate, my father drove up the road, avoiding the worst of the ruts, until we came to the front gate for the power plant.

In a field across the street was a great lot of activity. Bulldozers and tractors of all shapes and sizes plowed down the trees and scrub brush and leveled the ground. Off to the side, stacks of pipes of different sizes awaited installation.

My father whistled soft through his teeth. "My, looks like something big and important."

My mother leaned across him and peered out through the side window. "What do you think it is, Henry?"

"Don't know, Mom." He turned around to where I was sitting in the back seat, all eyes and ears. "What do you think, Richard?"

"Well, that's water and sewer pipes over there."

My father nodded. "Right."

"Maybe houses?"

"Not likely. Too far from town. And who'd want to live next door to the power plant?"

He had a point there. I shrugged. "Maybe a school?"

"Victoria already has a perfectly good elementary school and a high school."

True. "What else?" I was stumped.

"Maybe something to do with the war?"

I bounced in my seat. "Maybe a training base?"

My mother chimed in. "An airport?"

My father, always active in his church, added his opinion. "Perhaps an orphanage to handle all the war orphans."

I liked my line of thinking better, although an airport would be a cause for excitement, too. An orphanage wasn't exactly up to par when it came to wartime construction, at least not to my mind. "Why don't you ask the man standing outside the gate?"

He put the car in gear and we rolled forward. "What a good idea. Simple, too. The worst he could do is say he can't tell us."

During war, secrets abounded. Sometimes I thought all the secrecy was overdone. After all, if you couldn't trust the people you knew, how could you trust anybody? I don't think the people of Carbonear subscribed to the saying we saw at the movie theatres newsreels, "loose lips sink ships", but maybe the folks in Victoria did.

Whatever the reason for not being able to tell us about the construction before had evaporated, and the man at the gate seemed only too glad to tell us what was going on. He puffed out his chest and hooked his thumbs in his belt, swaggered back on his heels, and filled us in.

"We're building a prisoner of war camp for the Germans." He spoke as if he was out there personally hammering nails into boards, when in reality, he was only a man at the gate. No gun in sight, and the gate wide open, anybody who wanted to get in only had to drive past him and he couldn't have stopped them. "For the pilots and such what get shot down over England, you know."

Well, of course I did know about those dratted Krauts who were bombing England and sinking ships, and I thought a camp in Newfoundland was too good for them. I wanted to ask more questions, but my father seemed satisfied with that information and backed up the car to leave.

I tossed a final question toward the man at the gate. "When will we see the first prisoners?"

He shook his head. "We're hoping the war doesn't go on long enough for them to send any here, of course." He stared toward the east, a pastime more people had taken up, as if they stared long enough toward England they might actually see it. "But we think we'll be ready in about eighteen months."

A year and a half seemed like an awful long time to make ready, but I suppose there was a lot more to be done than to just throw up some buildings and bring the prisoners in.

On our drive home, I pestered my father about the camp and what kind of horrible conditions we might come up with to punish the Germans for their bad choices in life. I'll never forget his reply.

"Richard, they had no choice in being born German, any more than you had a choice being born a Newfoundlander."

I pondered that for about two heartbeats. "But—"

"No 'buts'. They think they're doing the right thing as much as you would if you were old enough to join the army or the navy. You'd go over there and drop bombs on them if you had the chance."

"Darn right I would, Dad."

"And they would think you were a bad sort." He glanced at me in the rearview mirror. "Are you a bad sort?"

"I don't think so."

"And neither do they think that of themselves. War is never only about right and wrong. There's a lot of other things to consider. And both sides always think they're doing the proper thing. Both sides, if they believe in God, think that God is on their side."

"How can that be? How can God be on our side and on the German side, too?"

He gripped the steering wheel and made the turn back onto the highway. "I don't know. The only thing I do know is that we must be careful how we treat others. We must always treat them better than they treat us."

I'd heard some of the horror stories of the Allied forces taken prisoner, of how the Germans were mistreating them, not allowing the Red Cross in, not allowing them letters from home. I'd pictured the Germans as being uncivilized, uncaring people.

And here I was, thinking how, if I was in control, I might do the same thing back to them.

Made me no better than they were. And that was a sobering thought, to think I was no better than a people I hated. A people I'd never met.

Some of my hatred for the German people slipped away that day, to be replaced by a hatred for war and conflict in general. I think I grew up a little.

As it happened, no German prisoners ever inhabited the camp in Victoria. By the time the camp was built, the people in control came to the realization that having a camp near a power plant, although its proximity solved the problem of providing electricity, could also prove to be a magnet for German espionage. By the end of 1943, workers and security guards carried firearms because of the threat of attack. The people in the know also conjectured that this camp, once filled with German officers and airmen, might be a reason for their comrades to invade the area and then the island, and that could have proven disastrous, given the large British and American military contingents in St. John's and Argentia.

While it surely seemed as though life as we knew it stopped so the war could take its course, in reality that didn't happen. In fact, with a few inconveniences such as rationing and boys going off to fight, we were practically untouched by the war taking place in Europe and the Pacific.

That doesn't mean we didn't lose men—we did. And it doesn't mean we were living in some kind of dream where the world went on around us—we didn't. We felt deeply the loss of our men, and several did die. More were injured. And those who came back weren't the boys we remembered. Most struggled for many years to find a way to fit back in.

I remember T.J. telling me some of the stories his brother Wilson told him, about sailing over on a big ship. Of being seasick for days. Of the bad weather and high waves. Of being certain he was going to die.

And then of seeing the shores of England for the first time. The streets of London lying in shambles from the German Blitzkrieg. Seeing the beautiful buildings and churches destroyed, people killed, children left without parents. Wilson told me a story that put everything in proportion for me as it did for him.

We were sitting on Harbour Rock Hill one afternoon in late October, T.J., Wilson, and me. School had let out for the day, and we'd met there to talk. Ever since Wilson came back, I'd been dying to ask him questions.

But this day, just sitting next to him, I was struck dumb. Here was a man—he'd left a boy, and come back a man. A man who'd fought in a war, in a foreign land, wearing a British uniform. What could I possibly ask him that would show how much I knew about the war, when he'd been there? So I waited for him to tell me in his own good time, as I knew he would.

He chewed on the end of a stalk of grass and stared out at Carbonear Island. "We were on the ocean for twelve days, you know."

I hadn't, but I nodded as if I did.

"I hadn't eaten for four days. Couldn't even keep a cup of tea down."

I'd been out in an open boat a few times when the waves swelled up and I wasn't sure I was going to get back to shore. And I'd gone pan hopping where I'd nearly been blown out to sea. But not for twelve days. I knew nothing about what he'd been through.

"And just when I thought I couldn't stand it any longer, when I was trying to make a deal with God to just wash me overboard, I heard the man in the main staff call out that he saw land ahead. We all crowded to the railing, trying to see through the fog, past the twenty-foot waves. Then we plunged down into a trough, and all I could think was I was going to die just when we spotted land, and I thought that was damned unfair."

His curse caused my heart to pound. I didn't often hear a curse word, and when I did, there wasn't usually this amount of emotion behind it. And I thought it damned unfair at that moment that he might die, too.

"And then we rode that wave all the way to the top, and I saw a dark shape about ten miles past us. And I saw a light flash, and I knew it was a lighthouse, and it was land, and we were going to be all right. As quick as that, I knew we would be all right."

He sat back, his elbows propping his upper body up, and stretched out his legs, crossing them at the ankles.

I waited for him to continue, and when he didn't, I thought maybe he'd fallen asleep. "What happened then?"

He mock-punched my arm and grinned. "Why, we won the war and came home."

I swatted back. "Come on, Wilson, tell us."

T.J. and I jumped on Wilson and wrestled until we were breathless. He tossed us aside like a couple of rag dolls, and I stared at a black drawing on the lower part of his arm. I know that wasn't there when he left. I'd seen tattoos before, of course, on the sailors who came to Carbonear from the Russian and Spanish fleets. But I'd never seen one on anybody I knew.

"Where did you get that?"

He stared at the drawing of an anchor a long moment as if seeing it for the first time, then shrugged. "Oh, I don't know. Some little shop along the waterfront in London."

T.J. poked his brother in the ribs. "Tell us what happened next, Wil."

Wilson selected another piece of grass and chewed a moment before continuing. "We got off the ship, and let me tell you, I was never so glad to be on shore. You know me. I love the sea. Love being out on the sea. But not after that boat ride." He tossed the stalk aside. "They took us on buses to a place outside the city where they kept their army. Gave us uniforms and guns. Showed us how to use them. Taught us how to march and stuff." He shrugged again. "Just army stuff."

T.J. bounced where he sat. "Did you get to shoot some Germans?"

Wilson shook his head. "Not going to talk about that. So don't ask me."

I wanted to keep at him until he talked, but T.J. gave me a funny look, so I backed off and waited. Maybe T.J. knew more and would tell me later.

Wilson stared past us out to sea. "One day I was on patrol in London. Downtown. Or what was left of it. All around us, the buildings are laying nearly flat. Smoke and gas and the smell of the dead—" He stopped and looked at each of us. "The dead dogs. And sewer is running down the side of the streets."

"Ee-yew. Must of stunk." T.J. pinched his nose in disgust.

"Yes, it smelled something awful. It was all we could do not to turn around and go the other way. And we came around a corner, and there in the middle of all this destruction was a little girl. She was kneeling in the dirt in front of what used to be her house, and she was pushing the soil around the base of a rose bush." He shook his head slowly. "I don't know how she or the rose bush managed to survive. She was covered in ashes, her face was filthy, and she didn't have any shoes on."

T.J. leaned forward. "What did you do?"

"I walked over to her and squat down beside her. She looked up at me, these big round blue eyes staring at me. I asked her her name."

Now it was my turn to press in. "What did she say?"

"She didn't say anything. She just went back to pushing the soil around the bush. She scraped at the ground, and it was frozen and icy, not much more than gravel. Her hands were bleeding, and her hair was so messy."

"Then what?" I asked.

"Then she stood up and walked away. She just walked away. She never said a word. She didn't look back. I don't know how long she'd been there. I saw a woman in the next house that hadn't been so damaged, and I asked about the little girl. The woman told me she didn't know the girl but saw her there every day, tending the plant."

T.J. grabbed his brother's arm. "Did you follow her?"

"No. Never saw her again. Everywhere I went, I asked about her, but nobody knew her. They'd all seen her, but she never talked to anyone. I started thinking I'd seen an angel."

I didn't understand. "An angel?"

"Yes. I needed to see some hope in what we were doing. And if one little girl could come back and tend a rose bush after all she must have gone through, then I could keep going and do what I needed to do to get through this war. I did some things I hope I never have to do again. I ate some things I wouldn't feed my pig. I slept in some places my dog would leave. And I did it because if that little girl could keep going, so could I."

At that moment, I knew a certain truth: Wilson Royal was a hero.

And I knew another truth: I could never have been the man he was.

And for the first time, I was glad I hadn't gotten a chance to fight with our boys.

Chapter 6

My anger toward and hatred for the Germans was rekindled about two years after my conversation with my father about German prisoners. Just before Christmas, when we were settling in for the winter and the season of peace and joy, we got news of a terrible fire in St. John's.

Our initial concern was family and friends in the Capital, and my father spent most of the morning of December 13th on the telephone, making certain everybody was all right. The Knights of Columbus hall had burned down, killing ninety-nine and injuring more than a hundred people. The place had been jammed with servicemen from Canada, Britain, and the US, with many Newfoundlanders present, either as military or civilians.

Over the next few days, we stuck close to the radio in the evenings, listening to the updated list of the dead, breathing a sigh of relief when we didn't hear anybody belonging to us. Uncle Reginald talked to several of the policemen who patrolled the streets that night, who said they suspected a Gerry was responsible.

One of the girls had an older sister who went to the dance was so badly burned that even her own mother didn't recognize her when they carted her home. The younger one, Grace, went to school with Maxwell and told him her sister Mary's experiences of that night, and he told T.J. and me the next time he came out.

He was as excited as if he'd been present himself. "Mary said they were having a grand old time that night, dancing and carrying on."

The only experience I had with dances was in physical education class at school or the sock hops we had once a year which I always hated because the boys would line up on one side of the gymnasium and the girls on the other side, each waiting for the other to cross the room to start the process.

I couldn't see how they could have been having any fun but I wanted to hear the rest of the story. "Go on."

"Well, Uncle Tim's Barn Dance crowd was playing, and folks were dancing when Mary said she thought the room seemed like it was filling with fog or something. She didn't hear anything, didn't smell the smoke, until a soldier who was heading for the lavatory came running back into the dancing area shouting, 'Fire! Fire!'."

By this time, I was sitting on the edge of my seat as I envisioned the place. I was never in a building that caught on fire, but I knew how bad it could get sitting around a campfire when the wind blew the smoke into your eyes. I waited and he continued.

"Everybody started running, trying to get away, except all of a sudden it seemed the fire was coming from every direction." He looked left to right and lowered his voice as if telling us a great confidence. "The windows were barred, and they couldn't get the doors open. Mary said she got knocked down, and when she came to, she was outside in the alley looking toward the CLB."

I'd heard my parents talking about the event. "Dad thinks the Germans set the fire."

Maxwell nodded. "My father said the same thing. There's going to an enquiry into the whole thing after Christmas."

T.J. smacked his fist into his palm. "I wish I could go find whoever did that."

I stood and paced the room. "Me, too. They shouldn't get away with it. None of those people ever harmed them."

Maxwell, being a little older than both of us, knew much more. "Some of those boys who were killed were here on leave from fighting in Europe. So maybe they didn't do any harm to the person who set the fire, but perhaps they did to someone in his family. Or a friend."

T.J. and I sat down. I was sobered by his words, remembering something similar from my father not too long before.

No matter what side we fight on, we always think we're on the right side.

And that German who set the fire, he'd always have to live with knowing how many people he killed.

In some strange way, I hoped he always believed he did the right thing.

Otherwise, that was a terrible load to carry on his conscience—and his soul—for the rest of his days.

Less than a week after this news about the fire in St. John's, Carbonear had its own fire. Nothing so exciting—in that terrible way of fires despite the loss of life and injuries—but big in our minds.

On December 18th, 1942, a mere week before Christmas, we awoke once again to the smell of smoke and ashes in the air. After hurrying down our breakfast, I walked down the street with my father to see what was going on. Along the way, we met up with T.J. and his father, so we broke into pairs and chatted as we made our way up to the post office.

T.J. and I speculated on what had burned during the night, but our minds were soon stilled as we came around the last turn and spied the mess before us. Not the post office—to which we all breathed a sigh of relief—but several buildings across the street were nothing but a pile of smoldering ashes.

Garland's storefront had singed boards and broken windows, but appeared to be otherwise undamaged. Mr. Garland and his clerks were loading stuff from the shop into a wagon hitched outside the delivery door on the side, and my father and Mr. Royal stopped to talk to him. Anything to do with business in our town interested my father, and while our shop might benefit if Garland's was shut for any length of time, he would never rejoice in another's misfortune.

T.J. and I walked on to the wreckage on the other side of Garland's, the spot where Carbonear Hotel and Restaurant used to stand. Apart from the foundation and a sign, which lay askew on the street, there wasn't much left to show the business had stood there for many years, a going concern at that. A couple of chimneys crawled halfway up to the sky, but even these had bricks missing.

The fire brigade was still dousing small fires in the building next door, the residence and shop of T.P. and W.B. Blackwood, two brothers in the shipping business. The brothers watched from the opposite side of the street as the firemen knocked down a wall, sending up a cloud of smoke and soot. Their white shirts stood out in contrast to the blackened snow around them.

Something was strange about that, but I couldn't put my finger on it at the time. I waved to our friend Matthew, and he came across the street to stand with us. Soot streaked his face and excitement sparkled in his eyes. Matthew lived just up the lane from the post office, and probably had a bird's eye view of the fire, the lucky dog. I knew it would just be a matter of minutes and he would fill us in.

He didn't disappoint us. "I woke up around three this morning when I smelled smoke." Despite being December, Matthew always slept with the window open. "I looked out and saw the flames shooting up out of Blackwood's shop, in the basement."

"See anybody?" T.J. knew better than to interrupt, but sometimes he let his tongue get ahead of his brain.

Matthew looked around as if making certain nobody was eavesdropping. He motioned us closer, and we stood in a huddle, our heads close enough to touch.

"Not then, but before."

I couldn't help myself. "Before when?"

"Last night about nine, when I was going to bed, I was at the window, opening it, and I saw T.P. coming out his basement door with a box of something heavy. At first, I thought that was odd. Moving stuff so late at night."

T.J. and I waited, and Matthew continued.

"And as I watched, W.B. came out with a box, too." He crossed his arms over his chest.

He had our attention. But I still wasn't sure why this was important or unusual.

"W.B. hasn't lifted anything heavier than his wallet in years, not since he fell off the wharf onto the rocks and hurt his back."

Ah, now what Matthew was saying made sense. In fact, W.B. was famous around town for having a "bad back", and nobody risked a lawsuit by asking him to lift anything.

I straightened, and the other two followed suit. "What did you see then?"

"They made another couple of trips each, loading what they were carrying into a truck next to their shop. Then they carried a couple of chests out of their house, and those looked real heavy, too. They drove off, and I went to bed."

I really needed to coach Matthew in his storytelling techniques. You don't just end a story like that. Still, I wasn't getting the connection. And I said so.

Matthew huffed. "Don't you see? They were getting out their valuables so they could set the place on fire."

"That's a bit farfetched."

"Now, Richard, don't put down my idea. You got any other explanation for what they were doing, sneaking around at night, loading stuff in a truck and driving away?"

I had to admit I didn't have any other suggestions.

T.J. shook his head. "That only works if they have insurance."

This was exactly the opening Matthew was waiting for. At least, if I had the information he had, it's what I would have done. "They have insurance. On the house, the shop, their furniture, and all their stock and equipment."

Now this was news. Not many people in Carbonear at the time carried full insurance. Some insured their businesses, some even had their stock and goods insured. A few homeowners had their houses covered, but most folks just considered their personal goods and furniture of no value and didn't want to pay the additional premium. I'd heard my father and mother talking about this one evening.

T.J. wasn't buying it. "How do you know that?"

"Heard my father talking to Mr. Cochrane, the insurance man. Mr. Cochrane said the Blackwoods already had insurance on their shop, but just added insurance on the rest. 'Good thing they did', he said, 'or they'd have had a big loss.'"

This was certainly more interesting. "What else did you hear?" I wasn't always sure I could believe everything Matthew said. Sometimes I think he made stuff up just to fill in the gaps.

"I heard the Constabulary has been down asking questions. The fire chief thinks it's queer that the fire started in the basement."

"Why?" I shifted my feet to fight off the cold seeping up through my shoes. I should have worn my boots.

"The wood stove is on the main floor, so there was no reason for a fire to start down there."

"Maybe they left a lantern lit?" If they'd had a cow, maybe she'd kicked it over. Seemed like cows started a lot of fires. Or at least, got blamed for them.

He shook his head. "The basement was dark after they left. I saw it."

Since he didn't have anything else to add, and no other rumors to start, T.J. and I headed back to where our fathers stood at Garland. After we left T.J. and his father off at their lane, Dad and I continued home.

I had questions. "Dad, is it illegal to burn down your own house?"

"I suppose that depends on the circumstances."

"Like what?" My breath carried off on the breeze.

"Like if you plan to make an insurance claim. Or if you put another property at risk. And there is always the fire brigade to be concerned about. If one of the firemen is injured fighting a fire you set, the law says it's the same as if you injured him personally." He peered at me, his eyes buried deep beneath the brim of his cap. "You're not planning to set fire to the house, are you?"

I heard a laugh in his question, so I chuckled at his suggestion. "No, I was just wondering, that's all."

"Terrible about this fire. The hotel and restaurant will take months to rebuild, and Mr. Parsons doesn't have enough insurance to cover everything. He'll be out of pocket a lot of money."

"If you set a fire and you don't mean for someone else's house to burn down, are you still responsible?"

"Yes."

"What if you set the fire accidentally? Like you tipped over a lantern?"

"Like Mother Murphy's cow?"

Sometimes we thought so much alike it scared me. "Yeah, like that."

"I guess if it really was an accident, nobody would blame you. But if that ever happens, you should raise the alarm and fight the fire right alongside everybody else."

That was the thing about the Blackwoods that struck me funny.

"Clean white shirts."

"What's that? Speak up."

"The Blackwood brothers had clean white shirts. They didn't help fight the fire."

My father nodded. "I noticed that, too. As did the fire chief. Almost as if they didn't want the fire stopped. And it was their house and shop, too."

I didn't want to tell my father everything Matthew had told me because I wasn't sure it was all the gospel truth. But I understood that my father—and the other adults—understood there was more to this business than met the eye.

Chapter 7

For a small town, Carbonear always had its share of excitement as boys of nine to fifteen would describe exciting—plane crashes, disappearances, and deaths. Sometimes these events were outside of our area but still belonged to us in a sense because we knew somebody involved. And more often, life happened.

We didn't see many airplanes in Carbonear. Most of the flights landed either at Gander or St. John's and seemed reluctant to share any of that with us. On this one night in September 1943, however, nature and circumstances worked together to provide one of the most exciting—and bizarre—landings I ever saw.

Just after tea and right before dark, I was in my room doing homework, when I heard what sounded like an airplane engine right over the house. I leaned out the window but couldn't see anything, and the sound died away. A few minutes later, I heard the sound again, except this time it wasn't as strong as an airplane engine should be. In fact, it was coughing like a colicky old horse.

I strained my eyes staring into the blue-black sky, and caught a glimpse of a lighter color passing over the Orangemen's Hall next to our house, headed away from the harbour and up toward the back road. A couple of more coughs, then nothing.

I listened and was about to give up and get back to my third grade history essay when I felt the house shudder. I say 'shudder' because that's what it felt like. A shiver from deep in the basement.

The next thing I knew, T.J. Royal was pounding on our front door, calling out my name. I raced down the stairs and got to the door just ahead of my father, who'd come from the kitchen where he'd been enjoying his newspaper and the heat from the stove after tea.

"Richard, come quick! A plane crashed!" His face was red from running, and he could barely get the words out.

I looked back to my father, who nodded as he shrugged into his overcoat. "Annie, we're going up the back road."

I grabbed my jacket and pelted down the steps and around the corner, my father close on our heels. Captain Frank's Lane isn't particularly steep, but after eating four biscuits and jam and two cups of tea, the journey took every breath I had in me.

We rounded the top of the lane and wheeled along the road. In the distance, a ball of smoke pointed us in the right direction as surely as the Star of Bethlehem led the magi to the manger. I just hoped the thing hadn't completely burned up before we got there.

A couple of doors down from Meaneys', we slowed to a walk. My father was about done in, and I was for sure. T.J. fretted that he had to take his time. He hadn't had tea yet so he had nothing slowing him down.

A crowd had started to gather around, so we went straight to that area. Mike Meaney always had a grand garden. He needed it. He was a Roman Catholic and had nine children, and he worked in the woods, which meant he didn't always have work. He grew potatoes, carrots, cabbage, turnip, beans and peas, and had a large section of raspberries and rhubarb off in one corner.

Lucky for him, summer came early and the rain fell when needed, so most of his garden was done for the year.

What wasn't, was surely done now.

Because a single engine airplane sat smack-dab in the middle of his potato rows, and Mike Meaney stood next to the plane, alternating between cussing the thing out and trying to move it by rocking it back and forth. A man came out by a small door, his goggles knocked to one side, his step as unsteady as if he'd been drunk. Another man followed carrying a leather satchel in one hand and a thermos jug in the other.

Mrs. Meaney stood in her back doorway using her body to keep the kids inside, but she was fighting a losing battle and eventually gave up. Instead, she spent her time rocking one infant on her shoulder as she watched the goings-on.

Within a couple of minutes, the fire brigade showed up, the lights flashing on the old truck as it groaned to a halt. Apparently, the old thing had found the lane as steep and demanding as we had done.

The firemen reeled out their hoses and hooked up to the pumper tank, but since there weren't any flames, they just stood by and waited. A couple pulled out cigarettes and lit up, while the fire chief puffed on a cold pipe.

What we'd seen coming up the road wasn't smoke, apparently, but steam created by a ruptured cooling system when the plane had clipped the top of Meaneys's barn before landing on his taters.

Mike Meaney approached the fire chief and pointed toward the barn which was now missing about half of its top peak. Then he gestured to the garden, his hands helping him get his words out. The fire chief nodded and made a few notes on a piece of paper.

Mike answered some questions, then threw up his hands in disgust.

He looked toward the crowd gathering at his garden gate. "Insurance! He wants to know did I have insurance." He stalked up to the fence and many people took a step back. "Do I look like I have money for insurance? Nine young'uns and another on the way doesn't leave money for insurance."

Apparently this news about another Meaney child was news to most of the people gathered there, particularly the women, as several stuck their heads together and chattered on about babies and don't the Catholics know how to stop making them. Mike glared at them until they quieted, then he stomped back to his potatoes.

I sidled over to where the fire chief now talked with the two men who'd come out of the plane. Apparently one was the pilot and the other the passenger. Neither were hurt, which was good news. The other good news, for Mike Meaney, at least, was that the owner of the plane carried accident insurance, so he'd be paid for the damaged barn and lost crop.

Which he'd have gotten even if he hadn't gotten in a tizzy.

The three men discussed how to handle the airplane, and finally the pilot said that the easiest thing to do was to remove the wings and ship the entire contraption back to St. John's on a flatbed truck for repairs. I thought that was a fascinating idea, and wanted to hang around to see how they'd do it, but my father had other ideas.

"You've got homework to finish, and tomorrow is a school day. Time to go home. We can't help here."

My father felt that if you couldn't help, you were only in the way.

The next day after school I ran all the way back to the crash site, but the only evidence of the accident was a flattened area in the middle of the garden and a lot of trampled earth.

The plane was gone, along with my chance to be a first-hand witness to the wonders of scientific innovation.

Living near the sea and working in the woods is bound to bring about injuries

The Physics of Love

and death, and like most small towns in outport Newfoundland, we were no stranger to either. My parents, unlike many others, took no joy in reporting deaths, and never participated in the rumor mills that inevitably sprang up when a person died suddenly.

In March of 1946, a cousin of my father's, Hayward Cameron, was working in the woods, hauling in a load of firewood. The winter had been longer and colder than anticipated, and he'd run short and had to make a quick run into the forest. His son was down with the grippe, according to the story, and couldn't go with him, so he went on his own.

He took his horse and sled, and a couple of other woodsmen passed him on their way deeper into the woods. He'd called out to them and wished them a good day. One of the men said he was leaning against the sled as if he was tired out, except that was early and he had nothing cut or stacked at that point.

Around one o'clock, another man happened by, and Hayward was lying in the snow, face down. Concerned, that man called John Dawe from Carbonear who was cutting wood nearby, and together they went over to the spot. John Dawe recognized Hayward, and after they turned him onto his back, they could see he was dead and had been for some time.

Since they couldn't do anything for him, the first man unhitched his horse from the sled and rode to Victoria to notify the Constabulary, and John rode his horse back to Carbonear. He came into the shop and told my father, who promised to let other family and friends know. Leaving the clerk in charge, my father went out to the woods to make certain of the identification, and I ran alongside him, struggling to keep up in the knee-deep snow.

I'd never seen a dead person before, and wouldn't have this time only for my father turned his back on me and I slipped past him. I don't know why I thought I wanted to see poor old Hayward in his present condition, but once I did, I turned right around and stuck to my father's side for the rest of the afternoon.

After about an hour, we made our way back home. The shop clerk said she'd spread the news far and wide, and I know she spoke the truth. She was better than a telegram and a telephone combined. At least this time, she had her story right. Not like the time she overhead my parents talking and thought she heard them say my mother was expecting twins in a month's time. That story was all over Conception Bay within the day, and women traipsed into the store bearing gifts and berating my mother for not sharing her good news sooner.

The truth of the story was my mother was expecting a set of tins from a cousin in Boston, who'd just shipped them and hoped they'd get there in a month. The clerk's hearing wasn't as good as her tongue.

At any rate, someone thought to tell Reverend Perry, and he went down and broke the news to Mrs. Cameron, although how she'd not heard yet is beyond me. Folks were real sensitive about having a clergy tell someone of the death of a close relative, so I guess they had to work extra hard to keep her from knowing. They didn't want to leave him out there, so later that day, the body was brought back to Carbonear, and taken to Clarkes, the undertaker.

There was a lot of talk going around about how he died. I can tell you I didn't see a mark on the body, although the rumors went around that maybe he'd taken his own life out of despair over something that nobody could quite put their finger on. I guess that's one reason why my parents hated gossip. Half-truths clothed in lies is how my father describes the way people around here talk. At one point, they'd had enough iterations to the story that Hayward was one of the men involved in the Great Train Robbery in England. We never saw any evidence of that in his life, and I don't think he was up to something of that magnitude either in smarts or in his lifestyle. I think it's more likely he just keeled over from a heart attack, since he was overweight and not used to doing hard work like that by himself.

Then in March, Samuel Dinn went missing. He had gone for a walk on a Wednesday, and was never seen alive again. The last time anyone noticed him he was down by the public wharf, so they did a big search down there and held a couple of public meetings to see if anybody could come forward with information.

By this time, I was twelve years old, and could help out on a simple land search like this one. T.J. Royal and I went door to door in our neighbourhood, checked in barns and sheds, went down in basements, and made sure to look down any wells we found. After my experience with Hayward in the spring, I wasn't too keen on finding another body, but T.J. convinced me we might be heroes if we found him alive, so I went with him.

At the second public meeting on the Saturday after he went missing, Mrs. Dinn appealed to everybody there. "My husband has a heart condition and diabetes. He takes medicine, and he needs it every day."

Truth be told, I didn't give him much hope for being found after that. After all, it had been three days since anybody saw him, and if he needed medicine every day, he was already living on borrowed time.

On Sunday afternoon, four search parties formed up again. I was laid up this time with blisters on my heels, and T.J.'s father didn't want him going out without me, so T.J. was out of commission as well, and not very pleased with me. I think he figured I was just playing at having blisters because I didn't want to go out. That wasn't the case, but I wasn't displeased with having to stay home, either.

Just before tea, a shot rang out, and we knew the search was over, for better or for worse. I hobbled down Water Street with my father, and joined up with T.J. and his father. T.J. eyed me over and seemed satisfied that I wasn't exaggerating my ailment. We all congregated at the public wharf where the shot had been fired from.

The search team dragging the harbour near the shore hooked on Hayward's coat and pulled his body to the surface. I stood back from the edge, letting others more curious than me see firsthand. A splash when he cleared the water, a gasp from several in the crowd, and then I was squished between layers of people as they stepped back to let others in front for a better view.

My stomach lurched, and I wondered at this pre-occupation with death. At least to my mind, that's what it felt like. My father laid his hand on my shoulder, and I looked up into his icy blue eyes that conveyed a warmth and understanding like I'd never noticed before.

"Ready to go home?"

I nodded and turned to press through the crowd. He never let go of my shoulder.

As we walked back the street to our house, he startled me by speaking. "Don't think harshly of them. Some of them have never stared death in the face before."

I thought back to how brave I felt in March, before I'd seen Hayward's dark face and blue lips. I nodded. "Once you do, you're never the same, are you?"

He patted my head. "I would do anything to spare you from that, but I can't. God created everything to live and to die, and that's the way of the world."

I understood that. I'd seen my dog run over by a wagon. I'd had relatives that died. It wasn't the death that scared me.

It was the suddenness of it all, the dealing with what was left behind. The body, the funeral, the crying.

The memory of a dark face with blue lips that never seemed to leave my memory.

He seemed to read my mind again. "Right now it seems like every time you close your eyes, you see his face."

I hadn't known that he knew I'd seen Hayward, so I stayed quiet.

He went on, "But one day you won't remember that unless you want to. That's another thing God created. Forgetfulness."

The funny thing about death—if there is anything funny about it at all—is that it touches us all in one way or the other. Hayward Cameron was a relation who died on an everyday, ordinary trip to the woods to collect firewood, an ordinary, everyday event in the lives of the people of the town. Samuel Dinn, ill in health and possibly in mind at the time, had taken a walk and either fell or jumped off a wharf, leaving behind his wife and four children to pick up the pieces of their lives. His youngest, only five weeks old, would have no memories of his father except what others told him.

And then there was Jump White. I don't know why people called him that. He didn't have a bump on his head, and he wasn't clumsy. He was just a strange old man who lived in one-half of a house and let a friend live in the other half, never charging him a cent of rent.

And while pretty much everybody in Carbonear knew and loved old Jump, this friend who received the most from him and had the best reason to keep him alive, hated him.

At least, that's the story we heard after the fact. If you can believe stories.

Old Jump didn't have much money, at least he didn't live as if he did, but he was always willing to lend a hand to help a person out. I recall one time my father and I were working in the garden, and I was carrying a load of rocks down the lane to dump them on the beach. When I got halfway there, the wheel on the barrow worked itself loose. The barrow tipped over, dumping the rocks on the side of the road.

Old Jump was in his garden a couple of doors down, and he heard me cussing up a blue streak. Well, he set his hoe down and came to see what was wrong. When he saw me there, my knees skinned and my face red as a beet, he pulled a bolt and a nut from his pocket, and while I sat there feeling sorry for myself, he attached the wheel, uprighted the barrow, and loaded the rocks back in.

He pointed to the handle nearest me. "Take that side and I'll take this."

I did as he said, and together we wheeled the rocks down and dumped them on the beach. I thanked him, and he waved off my words.

"Just helping a neighbour."

I guess that's how he looked at things, but I never forgot his kindness to this boy.

At any rate, mid-November of 1946, Jump and his friend had some kind of a tiff. Not a real falling-out. Just a disagreement about something trivial, like how many cords of wood they needed for the winter. Jump said two, his friend said one. Or something like that, because nobody actually heard them arguing. Nobody even saw them together that day.

My father had seen Jump in the shop that day, and he knew something wasn't right, but when he tried to ask, Jump answered him shortly and left the store. Mr. Royal saw him later that day working in his garden, but the wind was blowing too hard for Jump to hear when he called out to him.

The last time anybody saw Jump was around eleven that night. Jump didn't have the city sewer come to his house, and his septic tank hadn't worked in years, so Jump used what we used to call a honey pot, and emptied it each morning down off the lane that goes to the ocean. He was carrying that pot and whistling to himself, according to what Tom Rowe told me later. Happy as if he didn't have a care in the world.

Or maybe he'd made up his mind about a tough decision. I know that always lifts a huge weight from my shoulders.

The next morning, a couple of kids found Old Jump down on the beach, his honey pot thirty feet above him on the bank. They ran to tell their parents, and somebody called down to Victoria to the Constabulary while somebody else went to tell his friend.

His friend wasn't anywhere to be seen.

The police came and looked around, but they couldn't tell if he'd fallen or was pushed. Lots of people went to that bank to dump their honey pots, so there were plenty of footprints around. Tom's father made him come forward and say how he'd seen Jump the night before, but Tom couldn't tell them anything else.

And the friend was nowhere to be found.

My parents went to Bump's funeral, but I didn't want to go.

I wanted to remember him like I saw him that day, helping me carry the load of rocks to the beach, hale and hearty and full of joy over helping a neighbour.

Chapter 8

There was no doubt in my mind that my mother loved me, even when she complained to the other women about how bad I was. I recognized her affection and concern toward me, and never wondered whether her words or her actions carried a hidden meaning. I was a lucky boy.

One evidence of her feelings for me was demonstrated when I asked my father for permission to use the attic of the house as a workroom. At dinner one evening, I broached the subject. I was about twelve years old at the time. I waited until dessert because I knew we were having blueberry duff, a favorite of my father's, and he would be in a good mood.

"Dad, I was up in the attic the other day."

He took another forkful of pudding and washed it down with a sip of tea, staring at me over the rim of his cup. "You were, were you?"

"Yes. It's a fine lot of room up there."

He nodded. "Yes, I know."

I swallowed hard. Much depended on how I presented my case. I decided just to plunge in and speak my piece. "I'd like to have more room to work on my stamp collection. You know, a table so I didn't have to put my things away all the time."

My mother tossed in her two-cent's worth, and I hadn't even rehearsed her part. "Henry, what he says makes sense. Then he could do his soaking up there instead of in his room."

My father raised an eyebrow in question. "Soaking?"

"Yes, Dad, where I take the paper off the stamps. I could have a proper basin up there instead of carting water up and down the stairs. And I could have a light on the table, and I could take the encyclopedias up there so I can look up the geography and history."

My mother set her fork aside. "He said he's learning about the countries where the stamps come from. Like India and China. And Alberta."

I stifled a grin. She spoke as if Alberta were as exotic and afar as India.

"What else do you want to do up there?"

I thought for a minute. If I wanted the room, I'd need to convince him that the space was going to serve more than one purpose. My father didn't believe much in spreading out, and believed less in spreading yourself too thin. Even to my own ears, my reasoning sounded weak. "I suppose I could do some other schoolwork up there."

He shook his head and turned back to his pudding.

I was losing his attention. "I could have Frank up there when he comes so we aren't under Mom's feet."

She smiled across the table at me. I don't know how many times she'd complained about me and Frank, or me and Maxwell, or me and T.J. Royal, being under foot when she was trying to clean or beat the rugs or do the laundry.

He pursed his lips. "That's an idea. Should always have more than one purpose for a thing that you intend to invest time or money in, so that when one use is done, you haven't wasted your time."

I really hadn't given much thought to what I would use the room for beyond setting up the stamps, but I suddenly had a brainstorm.

The only problem was, I knew my mother would be dead set against it.

And I wasn't so sure my father would agree, either.

No, if I wanted to use that room for anything other than stamps and entertaining friends, I'd need to keep that under my hat.

At least until I had the deed accomplished.

The attic took some time to set up, mostly because debris cluttered the room. I spent the next week or so after school every day pushing broken rockers, old wooden chests, and dozens of boxes into the eave area, leaving the center of the room clear. The floor of the attic was finished with plain wood in the lower parts, and with wainscoting in the center where I could stand up straight.

One of the best finds up there was an old kitchen table with one leg missing. I didn't let that stop me, and fashioned a rough leg out of piece of stair bannister, and nailed it into place. The leg was about a half-inch shorter than the original legs, so I shoved a sliver of old linoleum underneath to level it out. Otherwise, my pen kept rolling off the edge.

Another find was a sideboard with cabinets and drawers. I think perhaps the piece belonged to Louise Abbott Cameron, and when my mother married my father, she had most of Louise's things moved to the attic. A tall stool and a table lamp completed the furnishings, and I made a couple of rough shelves between the upright wall studs to hold my books and supplies. A stained and slightly chipped china chamber pot served as my soaking bowl, and I patched up an old bucket to carry water up the stairs. The used water I could dump out the small eave window.

Once I had everything in place, I carted my stamp books and Book of Knowledge volumes up to my room, because I had come to think of it as My Room, and organized my new little world. I felt like a business tycoon surveying his factory, or like Henry Ford opening a new assembly line.

When everything was put away—a place for everything and everything in its place even at that age—I invited my parents to view my accomplishments. My mother declined, as I knew she would. She might have come up that rickety ladder to save me if I was unconscious and the house was burning down, but other than that, she'd never been up there and had no intention of altering that status.

My father came up far enough so his head was inside the attic and looked all around. His only comment was, "I hope you didn't damage anything when you moved it."

I assured him I hadn't, and he was satisfied, never showing his face there again.

Which worked well with the next step of my plan.

I had a fascination with chemistry, physics, and electricity, so the logical thing was to set up a laboratory where I could conduct experiments and further the cause of science.

My school wasn't offering classes in these sciences, so I took it upon myself to teach myself the things I figured I would need to prepare for future schooling or a career. I wasn't quite certain what I wanted to be when I grew up, but knew that electricity had to be at the center of my job.

My first series of experiments centered around preventing electrocution in humans. At that time, electricity was in many houses and most businesses, but people were still nervous when it came to handling electrical appliances. I thought that if we were going to make full use of the power of electricity, we needed not to be afraid of it, and if we could provide some way to prevent electrocution, that would go a long ways to assuring people of its safety.

I wasn't certain how I was going to accomplish my goal, so I studied the works of Thomas Edison. He had tried several hundred different materials before finding the one that could generate light without burning up instantly. I decided to emulate some of his processes.

I started with mice. I felt that if I could inject something into mice that would inhibit the passage of electrical current through their bodies, I could prevent electrocution.

The main problem was that I didn't have a supply of mice.

I needed live mice, and the only traps I knew provided dead mice.

So I designed and constructed a trap that would capture several mice at a time without harming them, and proceeded to set my trap in and around the house, disguising it since I knew if my mother figured out what I was doing, my mad scientist days would be over. The idea of catching mice that were already in the house and keeping them there, or bringing in mice I'd caught elsewhere, would not have pleased her.

And I didn't want to displease my mother.

I found an old pair of leather gloves—the mice kept biting me—and scrounged up the other materials I needed, including a syringe and needle and some samples of various metals suspended in liquid, and kept a careful journal of all my experiments.

Despite all that, my test subjects kept dying. And not when I subjected them to the electrical current. I never got to that point. They always died after I injected them. I tried everything, including diluting the solution with saline, diluting smaller amounts more often, and still they died.

After several months of sneaking mice into the attic, of sneaking food into the attic to feed them, and then hiding the bodies in other trash to take them to the trash barrel to burn, I gave up.

I decided to turn to more useful experiments, including coming up with a more efficient formula for gunpowder. But to do that, I first needed to create some gunpowder using the generally accepted formulation. I had a friend in the local pharmacist who didn't mind supplying me with some of the chemicals I needed, and the rest could be bought at the local farm supply store and the drug store.

I mixed up my first standard batch and was pleased at how easily the ingredients blended together. The only problem was I missed one important step, which was that the nitrogen had to be mixed into the glycerin.

Instead, I poured the two ingredients into a separate beaker, which created an entirely different chemical reaction and resulted in building up too much pressure in the glass container, which ultimately caused an explosion. Luckily, I had on gloves and was using tongs, or folks might have started calling me Three-Fingers.

When the explosion shook the china in the dining room cabinet, my mother put an end to my experiments. At least, she tried to.

Using my stamp collecting as a cover, I still did some minor experiments that didn't involve smelly gases or explosions. Not as exciting, of course, but I managed to maintain the peace of the household while not completely obeying my mother.

Chapter 8

Life wasn't all about disasters and death, although sometimes it could certainly seem that way. When life is hard, death is a constant neighbor, which makes the good times all that more important. To keep your sanity, you have to believe better times are coming, even as you struggle through the present.

One time my family took a family vacation out to Trinity Bay around 1948. The war was over and once again we'd settled down into the routines of life in a small town. My father rarely took more than a few days off from the shop, so for us to go away for a couple of weeks was a real treat. We drove over there in our own car along with my best friend T.J. Royal and his parents, and I don't think we gave the adults a moment's peace the entire way.

We gave up asking how much further about ten miles from home, but there was always something new and exciting to see along the rutted dirt road. July was a fine month of weather, and as we moved down along the bay and up the other side, the sun shone bright and we just knew the coming fourteen days were going to be filled with adventure and excitement.

I think our parents were hoping their vacation was going to be full of relaxing and not too much going around, although they talked the entire trip out about what friends and family we would visit, and which ones we'd try to avoid, because, as always, there was some we wanted to not spend time with.

As with most Newfoundlanders of the time, the Camerons and the Royals, as well as the Rowes and Mrs. Royal's family the Mahoneys, had relatives, no matter how tenuous or obscure the connection, just about everywhere. And if they didn't, they had friends, or friends of friends, as the case may be.

After a while, T.J. and I tuned out the adults' talk and made our own plans. We were hoping to get in some fishing, and I had a new rod and line and some flies my father had gotten from his shop that I was itching to try. We also planned to camp out a few nights, away from the adults, so we could talk about stuff. I don't think we really knew what topics we were going to cover, just stuff.

And then there was the lighthouse. When my friend Tom Rowe heard we were going to Trinity, he was some jealous.

"Richard, you're going to see that lighthouse while you're there, aren't you?"

We were walking along the back road that day, and we stopped to look out over the harbour. "I don't know. What's so special about a lighthouse? Seen lots of them before."

"I heard they brought that one over from England."

I couldn't picture taking the trouble to transport a lighthouse from England over to Newfoundland, and I said so. "Besides, don't we already know how to build our own lighthouses? We've done it often enough. Good ones, too." As if importing a lighthouse somehow meant our construction wasn't up to standard.

I wasn't convinced that this lighthouse was anything to write home about, but I wanted to keep an open mind. We arrived in Trinity just after dark and checked into the cabins near the shore. T.J. and I carried suitcases and bags into the rooms until we were worn out. And then we carried in boxes and bags of food, since each cabin had a small kitchen area where our mothers could prepare our meals.

Then we all sat out on the verandah in the front of the cabins and watched the moon rise over the harbour. T.J. and I cast sideways glances at each other, and when the adults seemed like they were going to talk all night, I stood, stretched, and yawned.

"Well, T.J., I'm tuckered out."

He followed my lead. "Me, too. Good night, folks."

His mother jutted out her cheek, and he landed a quick peck on the powdered skin before ducking into the cabin he shared with his parents, and I went into the one I shared with mine.

We already had a plan in place.

Once the adults were snoring in their beds, we met outside. During our walk the previous evening, we'd spotted an old dory tied to a buoy about twenty feet from shore, and another one tied to a wharf. We grabbed the first set of oars and waded out to the second boat, which had oars lashed down to the locks. After untying the rope, we set out to row to the lighthouse across the harbour.

One thing we hadn't taken into account was the distance. In the waning light of the day, we thought the lighthouse was 'just there'. We hadn't talked about how far, but I know I didn't think we had to go more than a mile or so.

However, an hour later, we were no closer to the flashing light than when we started. And, since we were rowing backwards, we had a job to keep our little boat lined up with the target. So we tucked in and rowed all the harder, trying to muffle our grunts as the sweat flew from our foreheads.

When I couldn't lift the oars one more time, I sank against the side of the boat. "I can't go any further."

T.J. poked me with an oar. "You can't give up out here."

I drew a couple of deep breaths so I could talk sensibly. "Maybe if we wait until morning, someone will come by and see us."

He shook his head. "No way am I going to sit out here like a sissy waiting to be rescued."

I hadn't really thought about that, and he had a good point. I picked up the oars again and dug into the water. Pretty soon all I heard was the dip and splash of the wood in the bay. I was going to get to the lighthouse if it killed me.

An hour later, and the moon disappeared below the horizon. The sun was still a couple of hours from showing its face, and the harbour all around us was dark and calm. I tried not to think about the sea creatures lurking beneath the surface, except the more I tried not to picture them, the more I felt a bump against the hull, or smelled something dead and rotten.

I checked over my shoulder again. We weren't any closer to the lighthouse and land, or at least we didn't seem to be. I wasn't certain how much further I could row. And if we wore ourselves out getting there, how would we have the strength to get back?

"Uh, T.J.?"

He grunted in reply. Seemed he was as tired as me.

"Maybe we should turn back?"

"If we give up now, we mightn't get another chance."

I knew he spoke the truth. "Maybe we could try again tomorrow night."

He shook his head. "I don't think I'm going to be able to move after this. I'm completely bagged out."

"Let's turn around."

If I thought rowing partway across the harbour against a headwind in the dead of night was tough, I didn't know the half of it. Beat out already, having had no sleep, hungry, thirsty—we hadn't planned our trip very well.

And then a westerly wind blew up and threatened to push us further off course. We lined up the nose of the boat with the wharf we'd left from, but by the time we'd fought against the wind, the waves, and the tide, we were more than a mile off course.

Bone-weary, we landed our craft just as the sun peeked over the horizon. I glanced back at the lighthouse. The first light reflected off the glass panes, taunting us in our failure. Add to that the place where we landed was more shallow than at the wharf, which meant we had to jump into thigh-deep water about fifty feet from shore, and you can be sure we were a couple of frustrated sailors.

We tied the boat off to a large rock and lashed the oars back in place, then took the extra set of oars and set off for the cabins. About a quarter mile away, we spotted two familiar forms walking toward us.

Our fathers.

A quick look at T.J. confirmed he was thinking the same thing I was—we were in for it. Not even seven o'clock, and already Dad and Mr. Royal were out looking for us. I could only imagine how worried Mom was, and suspected Mrs. Royal was pacing the floor or staring out the window, too.

What were we thinking, setting off like that without telling anybody?

We could have been drowned.

Or swept out to sea.

Before we drew within earshot, I'd already given myself the lecture I knew was coming. The only thing left was the punishment.

But life can throw you a pleasant surprise once in a while.

When we got closer, each of us carrying an oar over one shoulder, Dad raised a hand in greeting. We waved back. They waited for us and we stepped in next to our fathers. Mine took the oar from me and transferred the scarred piece of wood to his shoulder, laying his hand across my shoulder.

We walked for a while without talking. At a slight pressure on my shoulder, I slowed and let T.J. and his father go on ahead of us. Although by this age, I wasn't much shorter than my father, I still recall him looking down at me, his eyes shaded by the brim of his cap.

I opened my mouth to speak, to explain, to apologize, but I didn't get the chance. He dropped the oar and pulled me into his chest, wrapping his arms around my back. I responded and the tears fell. I couldn't talk past the lump in my throat.

We stood that way for days, or at least, that's how long it seemed at the time. I suspect it was really only about five minutes. But during that time, perhaps for one of the first times in my life, I saw my father's heart. Sure, I knew I'd get a lecture later on. Probably some kind of punishment, too.

At that moment, he couldn't have done anything more to hurt me than to cry over me.

And at that moment, he couldn't have said any more eloquently that he loved me.

Chapter 9

When I got the results of my final examinations in high school, I learned I'd failed and would have to repeat my final year. I asked my father to let me go to St. John's to take my Grade Eleven over, and to be able to drop history and social sciences and pick up chemistry and physics in preparation for future schooling.

My father and mother weren't convinced that spending a year in St. John's was the best thing for me. First and foremost, housing was a concern. Next, they would lose my help in the shop except on weekends when I could come home.

But the real reason came out one July evening when we were sitting around the kitchen table after tea discussing the subject. I'd already spoken with Aunt Maggie, and she was happy to have me come live with her and Uncle Morris. She still had a couple of my cousins living at home, but there was plenty of room for me.

I promised my parents I would come home every weekend unless the weather or my studies kept me away. My father looked over the tops of his spectacles at me as I laid my case before him, stressing the importance of getting chemistry and physics done if I was to stand a chance of getting in a college or a technical school. None of the schools in Carbonear offered chemistry or even had a lab. While my lab in the attic was good, it would not take me much beyond what I already knew.

My father had always hoped I would join him in the shop, but I think as the years went on, he saw that my heart just wasn't in it. Also, I'd done a lot of reading, and there was some talk about something called 'shopping malls', huge groupings of stores under one roof, that would soon replace the independent mom-and-pop stores. I knew I didn't want to spend twenty years of my life in a shop that was going to go under just as I was getting a family into the teen and college years.

And finally, as much as I loved my father, working under him was a strain. He was a strong-minded man, used to doing things his own way, and not much open to making changes. I could see that if I agreed to take over the shop, that wouldn't happen until he was good and ready to give it up, which meant I might be an old man before I was able to make my own decisions.

All in all, not a good situation.

Not to mention my interests in the sciences.

So once I'd addressed the concerns they'd mentioned, I waited. And waited.

Our tea grew cold, and the fire in the kitchen stove died down, cooling the room. The windows stood open and the back and front doors ajar to catch the evening breeze that was sure to freshen in off the harbour.

My mother glanced from me to my father and back again, fixing his eyes with hers. After a while, he nodded to her.

He fiddled with his teacup a moment longer, then cleared his throat, his signal he was about to say something important.

I leaned in, attentive.

"We don't think St. John's is the best place for a young person."

I wasn't sure if he was talking about me specifically, or young people in general. Surely he knew there were many young people who lived in St. John's and weren't harmed for the experience?

I waited.

"There's been some young people from Carbonear who went to St. John's and that didn't turn out well at all."

I was certain there were young people who'd had a good experience, too, but I wasn't going to argue with him. Not out loud, anyway.

So I came at it from another direction. "Whoever that was would likely have turned out bad even if they'd stayed in Carbonear."

My mother sniffed and I caught a hint of a smile on her lips.

What did she know that I didn't?

My father sat back in his chair. "That's as may be, but we're not sure this is the right thing for you."

I folded my hands on the table. "Dad, I'm old enough to drive. I'm old enough to get married. I'm old enough to join the army. Don't you think I'm old enough to make this decision?"

My father stared at me for a long moment, his pale blue eyes penetrating mine.

I pressed on. "And if not now, when? Next year? Is nineteen the magic age to be able to decide what I want to do with my life? Twenty? Fifty?"

I knew my words cut into him, but I couldn't stop now. "I'd like to have this opportunity to prove to you I am old enough. If you don't like what's happening by Christmas, you can tell me and I'll stay home and finish the year here."

He thumped the table with his fist. "You aren't like others, son. You're different." He looked at my mother. "I say we give him the chance."

My mother's eyes brimmed with tears, and she shook her head as she whispered, "You remember what happened to—"

My father stood. "He's not Laura. He's proven himself different. And better."

I stared at each in turn. "Laura? What about her?" Realization dawned. "She went to St. John's, didn't she? And got in some kind of trouble?"

Father glared at me. "Nothing we ever knew about."

My mother finished his sentence. "For certain."

"You can't compare me to her. That's not fair."

All my younger years I'd spent living in Laura's shadow. She lived such a glamorous life, or so it seemed to a small boy from Carbonear. When I learned the truth about her, that shadow became dark.

And now I saw that perhaps that darkness wasn't limited to me.

"It's what parents do with their children. Only natural."

Perhaps. I wondered had Laura been comparing me with Edna all these years? And how much had I fallen short? Both of us raised as an only child. Did Edna know about her mother, and that I was actually her half-brother? I suspected the news would rock her world.

But that didn't matter to me now. What mattered was my father's decision to let me step out and prove myself.

I wouldn't disappoint him.

The following June I received my graduation letter in the mail the same week I met Catherine Lawrence. She had moved to Carbonear with her parents to take up residence in the old Salvation Army officer's quarters. Her father was to be the school principal in September. They lived across the street and up the lane from us, and the first time I saw her was when I was coming out of church one Sunday.

Our family pew, for which my father faithfully paid his pew rent each year, was three rows from the front, in the center aisle, a position of importance and prominence. However preferential this seating might be, we were always delayed in exiting the church because of the steady stream of congregants who wanted to shake the reverend's hand and thank him for the sermon.

On this particular Sunday, as usual, we were the last to leave, and by the time I exited, all my friends had gone home with their parents. I'd hoped to have a chat with T.J. and Tom and Matthew, but never mind, I'd catch up with them later on.

As I walked up the street toward home, movement at the Salvation Army church across the street from the house caught my eye, and I looked in that direction. A lovely dark-haired beauty stood in the doorway, half-turned as if talking to someone inside.

I was lost.

She was new in town, and nobody had thought to introduce us.

I stopped, and my father, who had been walking close behind me, bumped into me.

"Goodness, Richard. Watch where you're going."

Ordinarily I would have reminded him that he was the one who had run into me, but at that moment, my mind was elsewhere.

He followed my gaze. "Oh, that's the Lawrence girl. Her father is the new principal. I've been meaning to invite them to tea."

My mother, bless her soul, must have seen the yearning in my eyes, and although she was no matchmaker, and particularly not across denominational lines, she stepped up and did the right thing. "We've got a huge dinner at home. Invite them now."

My father blinked a couple of times as if he wasn't quite certain he'd heard correctly, then strode toward the Army temple as two adults stepped out. They exchanged some words, and the girl identified as Catherine glanced in my direction. When I say glanced, I'm probably exaggerating, and when I say in my direction, she was more likely looking at my mother who stood close behind me.

After much head-nodding, my father and the three Lawrences came in our direction. There was a fourth, a brother, but he was off with some cousins for the day. Introductions were made, and when it came my turn to speak my name, no sound would come from my mouth. Catherine smiled up at me, and the resolve I'd made after the Doreen fiasco melted away like butter in a hot frying pan.

I was lost. In a serious way.

Over the years I'd developed a mindset that I would change what I could and accept what I couldn't change. Finding out about Laura was one of those things I couldn't change. I could either accept it and get on with my life, or let it eat me up from the inside out.

I chose to accept. I never held it against my parents that they had withheld the truth from me for fifteen years because I felt they were in much the same situation I was in: they couldn't do anything to change the circumstances, so they did the best they could.

Laura, on the other hand, had lied to me every day of her life. Even after I knew who she really was, and she came to Carbonear for a visit, she acted as if nothing had changed, even though I told her I knew. She kept a close eye on me whenever I was around Edna, perhaps afraid I would say something to her daughter. I never did. I didn't see any advantage at the time.

I told Catherine all about Laura and Samson Baldwin. After living in Carbonear for just a few months, she knew who he was, even though they'd never met. He was working in Nova Scotia, married with a child of his own. I didn't even know whether he knew about me.

Catherine finished school in June 1953 and struggled with deciding what to do for a career. On one hand, she felt perhaps she should be a teacher like her father. Teaching was a safe, respectable job she could take anywhere.

But something held her back.

"I don't know, Richard," she said one night when we were walking on the beach, "I think my father has done wonderfully, considering all he's been through in his life."

Her father had taken to teaching as a second career. He used to be a house painter until he'd gotten ill when Catherine was really young and then he couldn't take the physical labor of house painting anymore. So he went to teacher's college and her mother worked to support them until he got his teaching license. And now he'd worked his way up to principal of the Carbonear school.

"I'd like to have a job where I could move if I wanted, but one where I wouldn't get transferred all over God's half acre."

I agreed with her. I didn't want to have to follow her all over every outport town in Newfoundland, either, but I didn't say anything about marriage then. We needed to work ourselves into that conversation. And we were still young. She was just eighteen, and I was only coming on twenty. Plenty of time.

"I think I'd like to be a nurse."

My heart soared. To go to nursing school, she'd have to live in St. John's.

I wanted to live in St. John's and attend a radio television program there.

What had been a burden on my heart for several months became a kite that took flight on its own.

I grabbed her around the waist and swung her around. She squealed in delight until I set her down on her feet again.

I cupped her face between my hands and leaned in, eyes closed, and kissed her, tentatively at first, then more passionately. She put her hands on my chest as if to push me away, and I slacked off, afraid I'd frightened her. This was not our first kiss, but it was different, as if we were sealing our futures together by the pressing of my mouth on hers.

Before we married, we decided we wanted to own a home instead of rent, but we didn't have a large income and couldn't afford anything decent in St. John's, so we had to look further afield. At the time, there was a small outcropping of houses near the Torbay Airport that had just been built. While not the first subdivision in the city, it was one of the first. When my mother and father came out to see it, they thought we were moving out of the country.

At any rate, we bought the biggest house we could afford, which wasn't very big. Still, two bedrooms on a little plot of land on a dead end street, the area was called Penetanguishene. The name never made sense to me, since I looked it up and it was from the Ojibwa tribe, and it meant "land of rolling white sands".

No matter how long you stared at the rocks and marshes around our house, you were never going to see rolling white sands. Plus I don't think an Ojibwa ever set foot in Newfoundland. I expect the developer had grand plans for this little section of houses, probably hoping to convince folks to move there just because of the name alone. It was a mouthful, to be sure.

The new year brought us a surprise—Catherine was pregnant. I was excited on one hand, but a little nervous on the other hand. Still, there wasn't anything to do but wait and see where we went from there.

Because Catherine worked at the maternity hospital, she knew the delivery room supervisor and the doctor. She asked if I could be there when the baby was born. The doctor thought that was a grand idea, but the nurse wasn't so sure. She looked me up and down, sniffed once or twice like I had something stuck to my shoe, then peered at me over her glasses. "You won't faint, will you?"

I assured her I would not, that I was used to seeing blood because I hunted and fished, and it seemed if I was there for the conception, I should be there for the birth.

She sniffed a couple of more times, her mouth puckered like she didn't know anything about babies and how they were made. I think I was the first man who'd asked to be in the delivery room. It just wasn't done. We were supposed to pace the hallway and hand out cigars.

At any rate, she couldn't think of a reason to say no, and she wouldn't override the doctor's decision, so I was allowed in.

Catherine went into labor early on a Friday morning. I drove her to the hospital where things progressed naturally. About eight-thirty I drove downtown and told my boss I wouldn't be in that day as I was at the hospital with my wife, and he told me to take the weekend off, too. I returned, and around noon Catherine delivered a girl.

And no, I didn't faint.

Chapter 10

We were settled into our jobs and our house and our family life, but it just felt like something was missing.

Maybe it's the gypsy nature in my family. I know Laura, my birth mother, struggled with that all of her life.

Maybe it's just that I didn't work well with others. I always preferred my own endeavours, didn't play well on teams, and didn't mind my own company.

At any rate, regardless of the reason or reasons, I rarely sat still, never put up with stupidity, and often found myself at loose ends as a result.

I dragged my young family to Toronto to attend a technical school. Catherine's salary wasn't enough to support us, so I made good use of my time before and after school and on the weekends.

None of my jobs involved going into an office or place of business and doing a prescribed job in a certain fashion. Perhaps the work I took on was a precursor to my eventual negative attitude toward being an employee, or perhaps that attitude was already there and just needed a way to be expressed.

At any rate, I did various things at various times.

At one point, I went door to door as a Fuller Brush salesman. I felt they had a good product line, reasonable prices, and it was a good way to spend several hours a day during the summer. I made some money, met some nice folks, but I knew early on this wouldn't be a career for me, no matter how many bonuses or incentives they threw my way.

We always had a supply of scrub brushes, clothes brushes, and dust brooms, however.

For several months, I took on the late night shift as a taxi driver. I worked mostly on Friday and Saturday nights, because I didn't have to get up for school the next day, and I still had enough time to get my homework done and spend time with the family.

As an off-shoot of that, I also started bootlegging liquor out of the trunk of the car. I'd buy up about ten or twelve bottles of various kinds of liquor before the liquor store closed. Then while I was driving someone to their destination, if the subject of alcohol came up, I'd slip in that maybe I knew somewhere to purchase more, for a premium. Since the liquor store was closed, the only other place to buy alcohol was a bar, and that was too pricey and they wouldn't sell you a bottle to take home, so I almost always made a sale.

Of course, I had to be careful not to get caught. And I never was.

And I rarely went home with any stock left.

Another job I took was long-distance truck driving. I had a buddy who worked for a company that did a late-night run from Toronto to Montreal. Again, I could only work on the weekends, so we'd head out about six in the evening on a Friday or Saturday. I'd drive the first leg which was about 350 miles and took about seven hours while my buddy slept, and he'd drive the next leg back. It was long and boring, but in those years, the traffic wasn't so bad on that stretch of highway, so it was a lot safer.

The Physics of Love

In between jobs, mostly on the weekends, I searched the want ads in the newspaper and then check the for sale ads. If I saw a match, I'd call the want ad, get more details to make sure I was getting the right product, then offer to deliver the item. This was almost unheard-of, so most folks were willing to commit to buying from me. Then I'd go pick up the for sale item, usually haggling them down a little, and make the deal with the buyer. I made a few dollars on every transaction, and if it was a large console radio or television or anything I knew I could fix, I'd leave the buyer with my name and phone number, telling them the item was being sold as-is, but I'd give them a deal on repairs if they needed them down the road. I had a few call backs and got several new customers from that for other appliances and electronics, too.

We always had enough money, and I never ran out of projects or customers.

Chapter 12

Once I graduated from technical school, I could take my pick of jobs. At one point, I ended up in Corner Brook on the west coast of Newfoundland. At first I felt a little like a fish out of water, but I soon made a lifelong friend in Gary Kingman. He lived on the same street where Catherine and I planted the mobile home trailer we'd had moved from Toronto. He also worked with me at Canadian Overseas Telecommunications Corporation, which we affectionately called COTC. This company later came to be renamed Teleglobe. Gary and I were technical assistants (TA's), and spent a lot of time traveling the western coast of Newfoundland.

This job was a good fit for us. Gary, who was originally from England, had a wife and family that fit in well with Catherine and the girls, so I knew they had company when we men were off on an extended road trip. Gary was great company, always ready for an adventure, and not adverse to camping overnight in the station wagon or cooking up our dinner on an old camp stove.

Another benefit of this working relationship was Gary's interest in coins and collecting. He was more of an entrepreneur than a collector, but that never stopped him from saying yes to my hare-brained ideas.

We would hop into the car on a Monday morning headed out for various transmitting stations and potential tower locations. At that time, telecommunications in western Newfoundland was limited to the larger cities and towns. Small outports relied on exchanges and translators to get their calls through, and often a smaller community had only one telephone in the general store. But with the expansion of communications, all that was about to change.

Sometimes on these journeys, we would suss out folks in the towns who might have a few coins they wanted to sell. Often these coins were squirreled away in a mason jar or a mayonnaise jar in a cupboard, kept there in the dark for years at a time. Many times the wife was the owner, having saved her pennies and such from her housekeeping money over the years, but the husbands always knew the money was there.

Gary and I would take a long weekend we'd earned by working overtime and head up the Great Northern Peninsula, as it's called, the wagon loaded down with camping gear to keep our costs down, and we'd go to some of the communities we'd visited the week before. We had a bank account where we both put in an equal amount of money, which made splitting the profits a lot easier. In those days, a hundred dollars was a lot of money. You could buy a house for five thousand, a brand new car for a thousand, so a hundred dollars of what we called "mad money" was a fortune. At any rate, we tended to buy in smaller lots, so the four hundred dollars we contributed was plenty.

At that time, the road up the Northern Peninsula—where it was a road at all—was gravel. Pitted and dotted with pot holes, just driving took a lot of skill and conversation. The only air conditioning we had at the time was an open window, which didn't make a lot of sense on a dusty road, particularly if you were following another car. I spent a lot of time trying to pass vehicles in front of us just so I could open a window and get a breath of fresh air.

There wasn't a complete through-road, however, so we would drive as far as Bonn Bay, take the ferry to Woody Point, and head north to Daniels Harbour, the first community of any size. As with most things, if you wanted to be successful, you had to learn the technique. And, in our case, the language. We thought everybody in Newfoundland spoke English, but as Gary would comment, "there's proper English, there's Newfoundland English, and then there's Northern Peninsula English". He was good at the proper English, I had a good handle on most of the dialects of the Newfoundland English, but the N.P. English, as we called it, eluded us for some time.

Not to mention the technique. It took us a while to figure out what worked, but we quickly learned what didn't. Barging into a community, usually starting at the general store, and announcing we were looking for gold, resulted in blank stares and cold shoulders. No amount of wheedling or walking around opened the doors, and many a weekend we came home empty-handed and disheartened before we figured out a tactic.

We learned that we had to drive up to the Government wharf—and pretty much every community had one—park the car, and wait. No matter what time of day we arrived, there was always a fisherman hanging around, mending nets, repairing lobster pots, chewing the rag, or smoking their pipes. We simply sat there watching the goings-on until the locals stirred up and ambled over to see what we were up to.

It went something like this:

Me: "how's the fishing?"

Local: various answers, but never would they admit it was good. To do that would jinx them, they were sure. Or have other fishermen following them out to their secret fishing grounds.

A long pause would follow this answer, since I knew they would not be rushed.

Local: "where be ye fellows from?"

Me: "Corner Brook." Of course, in truth we weren't. I was originally from Carbonear, and Gary was from England, but I knew they meant where were we living.

Local: "Oh, aye."

Long pause.

Local: "What be ye doing up yer?"

Pause.

Me: "Looking for old Newfoundland money."

Local: (Laugh) "Ain't any new money round yer, let alone old money."

Very long pause.

Local: "Think the missus have a few old coins tucked away somewhere." Long pause. "Drop by de 'ouse and see what she got."

We would then go to the directed house, sit at the kitchen table, while the missus brought out the inevitable mason jar full of old coins. I analyzed them one by one using my jeweler's loupe, exclaiming over the best ones like a proud grandfather praising his grandchildren, because this was expected. These old coins often had a history with this family, and to treat them as mere objects would be insulting. And once insulted, no deal was going to happen. Not in that household, not in that community. I knew enough about Newfoundlanders to know that.

I generally made an offer on the entire lot, because picking and choosing would imply some were better than others. Even a coin I wasn't interested in might be of interest to someone else, and if it didn't cost me anything in the total amount, I didn't care if I had a few extra. My offer was generally accepted because I offered more than face value, and to these folks, that's all the coins were worth. The missus might have some clue as to how much face value she had in the jar, and to learn I was offering her twice the face value proved to her husband and the community that she was thrifty, a trait much valued in the outports to this day.

Life in these communities wasn't easy. Dependent on the sea for their livelihood, their gardens and subsistence farms for most of their food, and their husband's hunting abilities for their meat, meant there was never much money. A wife might sell a few eggs or vegetables, if there was extra, to the general store. A talented wife might sew for others or sell a few crafted articles like home-knit socks or caps in the general store, but a lot of that depended on travelers coming through the town because every woman in town had the same skills and rarely paid for someone else's handiwork. A thrifty wife, however, saved her pennies and coins in a jar so she had money when she needed a couple of dollars for something special like a new pair of shoes or a tire for her husband's truck—something she couldn't make, grow, hunt, or barter for herself.

At any rate, word soon got around that these city boys were throwing their money away on buying up old coins, and so other neighbors dropped by and suggested that perhaps their missus might have something we'd be interested in. We'd often get invitations to half a dozen homes that day, which we didn't mind one bit. There was a good deal of banter and chit-chat, and we always got offered a cup of tea.

Word started to get along the coast, and soon people were watching out for us. In St. Barbe, some locals met us on the wharf with their jars, and we spent an hour sorting coins on the splitting table, the gulls soaring and swooping overhead, expecting fish offal to be tossed to them since there was such a crowd around the table. They were sorely disappointed, but we weren't. I remember swiping at the table before we started to get a fish head and some guts off the work surface.

At one small hamlet north of Port aux Choise, we had been directed to call in on a schooner captain who was alleged to have a hoard of coins. When we went to his house, which was one of the nicer ones in town, his wife said her husband and crew were out to sea but due back in a couple of hours. We said we'd come back then. By that time, it was late in the afternoon, so we found a spot overlooking the wharf where we parked the car, and I hauled out the Coleman stove and our supper makings. Soon we were enjoying a good meal and a hot cup of tea. We saw the schooner come in, her sails flapping in the breeze. The ship nudged into her berth like a baby settling into its mother's arms, and the captain and two crew came ashore and headed for his house.

Since it was starting to get dusk, we decided to go to the house, too. We didn't want to be too late heading back to Corner Brook that night, as driving that road in the daylight was bad enough; in the dark, it was like playing Russian roulette. You never knew when a moose might step out in front of you, and there's a good reason why they're called Newfoundland speed bumps. No matter how big a vehicle you're driving, if you hit a moose, nobody wins.

We got to the house and they invited us in. We inhaled the yeasty aroma of fresh baked bread. The missus already told her husband we'd been around, so he was kind of expecting us. Many things have changed in Newfoundland in the intervening years, but never the fact that if you show up at someone's house around mealtime, you're invited to stay and eat. Since we'd just eaten, we declined their invitation to sup with them, but we did get a cup of tea to warm our hands.

We sat in chairs by the wall with our tea mugs while the captain and crew sat at the table for their supper. Gary and I were both under the misconception that a fishing schooner crew ate fish. Well, we were surprised. A large plate of thick-sliced homemade bread, and a dish with Good Luck margarine, was placed on the table. Then a large dish of boiled potatoes was placed next to it. We expected to see a dish of fried or boiled fish to come out, but it never did.

The captain and crew helped themselves to large helpings of boiled potatoes smothered with Good Luck margarine, and homemade bread. No pickles. No meat. Not even a jar of jam.

And while I can't for the life of me remember what we bought from the captain—except I know we bought most of what he had, and he had many jars of coins—I still remember that meal. Gary and I talked about that night many times when we were cooking up our dinner on that old camp stove. And while we weren't religious men, we were thankful we had meat at every meal.

On another trip up the N.P., we went as far as Flower's Cove, which is way up north. The local merchant, William Genge, was also a ship's chandler, meaning he outfitted local and foreign vessels, providing the food, supplies, equipment, whatever they needed to go to sea. His family had been merchants in the area for over a hundred years. Up until the early 1920's, most trading with foreign vessels was paid for in gold, which was a standard and they didn't need to worry about exchange rates. For a few years after, gold was still used between individuals and businesses, circulating from one hand to the other and back again in the normal course of business. Before 1923, government-issued money was scarce because the government wasn't as involved in the everyday life of people as it is now. At that time, there were no pensions, no unemployment, no reason for the government to give a person money unless they bought something from them, which they rarely did. The largest influx of government money came in 1954 to 1965 when the government, under Joey Smallwood, decided to consolidate communities to make it easier to expand services such as telephone, cottage hospitals, and mail. This was called resettlement, and many small communities disappeared when the government basically threatened to cut them off by not keeping up the roads or ferries, not delivering their mail, and not providing law enforcement.

We had no idea what we were going to run into, and we got a big surprise. A good surprise, at that. It was a numismatist's dream come true.

One of the more scarce coins was the Newfoundland two-dollar gold. They were minted only in the 1880's and 1890's in small amounts, which made them much sought after by coin collectors. One coin was worth many times its face value or its gold content value. We had managed, on a couple of previous trips up the coast, to get a couple of these coins, but they were scarce. But that didn't stop us from asking. We went into Mr. Genge's store just as he was closing for the day. It was already getting dark, and we had the return trip on our minds once again. However, when he said yes, he had a couple of Newfoundland two-dollar coins, we forgot all about the drive. We'd sleep in the car if need be.

He wanted us to drop by his house later, and we agreed. So we spent the next hour or so cooking up our dinner in the station wagon, and talking about the possibilities of what Mr. Genge might have to offer. We never said the words out loud, but maybe he'd have more than a couple? Perhaps even a dozen? We could make a small fortune if that was the case. We also never spoke out the doubts lurking at the edges of our minds, that perhaps he was pulling our leg or misremembered what he had. Or would want more than was profitable for us to pay. None of that mattered. As Sherlock Holmes said, "the quarry is afoot", and our quarry was gold coins.

About an hour or so later we headed for Mr. Genge's house. Being from a wealthy and well-established family, the Genge House was the largest in the community. Over a hundred and fifty years old, large then even by modern standards, this house would rival anything in Carbonear, or Corner Brook, or probably even St. John's. But there was no electricity, as the electric wasn't widely available and was considered expensive and wasteful to these thrifty Newfoundlanders.

Mr. Genge invited us into his parlor, which was full of quality furniture which would have been considered antique even at that time, and we sat at a round table in the center of the room. An oil lamp was placed on the table, casting a yellowish glow over the surface that was covered by a thick, ornate table cloth. I groaned. The table cloth could be a distraction from the coins. Maybe the old fellow was smarter than he let on. I wished he'd take the cloth off, or that I had thought to bring a plain piece of black velvet, which always shows coins and jewelry off to its best advantages. That's the reason you see so much of that kind of material in quality coin and jewelry shops.

Mr. Genge left the room and came back a few minutes later with a velvet drawstring bag, about eight or nine inches square. Gary and I held our breath as he loosened the string and tipped the bag out over the table.

A hoard of golden coins, probably around eighty in all, tumbled onto the table, their clinking muffled by the table cloth. A veritable pirate's treasure. Gary and I were mesmerized, looking at those golden circles glinting in the light from the oil lamp, much as they would have looked when they were minted over eighty years ago. A hush fell over the room, and I looked first at Gary, who stared at the coins like they were going to jump off the table and run away. I pressed my hands together under the table to resist picking them up and letting them sift through my fingers like sand. No point in showing too much interest too quickly. If Mr. Genge realized what he had, we'd be priced out of the market.

We spent the next two hours listing the coins. There were a lot of American gold coins, many British sovereigns and half-sovereigns, four or five Newfoundland two-dollar coins, and one Australian sovereign. Mr. Genge said these coins had been locked away in a safe since 1923, when most countries went off the gold standard and starting using government-issued paper money. Gary and I spent some time discussing the price while Mr. Genge went out of the room for a few minutes, and when he returned, I swallowed hard. We wanted to offer him a fair price, one that would allow us to make a profit. We didn't want to offer too little, because once the words were out of our mouth, he'd have an idea of what the lot was worth and might decide to hold out for a higher price. We also didn't want to insult him because he might have a sentimental attachment to this lot, seeing as how his father had a hand in collecting the coins.

We offered him twelve hundred dollars. That was a small fortune. I could have bought a new car, or paid off my mortgage with that amount. It was as much as I made in a year.

We held our breath.

Mr. Genge accepted the offer, and the deal was sealed with several tots of rum at the table while the hoard of coins sat in front of us.

We cut short our trip and drove back to Corner Brook at breakneck speed, leaving Mr. Genge with the assurance that we'd be back inside of a week. Our only problem was we had four hundred dollars in our Coin Collecting account.

We had to come up with eight hundred dollars in short order. There were no credit cards or lines of credit in those days.

Gary had a very good friend, a widower, who worked in the pay office at the Bowater's Mill. I thought Max Atkins, who was very well off, might be interested in coming in as a partner on this deal. He was. Within a week we were back to Flowers Cove and retrieved our gold. This time, when Mr. Genge tipped out the bag, five additional coins, which must have been caught in a corner of the bag at our previous viewing, tumbled onto the table.

I didn't blink an eye. I said, "Quite in order", scooped up all the coins in a flash, dumped them into the bag, and we departed with our treasure in hand.

And we knew we had a treasure. The Newfoundland two-dollar coins were selling for sixty to eighty dollars, depending on condition, so we'd never pay more than forty dollars for them. All the other gold coins were purchased at bullion value, which at that time was thirty-five dollars US an ounce. British sovereigns and the US ten-dollar coins had about the same gold content, and we figured them at face value times 2 times .09, so a ten-dollar coin was worth about eighteen dollars.

While it might sound like all of these trips were about money, and, some might even allege we were stealing from folks who didn't know the true value of what they had, I hope to redeem myself with this true story. We were up the coast on a cold and miserable day in an equally cold and miserable settlement, trying to make a few good deals. The folks were so poor, they didn't even invite us in for a cup of tea, and it was raining so bad, we didn't want to get out of the wagon to light up the stove.

So we sat in the car and waited for folks to come to us. Needless to say, customers were few and far between, most folks preferring to stay in by their stoves that day. But that didn't stop the locals from sending their children out to see us and offer what they had.

There was one young fellow of about nine. He was thin, wearing old clothes too big for him, a worn pair of shoes his father had probably handed down, scuffed, falling apart, no laces and no socks. He stood shivering in the rain, water running down into his eyes, his red hair plastered to his head. He presented an old Newfoundland ten-cent piece, worn and almost faded. The coin had no value to a collector, as dimes in good condition were very plentiful, and this one wasn't even in acceptable condition. Still, I pulled out my jeweler's loupe and spent some time checking it over, commenting on its characteristics and good qualities. I looked up and caught the lad staring at the coin.

At that moment, my mind flashed back to the story my father had told me of how he and my mother had come to Uncle Richard's house when I was about eighteen months old. I was dirty, in a dark room, dirty diaper, no clean clothes, thin, snot-nosed. My father had gathered me in his arms and said, "You're coming home with us, my son." And that decision of his forever changed my life.

I stared at the boy's too-large clothes. He'd likely never owned anything new. His shoes looked ready to walk off with him, and his bare legs were covered with goosebumps.

"I'll give you a dollar for it."

The wind threatened to carry my words off. The youngster stared at me, blinked a couple of times, and nodded. I handed over the dollar bill, and he clutched it like he'd never seen such an amount before. Likely he hadn't. He bobbed his head in thanks and sprinted for the house, slamming open the door and calling for his mother at the top of his lungs.

Gary nudged me. "Did you see something special in it?"

I shook my head.

Gary persisted. "It was barely worth a dime. Why did you give him a whole dollar?"

Once again who I might have been had I not been taken from that tough environment and brought into my parents' home flashed through my mind. How to explain all I was feeling? I shook my head again. "Did you see the shoes he was wearing?"

That seemed enough explanation for Gary. We both had kids of our own a little younger than this boy, and I know he was thinking the same thing I was: there but for the grace of God go I, or one of mine.

Chapter 12

We visited Mom and Dad in 1965, and I took the opportunity to have several long talks with Dad, as his health had been fragile for a couple of years. During this visit we discussed what I knew about my biological father and that whole situation. He didn't really want to elaborate, and implied I would find out in due course.

Dad passed away in February 1966. That was a tough time for me. One of the few people I'd known all my life was gone. I couldn't imagine living the rest of my life without him, to be honest. It just seemed overwhelming.

Catherine and I decided to move back to St. John's. I guess I was feeling less of a gypsy by then, with a wife and three children. I'd had a grand time traveling the country and Europe, and now wanted something more stable.

Work with Hydro, or the Power Commission, as we called it, was exciting but time-consuming. The power grid in Newfoundland was just being developed, and sometimes we worked from early morning until dark and then started up again early the next day. Sometimes we worked seven days a week, many times traveling out of town on a moment's notice, returning Sunday long enough to get a home-cooked meal and clean clothes, and then we were off again to the Stoney Brook Terminal Station by supper time. But the guys I met and worked with were great.

In 1967, we hit the road to install equipment. Today, there are about fifteen union men involved in these installations. Back then, it was up to whoever was there. We uncrated the equipment, drilled floor anchors, physically mounted the 500-pound racks on location, assembled battery banks, mounted chargers, ran the power, status, and co-ax cables, fired up and successfully commissioned the equipment. A lot of this equipment was prototypes, which meant they were like samples or ideas of what should work, and we were expected to troubleshoot and maintain this equipment at the component level.

If it didn't work, we went to Massey Drive in St. John's to get some test equipment, dragged it on a sled over snow banks and walked up to hilltops and microwave sites or waded out to Noel Peter's Brook to figure out what was wrong. And the problem was never in our installation. Always the fault lay in the design or the components.

And while all this was hard work, the thing I really liked was these remote locations gave us the permission and ability to be out in the wilderness areas of the Island, to do as we wished during our off hours. We got the chance to suss out some of the best hunting and fishing spots in Newfoundland, and we were able to go there on our trips, driving roads that nobody else knew existed. This was part of my secret for never coming home empty-handed from a trip.

No matter what the weather, we always moved when required, and maybe if I'd kept at that job, I wouldn't have survived. Everywhere we went, it was 100 miles an hour—not kilometers, miles. Between Whitbourne and Western Avalon, many is the time the highway was pure ice and we were going 100. That's wasn't driving. That was aiming a vehicle and trusting to luck, because we never had any concerns. Of course, the roads weren't so well-traveled then as they are now, and we could go hours and not see another soul. Especially at night, it was a good time to catch an hour's sleep while the other one drove. Our Transportation Department complained because the best set of tires they could buy at the time was the Firestone 500 Premium, and we couldn't get more than five thousand miles while other vehicles were getting in excess of 20,000 miles. I think there is still a bunch of tire studs somewhere in the woods at the Holyrood turnoff.

As full as my life was in those years, there was still something missing. If you'd asked me, I don't know that I could said what it was. I seemed to have everything a man of the 1970's and 80's could ask for—a wife, children, a career, good friends.

But even as a boy, I knew I lacked something.

So when the opportunity to lay hold of that something came, I grabbed with both hands, determined not to let go.

Book 3—Convergence
Our Story

con·ver·gence

[kuh n-vur-juh ns]

noun

1. an act or instance of converging.
2. a convergent state or quality.
3. the degree or point at which lines, objects, etc., converge.

Con·verge

[kuh n-vurj]

verb (used without object)

1. to tend to meet in a point or line; incline toward each other, as lines that are not parallel.
2. to tend to a common result, conclusion, etc.
3. Mathematics .

a. (of a sequence) to have values eventually arbitrarily close to some number; to have a finite limit.

b. (of an infinite series) to have a finite sum; to have a sequence of partial sums that converges.

c. (of an improper integral) to have a finite value.

d. (of a net) to be residually in every neighborhood of some point.

Verb (used with object)

4.

to cause to converge.

Origin:

1685–95; < Late Latin *convergere* to incline together.

Chapter 1
April 2004
Richard

"We often wondered what became of you."

I sat across from a woman who bore my eyes, my nose, my chin, at a social club dinner, marveling that we'd managed not to run into each other for nearly seventy years. My aunt Emily. A sister of my biological father, Samson Baldwin.

I said to her, "You're my aunt."

"Yes." She glanced at the woman sitting to my right. "And this is Catherine?"

I introduced them. "This is Mona. She's my second wife. Catherine died some years ago."

The two shook hands and greeted each other.

"Mona knows about my background. We've talked about the Baldwins."

Emily nodded. "I was there that day. The day Laura brought you. I wasn't the one who answered the door. But I knew what was going on. We all did."

I leaned in closer. "Tell me what happened."

She sat back in her chair as if trying to put some space and time between us. Perhaps this wasn't as exciting for her as it was for me, to discover and meet my biological father's family. I needed to move slowly until I learned which direction the wind blew.

Mona stood. "I'll get us another drink."

I nodded, feeling she'd picked up, as I had, that Emily preferred to speak with only me.

My aunt toyed with the edge of a napkin on the table.

I smiled. "I do the same thing."

She paused. "What?"

"Roll the edge of the napkin, or the placemat, like that. I have a daughter who does, too."

"Some family traits are strange, aren't they?"

"My daughter might think she picked the habit up from me, but I certainly didn't pick it up from you."

Emily resumed her nervous action. "No, that's for sure."

"Do I have brothers and sisters?"

She nodded. "One brother and three sisters."

At those words, my entire universe clicked into place. I *knew* there were others out there with a family relationship to me. Of course, there had always been my mother Laura and my sister Edna, and her two sons, but that bloodline was tenuous at best and rarely acknowledged. And I had my own five children and eight grandchildren.

But now I had four siblings from my father's side of the family.

I had a king's treasure.

We chatted for the next hours as I tried to catch up on the past seven decades of missed events. I'd kept tabs on my biological father from a distance for most of his career, and recalled seeing his retirement announcement in the paper. And more recently, his obituary.

None of which concerned me in the least, as I'd had no relationship with him.

And hope had begun to rise in me that perhaps the opportunity to meet my half-siblings may finally be near.

I dreaded asking the next question, because I wasn't sure I wanted to hear the answer. "Do you think they'll want to meet me?"

She held my gaze for a long time. "I don't know. I guess that will depend."

"On what?"

"On why you want to meet them."

Ah, the mother hen protecting her chicks. "I want no claim on the Baldwin family other than the fact I am Samson's son. I would like to meet his other children, for the sake of family connections and family completeness."

She studied me again before offering a tiny nod. Had I not been looking at her directly I might have missed it. "Fine. I'll contact Maureen. She'll know what to do."

I scribbled my name and telephone number on the back of a napkin, and she tucked the flimsy paper into her purse.

I almost laughed at the irony. My future held on a piece of disposable paper, meant to be used once and tossed away.

Like my mother.

Like me.

As with most things in my life, I had a decision to make, and I chose to let the matter go. I couldn't do anything to change the course of events. I had no control over whether Emily would do as she said and talk to Maureen. I couldn't force Maureen or any of her siblings to call me. The only thing I had control over was me.

Mona and I talked over the matter as we returned to our home in Bryant's Cove.

Mona started. "What do you think, Richard?"

"I don't know what to think. I had always hoped this day would come, but as the years went by, I wasn't sure I would live to see it."

"If they knew about you, why didn't they contact you?"

"I don't know."

"Would you, in their position?"

"I'd like to think I would."

"I knew of a situation just like this one." She'd been a teacher for over forty years. "In Old Perlican. A man found out he'd been raised by his grandparents, that his sister was his mother."

"What happened?"

"He was never the same. He couldn't handle it. He ended up killing himself."

I chuckled. "I don't have any plans of doing that at this stage in my life."

She laid her hand on mine. "Oh, I know that. Besides, maybe it was easier finding out when you were younger. He was in his fifties when he learned the truth, and by that time, his parents—or his grandparents, I guess they were—were already dead."

"So he never had the chance to talk to them about it."

I'd never spoken of the matter with my mother. I saw no benefit in hurting her. Since she'd been there the night Mr. Baldwin delivered me over to the man I called Father, she knew the whole story. I talked to my father about a year before he died. I didn't reveal who told me, or who I'd talked to, although he tried to worm it out of me. He finally simply said, 'Well, somebody must have told you'. I agreed, and said, 'It's out in the open as far as I'm concerned. A lot of people in Carbonear know it. Knew it at the time, and know it now. And people I work with in St. John's know. And in Grand Falls, too'."

"How did he take that?"

"I'm much like my father. He never lost a moment's sleep on anything he couldn't change. He simply nodded and that was that. It never changed how I felt about him and Mom, and he knew that, could see it."

When we reached the house, I could hear the phone ringing inside. I hurried in, dropped our grocery sacks on the kitchen table, and answered.

It was my half-sister. "Hello, Richard. It's Maureen."

I said, "I wasn't sure you would call."

"And why shouldn't I? You're family."

All the years of questions and no answers and half-truths and wondering where I fit into the big scheme of things melted away like wax.

I'd found where I belonged.

The first time I met my brother Bart and his wife Patty was in late 2000. I'd chatted on the phone with him a couple of times, and when he suggested we meet in St. John's, I was thrilled. I decided the appropriate and honorable location should be My Brothers Restaurant. I'd never had a brother before, so this was a special day and deserved a special place, one that we'd never forget the name of.

We had lunch, and I'll admit I wasn't quite as nervous as when I met Amelia, but still I was apprehensive. I wore a suit again, and a bolo tie. I don't know if I thought how I was dressed would get me onto their good side or what, but that was my mindset. As time went on and I met more of the family, I relaxed a little and didn't feel the need to prove myself.

But you must look at this from my point of view. I'd been rejected as an infant by this family, and rejected by my birth mother, so I've always struggled with feelings of inadequacy. As a result, I admit I'm an over-achiever and a perfectionist, a real Type A personality. While I didn't purposely treat my biological family as a project to complete or an obstacle to overcome, I did view them as people I thought I wanted to know, and I would put forth my best foot to persuade them to want to know me.

Silly, now, when I think back on it, but that's the way it was at the time.

Laura

As the years passed and I watched Richard from afar, I often wondered what it would have been like to truly be part of his family. To call him Son.

But that joy—and that privilege—was denied me. No, not exactly denied, because that would lay the blame solely at the feet of others. I'd had a huge part in the happenings. Nobody had forced me to do anything.

And so I spent the rest of my life trying to prove my father wrong. Working hard. Loving hard. Studying hard. Making more of myself than he'd ever thought possible.

And still I could never please him.

His letters he wrote to me in later years proved that: Worried about your soul. Troubled at the goings-on. How could you not have known he was already married? Ashamed to admit you're my daughter.

So perhaps I became the black sheep of our family so that he could be correct in his assessment of me. Oh, perhaps that label was never applied from anyone speaking directly to me or looking me in the eye. But I know what they were thinking.

And what of poor Edna, my daughter? She managed to finish college, find a husband, have a family, despite my inept mothering and her broken family. Because yes, as soon as I could scrape together enough money, I was gone from Albert Jamieson, and I never looked back.

In those days, the only way to get a divorce in Newfoundland was to petition the Lieutenant Governor.

Might as well have asked for a letter from God.

Because unless you had grounds—oh, I had grounds, all right, just nothing that was visible—divorce was almost unheard-of.

I saved enough to travel to Las Vegas, Nevada. Lived there for thirty days, and got my divorce. Mailed the papers to Albert—I'd have liked to been a fly on the wall that day, you can be sure. Then I returned to Canada and started a new life.

Except, not really. I somehow managed to repeat the same mistakes when it came to men.

Maybe my father knew me better than I know myself.

There was some satisfaction, though. As Richard grew up, I saw some of the same gypsy spirit in him that I possessed. He got into a lot of the same scrapes as I did while he was under my father's roof. So perhaps I had some revenge on my father as he lived through my childhood again—not to the same extreme degree, of course.

I once accused Richard of being like his father, and he thought I meant Henry Cameron.

I didn't, and I corrected him in his assumption.

"I mean, you are just like Samson Baldwin. You don't want to spend any more time in Carbonear. You want to be a big fish in a big pond."

He'd smiled at me, that slow smile that just tickled his mouth—again, just like his father—and nodded. "Nothing wrong with that."

"There is if people get hurt."

He shook his head. "People get hurt regardless. Besides, Samson Baldwin may have contributed some genetic material, but he isn't my father."

Honestly, I don't know which I preferred: that he was the son of the man who couldn't love me, or the son of the man who never loved me.

And truthfully, I couldn't tell you which man was which.

Chapter 2
Richard

When I worked with Newfoundland Telephone in the 70's, Samson Baldwin, my biological father, was on the Public Utilities Board, which regulates the utility rates of the power companies, telephone companies, and other utilities. He worked in the same building as I did, only on the second floor, while I was on the fifth floor. I had gone up and down in the elevator with him more times than I can count.

Each time we rode up or down, I wondered what he was thinking. I never caught him looking at me, like people sometimes do when they think they know you but aren't sure. Or in this case, I'm pretty certain he did know who I was. But he never spoke to me, and he never eyeballed me.

He knew I worked for Hydro, and my resemblance to my siblings is unmistakable. One day, my boss, Walter Dunne, came to me and asked, "How well do you know Samson Baldwin?"

I wasn't sure where he was going with this, and so I was cautious not to reveal too much information beyond what was generally known about the man. "Well, he grew up in Carbonear. And he is a member of the Baldwin family that lived not too far from where I lived. And he's on the PU Board."

"You don't know him any better than that?"

"Walter, what are you asking me?" I knew there was some reason he'd bring up this particular man right out of the blue. I mean, if he'd asked me if I knew Adam, I could have told him just about the same amount of information.

He leaned against the doorjamb. "Just curious."

I wasn't fooled. "Why would you ask me if I know Samson Baldwin? Everybody in Newfoundland knows the name Samson Baldwin. He works for the PUB."

Walter tried to look nonchalant. "Is he an engineer?"

I wasn't buying his act. "Of course he is." When Walter didn't respond, I decided to push him a little harder. "Walter, Samson has asked you to ask me some questions. Don't lie to me. You're not that good of a poker player." I had played poker with him for several years by that time, and I could always tell when he was bluffing. He had a little vein in his temple that bulged out when he wasn't being entirely truthful. I'd won some money from him once I'd identified that little tell. The vein pulsed right now.

"Well, we associate a lot, and our wives are in the same card club."

"Do you play poker with him?"

"He doesn't play poker."

I leaned back in my chair and folded my hands behind my head. "That's a nice piece of information to know. I play poker with you on a regular basis, and you don't have a good poker face right now. Come on, spill the beans."

He sat in the chair opposite mine. "Are you related to Samson Baldwin?"

I said, "Has Samson sent you to get information from me?"

"Well, if you're related to him—"

"Walter, don't beat around the bush. If Samson asked you for information about me, he gave you the reason he wants to know. So tell me what you know, and you may get more information."

"I don't know why he wants to know. I went to university with Samson. I didn't know him from before that, since he's from Carbonear and I'm from Deer Lake. We met at Nova Scotia Tech. Is Samson your father?"

"I have very strong reason to believe the is."

"Okay," he said.

I said, "Now, because I know one of your engineering buddies, do I get a raise in pay?"

He laughed and we never talked about it again.

I don't know for sure how all this came up. Maybe Samson got to wondering if I was "*the* baby", and asked Walter to ask me. Maybe Samson just asked Walter some questions about me, and Walter got curious about my connection to Samson.

Whatever the case, he'd put Walter in an awkward position. And me, too, for that matter. And I didn't appreciate it. But that was the only time it was mentioned.

But it's not the only time I was reminded of my connection to a family that seemed to want to have nothing to do with me, which is why when Maureen called me, I was so pleased.

And the funny thing is, the next time was also related to my time at Hydro. Over one summer, I had a student work for me who was doing his engineering degree, James Cahill. Frank's father and my next up the line supervisor, Arthur Earle, were engineering buddies, and Richard brought Frank in for the summer and assigned him to me.

After I came back to Carbonear, I went to the post office one day, and Michael Cahill, Frank's father, was there. As I passed by, I said, casually like, "Hello, Michael. Long time no see."

"Oh, yeah, Stuart."

I said, "You're only half right."

He looked at me, peering over his glasses. "Ah, yes, Richard Cameron."

"Yes, that's it," I said, and on I went.

There was nothing more to say about it, particularly not there, but it was obvious he knew all about it.

But somewhere, deep down, I was glad to know I looked like the rest of my biological family. Completed that connection in some way.

Laura

Finally, I've found a man who would not and could not hurt me. He is quiet. He is divorced—this time I asked to see the papers, and actually checked them at the court to make certain they were genuine.

He doesn't have the temperament to strike me or verbally abuse me in any way. God knows I pushed the limits of human endurance during our courtship.

I will keep this man for the rest of my life. I am a faithful wife, never looking elsewhere. He loves me unconditionally, and we enjoy many of the same things. Once again I find myself molding myself to his personality, and I like the changes I see in myself. I fret less. Hold fewer grudges. Forgive more quickly.

We travel to satisfy the gypsy within me. Perhaps because I feel I don't deserve nice things, we tend to rough it, spending winters in Death Valley without air conditioning, rationing water, living on little more than love.

Or perhaps I am merely proving my mettle, to myself and anyone else who looks on.

My father is gone now; I have nothing to prove to him. But Aunt Annie lives on, and I love to send her letters that I know will shock her sensibilities as I relate stories of large insects and venomous snakes, of traveling in a caravan, living with strangers who soon become friends, learning how to do beading so we can eke out a living at fairs and festivals.

I find I enjoy painting, and spend hours in the desert by myself trying various techniques to capture the savage yet sensual desert on canvas. I am only sometimes close.

And when the heat of summer threatens, we pack up and move west and north, following the crops, doing the work of itinerate pickers. I would not say we "become" itinerate pickers, for this is not our lot in life. Instead, we do this work because we can. We do this work because we choose to live a life free of constraints.

I do this work to horrify Aunt Annie, and, hopefully through her, my father.

Yes, I know he is dead and buried, but my desire to do whatever I can to shock him is only slightly greater than my desire to please him.

And since he's already proven I cannot do the latter, I will strive at excelling at the former.

Donna Schlachter

Chapter 3
Richard

"I did not know I was pregnant."

My mother stared back at me with that wide-eyed look of innocence perfected by Bette Davis, the actress, many years before.

And for a moment, I almost believed her.

Perhaps I wanted to believe her. Perhaps I didn't want to believe that anybody could coldly marry one man while carrying another's baby, hoping for—for what? That Albert Jamieson would simply accept this child and raise it as his own?

I don't know many men as forgiving as that.

And Jamieson wasn't one of them.

Her answer was in response to my question of how she could marry Albert knowing she was pregnant. And not by him.

I wasn't satisfied with her answer. "How could you not know? I mean, married in December, delivering in March?"

She waved off my words like a fly at a picnic. "Well, we didn't have pregnancy tests. I wasn't about to go to the doctor in Carbonear. Word would be all over town before I got home again. And after I married Albert, well—my visitor was never regular."

"Why did you go back to Albert?"

What I really wanted to know was how she could choose between her husband of four months and her child, but I couldn't bring myself to ask that question.

"I had no choice. I couldn't stay in Carbonear, so I went back."

"What happened?"

She looked at me with that blank look again as if I were an idiot. "Happened? I went back to Grand Falls. I cooked his dinner. He greeted me as if I hadn't been gone for three weeks or more, and then he laid down the law."

"Law?"

We sat across the table from each other in her apartment in Hantsport, Nova Scotia. She'd returned to live in the same town Edna lived in about five years before that. Since then, her third husband had died, and she was alone.

Again.

"Things were always done on Albert's terms. My responsibilities included keeping house, preparing meals, hostessing when he invited business acquaintances to the house. You know, the normal things the wife of an executive does to further his career."

"Doesn't sound as if there was much love."

She looked at a spot over my shoulder, somewhere far away. "No, there's wasn't. We slept in separate rooms."

"But you had Edna."

A hint of a smile tickled her lips before she shut it down and stared back at me. "Yes, I had Edna the next year. As I already knew, it didn't take much to get pregnant. For which I've always been extremely grateful." She looked at that spot again. "Your father, Henry Cameron, was a hard man. When his first wife died, he died, too. After that, he didn't have any love to give. Or if he did, he surely never gave it to me."

I leaned forward, elbows on my knees. "That's where you're wrong. He loved me. He taught me much of what I know. I saw him love Mom. He loved my kids. And yours."

"Maybe. But not me. Always trying to tell me what to do. What not to do."

"He cared about you."

"He cared for nobody and nothing but himself. His reputation. What his friends would say."

Richard shook his head. "Don't you see? That's how he showed love. He didn't have the words. He didn't have the soft hands or the tender heart. But he had a love for you that tore him apart."

She slapped the table. "All my life I lived with men who wanted to make me into something I couldn't—or wouldn't—be. That was one reason why I married Frank. I knew he could never hurt me in that way. Not that he wouldn't. He couldn't." She shook her head. "Henry Cameron loved only one person, and she died. And I spent the rest of my life looking for love and not finding it."

"Well, I've spent all my life looking for family, and I found it with the Baldwins."

She peered at me, a hard look that chilled to the bone. "You've always had Edna. She's your half-sister, too."

"You tried to keep even that relationship from me by denying my relationship to you and to her."

"Well, don't think the Baldwins are so high and mighty. They might accept you now, but it didn't happen until after their father and their mother were dead. Nobody to fight. Nobody to hurt. And one sister still won't accept you as family."

She was correct on that. I don't know what Krista was afraid of. Maybe she thought I'd try to lay claim to the Baldwin estate or something.

I don't know for sure. She never gave me a chance to explain.

But that's okay.

I'm still a rich man.

The next time Mother and I talked, I'd met my siblings and developed a relationship with them. On another visit to Nova Scotia, I decided the time had come to tell my biological mother what I now had—a second family related to me by blood.

This time we sat in the living room of Edna's living room. Laura, or Mother, as I now called her, sat in a wheelchair near the fire. She was nearing ninety-five, frail, and her blue eyes had faded as much as her memory.

I started the conversation and watched her for a reaction. "I've been in touch with my siblings on the Baldwin side of the family."

A sharp intake of breath from Edna broke the silence. I hadn't really given much thought to her feelings in this, to be honest. I was more concerned about Mother's.

Mother sat still as a statue, and for a moment, I wondered if she'd heard me. Mona stirred beside me and squeezed my hand, our private signal to wait.

So I waited.

After several long moments, Mother stirred. "I never thought I'd live to see that day."

I wasn't certain whether she was pleased or not, and I didn't want to ask. I was excited at discovering I had half-sisters and a half-brother. I already knew I had aunts and uncles, because I'd gone through school with my biological father's younger brothers and sisters, although none of them had ever said a word to me about our relationship.

She glanced at Edna. "I suppose the secret had to come out at some point."

Edna shifted in her chair. "I've known for many years, Mother, who Richard really is."

"Who told you?"

I spoke up. "I did. At least twenty-five years ago."

Edna's husband Gregory, an affable man with a deep belly laugh, put in his two cents' worth. "Laura, that was the worst-kept secret of all time. I knew about it, too, before Richard ever told me."

Mother looked down her nose at him. "I would expect you to listen to low-talk like that."

A rumble emanated from him. "Low-talk from all your high and mighty acquaintances from Grand Falls, Corner Brook, and Botwood."

She frowned at each of us in turn. "Who else knows?"

I shrugged. "What? That I'm your son, or that I'm in contact with my father's other children?"

"Both."

I thought for a moment. "Well, the list is long and not exclusive, and probably I don't know half the names, but I have told my children the details of my birth. I told them after Catherine died. Mr. and Mrs. Lawrence already knew because of talk around Carbonear. Catherine knew, of course. Some of Mom's family and Dad's. Carbonear."

Mother studied Edna for a couple of heartbeats. "What do you think of this?"

Edna leaned forward in her chair. "Mother, I think this is something you should have told me a long time ago. I was shocked when Richard told me, but I was also relieved. There was something gratifying in knowing we were brother and sister, instead of cousins. It's taken me some getting used to, but I think we're closer now than we used to be."

Mother nodded. "So where does that leave us?"

That was a good question. And one we couldn't answer at that point, because to answer it would then define what would happen next.

Instead, I came at if from a different angle. "I'm glad this is out in the open. I don't like secrets. I would like to feel free to talk to you about all of my family. My children, grandchildren, brothers, and sisters."

Mother thought about that for a while. "And Samson?"

"He's dead. Been gone several years now. I haven't seen him since I worked in St. John's. His wife recently died, which is why the family hadn't reached out to me before now." I paused. "She knew about me, you know."

"How do you know that?"

"Maureen told me. That's why her mother never came back to Carbonear when Samson went back to visit his parents. She hasn't set foot there since I was born."

I thought about that for a moment, how I might feel had something similar happened to Catherine. Would I want to know her child that was not also mine? I didn't know the answer to that question. "She doesn't know who I am, of course. She just knows you had a child and claimed Samson was the father. She's heard all the family stories, I guess. But she's never spoken a word publicly about the matter."

Mother tilted her head to one side. "What do you think of all this?"

I already knew the answer to that. "I'm thrilled to find out I have brothers and sisters. I don't see myself ingratiating myself into their family beyond that. I am quite content with my own children and grandchildren, and my Baldwin nieces and nephews don't know anything about me. I suppose Maureen might tell them about me. She's the ringleader of the family. I'll be glad to meet them, and have plans to do that soon, once I get back from the States in the spring."

Laura

I am a big believer in telling the truth. Lies are too difficult to keep track of.

But as the years have passed, remembering the truth has become much harder.

And so I have learned to tell the truth as I believe it.

And if I believe it, then it is *my* truth.

When Richard asked me about marrying one man knowing I was pregnant with another's child, he caught me completely off guard. To be honest, I never thought he'd have the nerve to ask such a question. Up until that point, only two others had asked the question: Albert Jamieson and my father.

And I felt such repulsion at the first and fear of the second that I couldn't answer them.

How Richard found out I never learned as fact. I suspect some big mouth in Carbonear spilled the beans. Probably someone jealous of me. One of the Butt girls, maybe. Perhaps even a Cameron. None of that family thought much of me.

As I sat there and listened to Richard, Edna, and Gregory talk about the matter as though discussing a soap opera or a low-budget movie they'd seen, I see their fascination with the topic has them energized as they surmise about people and situations.

But I was the one in the back of that 1933 Mercury.

I was the one tossed aside like yesterday's newspaper in favor of today's.

I was the one who had no choice but to make the best of the situation.

And although Richard might like to believe he's nothing like me, he is gravely mistaken.

Because as I've watched him over the years, I've seen him analyze a situation, consider his options, and make the best choice he could with the information he had.

Which was what I'd done at the time.

Options were few. Information wasn't encouraging. Choices were forever.

Had I known I was pregnant? Of course I did. Maybe in a tiny corner of my mind, sitting in the hospital room looking at my newborn cousin, I hoped I was wrong. But I wasn't.

I had underestimated Albert Jamieson's care for his public persona. Not only had he hated the notion of raising another man's get, he didn't want his friends and colleagues to think less of him for marrying a woman he'd "gotten in the family way". Which is what folks would have thought had he allowed me to keep the baby.

Instead, he bathed himself in the sea of sympathy engendered by my apparent miscarriage, and rejoiced with him when I delivered him a fine, healthy daughter less than a year later.

I never made the same mistake with Albert again. What other people thought of him was paramount.

But Albert would never admit to anybody else that I was pregnant when we wed. Except my father.

Before deciding what to do, he'd written to my father, accusing him of being the mastermind behind this hasty wedding.

My father soon set him straight, which, I think, destroyed Albert's love for me. Obliterated any chance that perhaps we could straighten things out.

Because then he knew for certain that I knew about the baby.

Not once in our marriage did he mention the child, not even during some of our knock-'em-down-drag-'em-out fights.

It was as if Richard didn't exist.

But he did. And on my few visits to Carbonear, I watched him as he played at Aunt Annie's knee, burbling and chattering to her, calling her Mommy.

And then later, when he and Edna played together, I compared them. But Richard walked sooner, talked sooner, was more energetic, excelled at school.

I never said anything to Edna, of course. I would not hurt my child as my father had done to me. I praised her constantly, and she, in turn, excelled in her studies.

I would not make the same mistake my father had made with me.

But his words to me that night had cut me to the core, and our relationship was strained from then on. I made certain not to spend any time alone with him, not to give him any opportunity to preach to me.

So he used his letters to me to fill in the gap. First paragraph, all the goings on and gadding about he and Aunt Annie had done since he'd last written. Second paragraph, chastising me for not writing sooner. Third paragraph, criticizing a gift or a package I'd sent them. They didn't need anything from me, and I should use the money to better myself.

And always, then, the sermon, about the immoral life I must be living, the people I associated with, how low I stooped in my work, the chances I took in living in Toronto, not to mention the loose women and immoral men I had as neighbors.

And closing with a paragraph about how worrying over me made him old before his time, and how glad he was my mother wasn't there to see what I'd done with my life.

Always with the mother card.

He knew how much I loved her. How much her death devastated me. How much I needed her.

And how badly he'd treated me in the years following her death.

And now Richard knows the truth, although I won't admit it. I'm old. I'm forgetful. I change the endings on my stories to suit myself.

But that doesn't change the fact that I have won.

I have come out on top.

At least in my own mind.

I am *not* unredeemable.

Richard

There are many parts of this story we will never know the truth about.

I've picked through everything, on paper and in my head, sifted through the accounts, and come to the conclusion that apart from finding my brother and sisters, the rest doesn't matter.

So whether Mother really knew she was pregnant or not, whether she hoped for a quick marriage to convince Albert to keep the baby, whether she ever gave me a moment's thought after leaving me at the Baldwin house, doesn't matter.

Because in the end, family is family, and nothing can change that.

I have a brother and sisters who were willing to take a chance on this Cameron fellow from Carbonear, to accept his claim as being their father's child, and to embrace him unconditionally as their own.

If that's not love, I don't know what it is.

Chapter 4
Richard

By spending time with my half-siblings, I came to know another side of my biological father, Clarence Powell, that I hadn't considered until then. Whereas I always pictured him as cold, indifferent, unfeeling—a person would have to be, wouldn't he, to leave my mother the way he did?—now I realized he didn't know about my mother's pregnancy and my existence until after the fact, and raising me really was no more of an option for him than it was for my mother.

No, I had really been raised by the best parents a boy could have. Mom and Dad loved me, gave me everything they had to give, and raised me to be independent, forward-thinking, logical, hard-working.

Who could ask for more?

Laura

Who could ask for more?

I could.

Oh, I know that from some perspectives, I've lived a glamorous life. I've loved a few times. I have grandchildren who love me. And someday I hope to have great-grandchildren who will climb up on my lap and chatter with me about their day.

I have no right to ask for more.

So I don't.

But that doesn't mean I don't want to.

Because I know I've missed out on a lot of things. A son who didn't call me Mother until the woman who raised him had passed away.

Grandchildren who still call me Aunt.

Great-grandchildren who don't know the truth of who I really am.

A girl-child who lost her mother at a young age.

A young woman who looked for love and found rejection and betrayal.

An older woman who would like to change history, but knows that if given the chance, she'd probably have made the same choices.

Chapter 5
Richard

Mother made it to 102. My biological father lived to well into his 80's. Analytical as I am, I figured if I split the difference, I had until at least 90.

But that was not to be.

Like everything in my life, I approached the end with the attitude that if I couldn't change the outcome, I'd make the journey as pleasant and easy as possible.

I took care of my affairs, as the doctors tell you to do when you only have two to four months to live.

And instead of looking at that diagnosis as a curse, I viewed it as a gift. You see, the truth is, we're all dying. Some of us just know the date, while the rest of you are left guessing. And wondering. And worrying.

That four months was such a gift. I made legal arrangements. Mended rifts. Saw folks I might not have bothered to see. Called friends I hadn't talked to in while. Napped more. Ate what I wanted, not because it was good for me, but because that's what I wanted at the moment.

And I made the most important decision of my life just three weeks ago.

I recommitted my life to Jesus Christ as my Lord and Saviour.

I know not everybody reading this book will agree with me, but it's my terminal diagnosis, my last days, my decision.

Although, it wasn't really mine.

As I wrote in my journal, *I came to Christ of my own choice, and not of my own volition—Christ brought me to Himself.*

Not The End

Other books by this author:

Mended By God series

Writing Encouragement

Short Stories

Devotionals

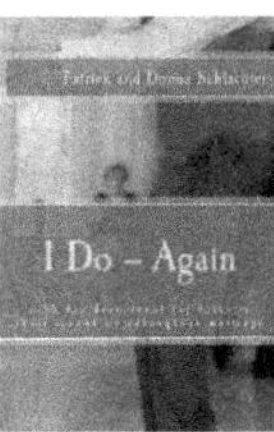

Books by Leeann Betts (pen name)

November 2018

All books are available at Amazon.com in print and digital formats

About the Author

Canadian by birth, American by choice, Donna grew up in Newfoundland but now calls Denver, Colorado home, along with husband Patrick, who is her first-line editor and biggest fan. Together they share two grown daughters and ten (and counting) grandchildren. She writes historical suspense under her own name, and contemporary suspense under her alter ego of Leeann Betts. She has published four cozy mysteries and a devotional for accountants under her pen name, and a collection of short stories, a book on writing tips, and several devotionals under her own name. She is currently under contract with Barbour Books in a novella collection on the Pony Express. Donna is a ghostwriter and editor of fiction and non-fiction, and judges in a number of writing contests. She will be teaching an online course for American Christian Fiction Writers in June 2017, *"Don't let your subplots sink your story"*. Donna loves history and research, and travels extensively for both. You can follow her on Facebook and Twitter, and online at: www.HiStoryThruTheAges.wordpress.com and www.HiStoryThruTheAges.com. Her books are available at Amazon.com in digital and print.